ROYALLY
Relinquished

A Modern Day Fairy Tale

HAYLEY FAIMAN

Editor: RC Martin, The Green Pen
Cover: Cassy Roop, Pink Ink Designs
Formatting: Champagne Formats

Fairy tales are stories of triumph and transformation and true love, all things I fervently believe in.
Kate Forsyth

CHAPTER
One

Caitriona

THE NAME THAT LIGHTS UP MY CELLPHONE SCREEN makes me cringe. It's my mother. I hit the ignore button and send the call to voicemail. I haven't spoken to her in years. She's not necessarily a *bad* person, but she's a user.

The last time she called me, it was for money. The time before that, it was for a place to stay. And the time before *that*, money—*again*. We've never been close, and I counted down the days until I turned eighteen so that I could run as far away from her as possible.

My entire childhood was a revolving door of men—men she could suck dry until they got fed up, or she'd used every ounce of what they had, then she would move onto the next.

I'm not even one hundred percent sure she knows who

my actual father is.

My birth certificate lists my father as—*unknown*. It's probably better that way; the caliber of men that my mom was able to snag were usually pathetic and mostly disgusting. I'd hate to think of where I actually come from.

It's been seven years since I've been back to see my mother, and I don't plan on going back to that little town anytime soon, either. I moved to Portland, Oregon with my two best friends on my eighteenth birthday, and other than the few phone calls I've had from my mother, I've never looked back.

I'm also fairly certain that I'm afraid of commitment, when it comes to relationships with men. I'm twenty-five years old and I've got no prospects, mainly because of my fears of turning into my mother.

What if I open that door and it suddenly turns into a revolving one?

I don't want to be like her, a woman who sucks men dry, who uses them and then moves on to another. A woman who screws anything with a couple nickels in his pocket.

My phone alerts me that I have a new voicemail. Reluctantly, I choose to listen to it.

"Caitriona Geneva Grace, this is your mother calling. I'm desperate. This time, it's real, Caitriona. I'm going to be homeless if I don't get some rent money. Call me back, or you can just deposit the money in my account. You still have the account number, don't you?"

Caitriona Geneva Grace—who names their baby that? *My mother,* that's who. The call ends, and without hesitation, I delete the message. She's been on the verge of homelessness her entire life. It's the same line she used on my grandparents before they passed. It's the line that she used on me the first and the third time she asked me for money. The third time I gave in, so I'm sure that's why she's calling me now.

I shove my phone into my purse as I walk inside of my best friend, Madison's, office building. Madison is completely opposite of me; she's always been that way. She's a successful attorney and married to James, who owns his own contracting company.

Madison, James, and I have been friends since kindergarten. Somewhere along the way, their relationship morphed from friendship to romance.

"Hey," I sigh as I sit down across from her at her big wooden desk.

I reach forward and set down the paper bag that contains her Philly cheese sandwich on the top of her desk before I pull mine out of my own bag.

"I think I broke James' dick," Madison blurts out as I take a bite of my sandwich.

I swallow the bite of food in my mouth harshly, trying not to choke at her words. Though, I'm not sure why I don't expect them. It's *Madison*. My best friend is outspoken, and sometimes I wonder if her words are for shock value alone.

"How?" I finally ask.

I try not to imagine poor James' dick bent in half, broken and barely hanging on.

"We've been having sex for months now, constantly. Last night, he told me that his dick hurt, that it was raw, and he needed a few days off," she explains before she lifts her head and narrows her eyes. "Who turns down constant sex?" she demands.

"A man whose dick is raw?" I point out. She practically growls.

James and Madison have been trying for a baby for the past six-months. She's past the point of calm and rational, and she's turning almost desperate. We're only twenty-five, but Madison has focus and drive that goes beyond anything I've ever seen before. It's how she got through school, then law school, then passed the bar and landed this fantastic position with her law firm.

"I need a vacation," she announces before she takes a bite of her food.

"You and James should totally go somewhere. What about Seattle?" I ask.

"I don't want to go anywhere with him. I want to get away from it all, just you and me," she says.

"I can't afford to go anywhere, Mads. I'm broke," I practically whisper.

I've been living in the same crappy apartment since I was eighteen years old, in one of the worst neighborhoods in Portland. I live paycheck-to-paycheck, scrimping and barely getting by. A vacation is *not* something I can just take when I feel like it.

"My treat, Cait," she announces flippantly.

"I can't ask you to pay for a vacation for me, or even accept it."

"I need some down time, a break from all this baby business. I want to relax by a pool, drink cocktails, and watch cabana boys walk around," she grins.

"Mads, I just can't accept that. You and James already do too much," I murmur.

They do, too. They've fed me so many dinners that I could never pay them back. Madison is always pretending not to want things, like clothes, furniture, and housewares, giving them to me instead. They've been my support system since we were only kids.

They're my only family.

"I'm taking you, you're going. Pack your sexiest swim-wear and a dress or two. We're leaving after work tomorrow," she announces.

Before I can object or ask anymore questions, her phone rings. She grins as she picks it up, and then she puts on her serious lawyer face and starts to talk business. I grab our lunch trash and dispose of it before I bend down and get my purse, throwing it over my shoulder and giving her a small wave as I leave her office.

"Hello, Caitriona," Robert Dayton, one of the partners at the firm, says as I close Madison's door behind me.

Robert is in his mid-forties and handsome; but he knows he's handsome, and that is a complete turn-off. He seems nice enough on the surface, and he's fit and dresses impeccably. He's a snake, though—a completely charismatic snake. Something about him makes my skin crawl, and he always seems to find me when I'm in the building.

"Hey, Robert. Are you having a good week?" I ask, smoothing down the wrinkles in my skirt.

Robert quickly loses interest in my face as his eyes zero in on my breasts, like they always do when he corners me. Another reason I don't really care for him; he always makes me feel a little uncomfortable. He's that guy you have to con-stantly stay on the defense around.

"Of course I am, Caitriona. I'm alive, I'm healthy, and I'm making a shit ton of money every hour I work," he laughs.

I scrunch my nose up at his words. He always tries to

work in how much money he makes into a conversation—yet another reason why I don't care for Robert Dayton.

"That's nice. I better get to work. Sorry to cut this short," I say as I begin to walk toward the elevator.

I feel Robert's cold hand grasp my bicep, halting my attempt at a quick getaway.

"Why don't you quit that pathetic excuse of a job at the MediSpa and come be my assistant? I'll double your salary," he leans down and whispers, his mouth almost touching my ear.

"That's, uh, very generous; but no, thank you," I murmur.

I wriggle out of his grasp and hurry away from him as fast as I possibly can, feeling his eyes watch me as I go.

Henrik

It's time to settle down, Henrik.

My father's words play on a constant loop in my head. He said them, he meant them, and he showed me the woman that I would choose while he did it.

Eugenie, the ice fucking cold bitch, looks back at me from a picture on the dossier he handed to me. It boasts of her familial lineage, her proper education, and her impeccable breeding.

Now I'm on a plane headed to Vegas. I need to unwind. I need to relax. More importantly, I need to get laid. Soon, I'll be tied down—tethered to and ice cold bitch. My cock will probably shatter the instant I try to fuck her.

I shiver at the thought.

"We'll be landing in just under an hour, sir. Is there anything you need?" the flight attendant asks, dropping her voice slightly.

I sink my teeth into my bottom lip, thinking about what she's offering. I could give her a quick fuck in the loo if I wanted. She's laying it out there for me to take, but I shake my head. She knows exactly who I am and that's why she's offering.

A year, even six months ago, I would have gladly taken her up on the fuck. Now, it doesn't seem as appealing. I want someone who wants me for—me. I know it sounds mental, considering I'm going to be getting married to someone else soon, but just once I want someone to want only me—not my title.

"No, thanks, luv," I murmur. Her face falls slightly before she walks away.

An hour later, I've landed in Las Vegas, my security guard, Hugh, flanking my side.

"When we get to the hotel, out of sight?" I ask.

"As always, your highness," Hugh mumbles next to me.

I roll my eyes at his use of my title. He knows it drives me crazy, and he does it just to piss me off.

"Hugh, I hope this sunshine relaxes your puckered ass," I grin.

I watch as he narrows his eyes slightly, but he doesn't say a word in response. He's such a tight ass, and so easy to fuck with; but at the same time, he's my best friend, aside from my brother. So I razz him because I can. He does it back, but in a subtler fashion, like calling me *your highness*.

Caitriona

After my lunch with Madison, I head to work. I'm a receptionist for a MediSpa. I schedule appointments, answer the phone, and file. It's not a demanding job, physically or mentally, but it pays the bills and keeps a roof over my head.

I wish that I could do something else, go to school and find a career, but I don't have the money or time for that. There's only one person who will take care of me, and that's—me.

"Have you thought about doing any *CoolSculpting* on your thighs and your ass?" Natasha, my coworker, asks me.

Natasha is the other receptionist in the office. I have to spend my days sitting next to her vile self, pretending not to completely dislike everything about her awful personality.

"No, I haven't," I grind out through a clenched jaw.

I don't look over at her. I continue to do my work, scheduling appointments for the next day and emailing the staff so they know what their day will look like tomorrow.

"You really should think about it. You know it freezes fat cells. I can tell just by looking at you, you could really use it," she says.

I can hear the evil smile in her voice, and I know she's just trying to goad me.

I ignore her, refusing to respond. She's not worth the wasted breath or energy. Natasha asks me at least once a week if I'm going to have work done. This week, it's *CoolSculpting*, last week it was Botox. Next week, who knows what she'll come up with.

Natasha sees flaws, in everyone, and she feels the need to point them out—not only to me, but to clients. I'm sure that she's sold a lot of services for the spa that way, but that isn't me.

I'm confident enough in myself to know that I don't *need* anything done. I might have something tightened, lifted, or filled later in life, but it won't be because I feel like I need it; it will be because I want it, because I'll want it for nothing other than myself.

I have curves. I like dessert, I love good food, and I like to drink cocktails, so I'm not perfectly toned and fit, and that's okay with me. I'm having fun and I'm enjoying life. I'm not trying to suck the fun out of everything along with all my excess body fat.

The rest of the workday is fairly calm. Natasha is too busy talking to everybody around her to focus on me for the remainder of the day, and I'm grateful for it.

I make my way home, thankful to be done with work and people for the day. Walking inside of my tiny, crappy, studio apartment, I'm too tired to even think about my mini-vacation with Madison tomorrow. I need to pack, though. I know that if I don't, she'll rummage through my closet and pack for me.

I throw my swim suit, a couple dresses, a pair of shorts, a pair of pants, and a few tops in my bag. Then I wash my face, shower, and throw on an old t-shirt before I crawl into bed. Tomorrow, I have to work for most of the day, then I'm off with my best friend.

CHAPTER
Two

Caitriona

I LOOK AT MADISON IN SURPRISE AS WE WALK UP TO THE check-in counter. *Portland to Las Vegas*. We're going to Vegas. I've never been out of Oregon before, and I'm giddy with excitement at what lies ahead. I've seen videos of Vegas, and pictures, but being there is going to be so amazing. I already know it.

While Madison is checking in our bags, my phone rings. I step to the side to take the call, glancing at the name first before I do.

It's James, Madison's husband.

"Hey," I say quietly.

"Take care of my girl while you're gone, okay?" he asks, sounding tired and worried.

He's stressed; he has to be. He and Madison have built this

wonderful life, but they're struggling emotionally right now, and I completely understand it.

"Everything will be fine, Jimmy. I'll keep an eye on her, and we'll have a relaxing time just hanging out by the pool. Take the weekend to relax yourself," I say softly.

"She needs this," he murmurs.

"You do, too," I say before I tell him *goodbye* and hang up the phone.

"Ready?" Madison says as she walks up to me.

I smile and nod, happily taking my ticket and following her to the TSA line. Once we make it through the checkpoint, we walk to our terminal and sit down. I'm anxious about flying. I've never actually been on an airplane before.

"Are you okay?" Madison asks.

"I'm nervous," I admit.

"Maybe you'll meet some super sexy guy while we're gone," she says, nudging my arm with her shoulder.

"I doubt that," I laugh.

It's funny because I haven't really dated in years. It's not that I don't want to find someone, it's that I'm too terrified of turning into my mother. I don't want to put myself out there, at all.

We board the plane, and I'm a little overwhelmed that we're sitting in first class. We're offered cookies and a cocktail, and I quickly take them up on the offer, needing a rum and coke to help me relax a bit.

"How are you not nervous?" I ask her.

"Why? I'm pretty sure the pilot doesn't want to die today, so he's going to do his best to get us to *Sin City* in one piece," she shrugs.

My eyes widen at her words. She's absolutely right, and

I've never thought of it like that before. I find myself completely relaxed by the time the plane takes off, and I even fall asleep for the duration of our flight.

Madison and I arrive at the *Aria*, on the strip. It's the nicest lobby I think that I've ever been inside of, in my life. Then when the elevator opens on our floor and we walk into our room, I almost faint. It's a two-bedroom suite. It's bigger than any place I've ever lived in before. It's huge.

There is a bedroom on each side of the suite with a living area, kitchen, and full dining room separating them. The first thing I do is slip my shoes off and feel the plush carpet against my feet. It's like walking in heaven.

The kitchen has marble flooring and matching marble countertops, along with all stainless-steel appliances, and even a full-sized fridge.

I hurry to my bedroom and squeal when I see it. It's as big as my entire apartment. The bed is a king size, and I'm a little afraid to lie down on it. It looks so plush that I may never want to leave. Then, I walk into the bathroom, and I let out an involuntary whimper at the infinity tub that is placed in the middle of the room.

"You can't lose yourself in that tub just yet, Cait," Madison says. "We're going down to the pool first," she announces before she turns and walks to her room.

Staring after her for a few seconds, I then shake myself out of it and walk over to my suitcase, grabbing my swimsuit and quickly changing.

My suite isn't anything special. It's a silver triangle bikini top that doesn't hide much and has silver bottoms that tie on the side.

I usually don't wear a swim suit in public places. Though I'm comfortable enough with my body, I don't like to show it off. I already know that I'm definitely not going to be the fittest girl at the pool, so I nab my little see-through cover up and put my long dark hair in a huge knot at the top of my head. I then slip on my dollar black flip flops and head into the common living area to wait for Mads.

Madison walks out wearing a leopard print wrap cover-up, and black high heels, along with a huge black floppy hat. She looks like a famous movie star, especially as she slips on her oversized sunglasses.

"You ready?" she asks, arching a brow.

"Yeah, let's do this," I almost groan.

Henrik

I watch her walk into the swimming area. Fuck me. She's an absolute knock-out, and she has no fucking clue, I can tell by the way she walks with her head slightly down, and her shoulders somewhat slumped.

She's walking with a friend, a slim girl, with blonde hair, in high heels. But blondie isn't my focus. I can't take my eyes off of the curvy brunette. Like a creep, I watch as she takes her cover-up off once they've reached their cabana.

My cock twitches at the way her swim suit fits her. It's a tiny little silver thing, and she's got so much skin showing, I want to throw a towel over her so that nobody else can see her.

Fuck me—she's stunning.

She talks to the waiter and smiles before she walks over and reaches for something. Her friend says something and walks away, but *my* girl, she lies down, unbothered by anything else, and begins to read what looks like a book, an honest to god *paperback* book, which surprises me. I can't remember the last time I saw a woman read a paperback book.

My eyes are glued to her; I couldn't look away if I tried. Then I see as she lifts her head before she stands and makes her way over to the pool where her friend is. It's when she arrives at the pool and sits on the edge that I notice two men with her. One eyes her and even licks his lips. I don't understand the rage that bubbles in my blood at seeing the man look at her.

When the one talking to her reaches out and grabs ahold of her bicep, yanking it in a way where she almost falls in the pool, I know that it's time for me to intervene.

I walk right over to where she is, standing right behind her, looking at each prick before I speak.

Caitriona

Madison calls me over to the pool, and I roll my eyes, letting out a breath before I stand. Madison is inside of the pool, chatting to two guys when I walk up. I slink down and let my legs fall into the water as I sit on the edge.

The guys she's talking to are full of thick, bulky muscle, and they look like they survive on whey powder and lean protein alone. They're pretty intimidating.

"Vinnie and Trey, this is my friend, Cait," Madison introduces as I sit down.

I smile and wave, trying not to roll my eyes behind my glasses.

"Hey, babe," Vinnie grins as Trey just lifts his chin in my direction.

"You girls gonna party with us tonight? We're going over to *New York, New York* to that Coyote Ugly bar," Vinnie announces, his eyes bouncing from Madison to me in question.

"We're really here for a girl's trip, but we might catch you there later tonight," Madison says, trying to brush them off.

I open my mouth to come up with some kind of excuse to *never* catch up with them when Trey opens his mouth, speaking before I can.

"You ladies gonna show off those sexy bodies tonight when you come?" he asks. I scrunch up my nose at his question.

"I think I want to gamble a little, maybe dance later, but gambling for sure," I say, trying to avoid both men's gazes.

"I'll take you dancing, baby," he says, reaching out and wrapping his hand around my bicep as he tries to pull me into the water.

I yank back on his hold when a shadow falls over the back of me. Trey releases his hold on my arm, and I take that moment to turn around and look up into the most beautiful pair of green eyes I have ever seen before—*in my life.*

"There a problem here?" he asks.

His accented voice washes over me. He's *British.*

"What's it to you?" Trey asks.

I can't even look back at the men in the pool because my gaze is focused, and my neck is craned back staring at this man standing behind me. He's so tall, and his board shorts hang loosely off of his washboard, *six-pack abs.* His shoulders are broad, and his body is packed with long, lean muscles. Everything about him is sexy, even the slight stubble on his face, and his aviator glasses that are pushed up on his head.

"You're bothering the lady. I could tell from across the way," he states.

"Stand down, fancy pants. These bitches aren't your concern," Vinnie announces.

My eyes widen at Vinnie's words, but *Mr. Sexy Green Eyes* doesn't show any type of response. In fact, he completely ignores both Vinnie and Trey, keeping his focus solely on me.

"You all right, precious?" he asks, holding out his hand.

I place my own in his waiting palm, and I swear as soon as my skin touches his, I feel sparks between us. Trying to ignore the instant pull toward him, I stand up next to him.

My breath hitches when he wraps his golden tanned arm and hand around my bare waist. My mouth drops open in awe, and my body sways slightly, off kilter from the heat that's rushing through me. He's *touching* me. This gorgeous *Adonis* is touching me.

"You coming, luv?" he asks, looking at Madison.

I turn my head slightly to look at her, and I swear I see her entire body do a shiver before she swims to the edge of the pool. She jumps up and quickly follows beside us to our cabana. He doesn't even ask us where our cabana is, he already knows. I'm too awe-struck by *him* to even question it.

"Thank you," I finally manage to whisper after we're in the shade.

I watch as Madison walks away to give us some privacy, and then my attention is back on this stranger in front of me.

"You really should be more careful who you engage in conversation," he warns, tilting his head and then looking toward Madison.

"How can I thank you? I don't know what I would have done had you not stepped in," I mutter, trying not to sound so damn breathless.

It's hard with those eyes staring back at me, and his body so close to mine.

"You want to thank me?" he asks, quirking a brow, "come out dancing with me tonight, precious," he murmurs, running the tip of his index finger along my hairline, down the side of my face and to my chin.

I want him to slide his fingers through my hair. His touch feels like heaven.

"Okay," I whisper, unable to meet his eyes.

He asks my room number and informs me that he'll pick me up at nine o'clock for dancing. I want to squeal, and I want to jump up and down like a freaking idiot teenager, but I try to stay as cool as possible and I do neither of those things.

Instead of acting crazy, I give him a shy smile and watch him wink before he turns and walks away from me. With my eyes glued to his firm ass, I suddenly realize that I don't know his name, and he doesn't know mine.

Then it hits me that I gave a perfect stranger my room number, and I agreed to go out with him *alone*. He could be a serial killer, and I just took the bait because he's pretty.

"You look like you're gonna be sick," Madison whispers in my ear.

I jump slightly and turn to her.

"I just agreed to go dancing with him," I croak.

"Holy shit," she grins like crazy.

"He could be a serial killer, Madison. I just gave him our room number," I bark as my heart starts to beat rapidly in my chest.

I can feel my body filling with anxiety. I'm going to have a panic attack; I can feel it coming on.

"You need to calm down. It's no different from an online date. You'll only be in public, and I know what he looks like. Nothing will happen to you. For once, Cait, please, be a little spontaneous."

"If I end up dead in the Nevada desert, it's all on you," I grind out.

"I can live with that," she shrugs.

CHAPTER
Three

Caitriona

I'M STANDING IN FRONT OF THE FULL LENGTH MIRROR IN my bedroom just staring at my reflection.

I'm wearing one of Madison's dresses. It's too short and *way* too tight. Madison is a good fifteen pounds thinner than I am, and her chest is a good two cup sizes smaller. I'm also at least three inches taller, at five-foot-eight.

Needless to say, my breasts are spilling out of the top just as much as my ass is hanging out of the bottom. I look like I belong walking down the strip instead of going out on a date with a stranger.

The dress, or lack thereof, is strapless. With my chest, I should never go strapless. But the dark teal fabric is stretched to capacity and leaves no room for a bra underneath; plus, it's so short, if I move the wrong way, my ass will definitely make an appearance. Also, because of the tightness, I can't wear panties with it, and I really don't like *that*.

I try to ignore the fact that I'm sans undergarments as I slip on the silver sparkly high heels that Madison forced me to wear. They're hers and, thankfully, though we aren't the same dress size, we *are* the same shoe size.

I washed my hair and left it to curl naturally, and it is a massive bulk of rings. Usually, I spend time straightening it, but I don't have the time this evening. Luckily, Madison knows how to style it when it's curly, and she always does the best job.

It looks so wild and sexy.

She always knows how to style my hair and how to accentuate my makeup to play up my best features. She does my makeup as well, and it's absolutely flawless. Mads should have really gone to beauty school.

My normally freckled spattered nose and cheeks are smooth, without a hint of the freckles that lie beneath the makeup. My dark blue eyes pop and stand out just as much as my light pink, glossy, full lips.

"Mads, I can't wear this," I announce, staring at myself.

"You can and you will. Trust me when I say that fine piece of man candy is going to flip his shit. You look outstanding," Madison grins.

"You're crazy. I look like I should be hooking the strip, not going on a date, and especially not with a guy as hot as he is. I should change," I murmur.

A knock on the door causes me to jump, and my eyes go from Madison to the door, frantically.

"Go," Madison says as she pushes me. I practically fall on my face, stumbling toward the door.

She's not going to give me the opportunity to change. She's determined to let me go out with some stranger, looking like a five-dollar hooker, and she gives not one single shit about it.

I take a deep breath and stare at the closed door, knowing that the beautiful stranger is on the other side, hoping that this night doesn't turn into a complete disaster.

"Open the door," Madison urges on a whisper in my ear.

I turn to her and narrow my eyes, but she's too busy smiling to care about my irritation. I sigh heavily before I open the door. When I look at the man before me, I swear my mouth waters at the sight of the nameless stranger.

He's dressed in dark denim jeans that hug his sculpted, long, lean legs perfectly. He's wearing a white button down shirt that is tailored to fit his broad chest, arms and waist. His hair is still a messy, wavy, dark mop on top of his head, and my fingers itch to run through it. It looks so incredibly thick and soft.

When my eyes finally meet his, I notice that he's taking me in as well, assessing me. I wish I knew what he was thinking, but his facial expression is extremely cool.

"Good evening, precious," he murmurs.

I let his deep voiced English accent wash over me. *Jesus, but that is hot.* I need panties. No, he would just melt them off. It's probably best I don't wear any at all.

"Hey," I whisper, clutching the little silver bag I borrowed from Madison to my ample, spilling-out-of-this-little-dress, chest.

"I never got your name," he says with tipped lips, his eyes staying focused on mine.

"Caitriona," I reply, all the while cringing.

I really hate my name. My freaking *mother*.

"Beautiful. I'm Henrik," he says with a grin.

Before I realize what's happened, he slips his arm around my waist and pulls me into his body. My chest pressing against his, all of my softness against all of his hardness—and good *gosh*, is he so freaking hard.

"Nice to meet you," I mutter in a daze, my eyes fixated on his lips, full and pink.

They look so soft, too.

I wonder what they would feel like—*everywhere*.

"You stare at my lips much longer, luv, and we won't even make it out of your suite," he murmurs, his voice rumbling.

I shake my head and lift my eyes up from his soft looking lips to take in his face again. *Shit*, he's pretty.

"Let's get dancing," he announces before he takes a step back from me.

"Bye, kids. Have fun," Madison calls out from the room.

I wave my hand behind me, too enamored by this man to even attempt to look away from him.

Henrik keeps his arm wrapped around my waist as we walk toward the elevators. Unfortunately, Madison didn't give me lessons in walking while wearing her unbelievably high heels, and I trip three times before we even make it to the elevator doors. Henrik has the good manners to pretend not to notice, though I'm not sure how. I'm a complete embarrassing disaster.

"I'm sorry, I'm not used to shoes this high," I admit once we're inside of the elevator car.

"They aren't yours?" he asks, arching his brow.

"Uh, no," I snort. "Madison dressed me, like her very own *Barbie* doll. Nothing I have on is mine," I laugh.

"I think I like Madison. No… I think I *adore* her," he chuckles.

I suck in a breath as his hand travels to the lowest part of my back. I feel his fingertips dance along the top of my ass, and it takes everything inside of me to keep from groaning.

All I want to do is to get on my tip toes so his hand would actually *be* on my ass. I can imagine how his fingers would dig into the thin fabric, and I shiver.

"She's a pain in the ass," I say with a smirk.

"How long have you known her?"

"I've known her and her husband, James, since we were all five," I say matter-of-factly. "Madison and James are my best friends in the whole world. We all met in kindergarten. Madison pushed James off of the swings and told him ladies got priority. Then he countered back and told her that he didn't see any ladies around. She tackled him and I separated the fight. That's been the story of our lives from day one. They fought and I mediated. Then, as we got older, I stayed out of their fights because they usually ended in sex," I announce, unable to stop myself from rambling like a total fool. Henrik chuckles. It's deep, rich and sexy as hell.

"Where are you from, then?" he asks as we continue to walk toward the dance club.

We're going to the one inside of the hotel, *Jewel*, which I'm thankful for. My feet are already starting to hurt from these freakishly tall heels.

"Portland, Oregon," I say.

Madison, James, and I moved to Portland when they started college. I couldn't wait to get out of my mother's home, so I tagged along. We're originally from a small town, a town of only ten thousand people; but when Madison and James were accepted into Portland University, we all ran as far away from small town life as we could. I've never been back, but they go from time-to-time to visit with their families.

"Where are you from?" I ask, knowing with his accent he must be from somewhere in England.

"London," he says as a look of confusion settles over his face.

He's looking at me with something I can't quite describe, but it's as if he thinks I should have already known. Then, as soon as it crosses his face, it's gone. He settles his features and he grins down at me before giving my waist a squeeze as we arrive at the club's entrance.

The music is loud, the room almost black, except for the burst of colored lights that are timed perfectly with the beat coming from the speakers. As we walk up to the security guard, he gives Henrik a nod before he lets us walk right in. Then there's another guard that meets us with a chin lift, and we follow him toward a roped off area where there's another guard waiting.

I wonder who exactly this man is?

I look around and see that there are several empty loveseats and tables, which have ice buckets set up with bottles of what look like champagne chilling inside. I don't know much about champagne, since I've personally never had any, but I don't think that this is a normal event.

I watch with fascination as Henrik walks over, pops a cork from one of the bottles and pours some bubbly liquid into two glasses that are empty and waiting.

Without speaking, he hands me a full glass before taking a swig from his own. I watch as the liquid works its way down his thick throat. I've never seen anything hotter in my life. I lift the glass to my lips and take a tentative sip. Unfortunately, I end up coughing as the bubbles make their way down my throat.

"Don't like champagne?" he chuckles.

"I've never had it before," I shout over the loud music.

"Never?" he asks, his eyes wide with question.

I shake my head, my mass of hair flying around my face and shoulders. I watch as he sets his glass down on the table before taking mine from my fingers and setting it down to join his. Then I feel his hands on my waist as he hauls me into his body. His head dips and his lips, just as soft as I imagined, touch my cheek before they press against my mouth.

"I've been wanting to kiss you since I saw you reading at the pool earlier," he whispers in my ear, his lips lightly touching my skin.

I feel his hands roam down my lower back and cup my ass, then his fingertips lightly touch the skin of my thighs, right below the hem of my dress. They're firm and his hands are warm, practically melting my dress.

I lift my arms and move closer against his body. I have never felt this way before with anyone, as if our connection is instant. We don't need words because our bodies speak what our mouths don't.

"You have?" I murmur.

"At the end of the night, I'll be doing much more than giving you a kiss on the lips, precious," he whispers against my neck before his lips touch my sensitive skin.

I shiver.

I've never had a one-night stand before, but with him,

I want to. I want to throw caution to the wind and let this gorgeous man claim me for the night. *I want him.*

"Dance with me," he rumbles.

I nod, knowing that he probably wouldn't be able to hear my response anyway. Henrik takes my hand in his and guides me down to the dancefloor.

I notice that the security guard that was positioned at our table has followed us as well. I want to ask Henrik why, but then his hands wrap around my ass and his hips start to move, which causes me to forget all stream of consciousness.

When the third song is over, Henrik lifts his chin and wraps his fingers around mine, tugging me behind him and toward the roped off area where we began the evening.

A waitress appears and he orders us rounds of shots and drinks. He sits down on one of the loveseats and pulls me down onto his lap, I fall with a giggle and bounce. His fingers wrap around the back of my neck and my thigh as the waitress appears with a tray full of drinks.

"This can't all be for us?" I ask with wide eyes.

"Fuck yeah, luv," he chuckles as his hand releases my thigh and reaches down to grab a shot glass.

He hands me a full glass before he takes one for himself. With a clink against my glass, he winks before he shoots the whole thing. I look at the clear liquid and throw it back myself.

I'm going to enjoy tonight *and* this sexy stranger's touch. We shoot two more glasses of liquor before we each take the cocktails he's also ordered and begin to drink those.

The conversation flows easily between us; we don't talk about anything of importance. We talk about music and movies as we continue to drink. Then we break from the liquor and dance in our roped off area, never making it down to the dancefloor before we shoot some more liquor.

Henrik's fingers skim my skin at the hem of my dress, again; but this time, they're traveling further, daring to intimately touch me. As badly as I want him to, he doesn't. We dance until two in the morning, before Henrik suggests we see more of the city.

It's two-thirty when we're stumbling from *Jewel's* doors and making our way toward the hotel's exit. We're drunk off of liquor and high on our own sexual tension. We make our way down the busy street, bustling with partygoers and couples just like us. My feet don't even hurt. I'm numb from the liquor, and too focused on his hand resting on my hip.

"What's your dream, Henrik? If you could be or do anything in the world, what would it be?" I ask as we aimlessly walk, going forward but nowhere all at the same time.

"I would be *anonymous*," he says, sounding even more mysterious than he already is.

"Why would you want to be anonymous? I think it would be impossible."

"Why's that?" he asks, lifting a brow.

"Because you're the most handsome man I have ever laid eyes on. You'll always be noticed for that and that alone," I explain.

Henrik stops in the middle of the sidewalk, ignoring the people who have to stumble around us to avoid running us over, since we were walking with the flow of foot traffic. He pulls me a little closer into his chest, one hand on my lower back, the other tangled in my mess of hair at the back of my head.

"I've never had so much fun, Riona," he slurs with a lopsided grin tipping his lips. "What's your dream, precious?"

"To be loved for me," I whisper, biting on my bottom lip with a cringe.

"Who couldn't love you, Riona?" he asks, using his nickname for me, something he just started calling me after he had a few cocktails.

"How could anybody love me when my own parents couldn't?" I ask, dampening our fun evening.

Henrik shakes his head and moves to wrap his hand around mine as he tugs me down the boulevard. It's warm outside, and loud from the traffic and the people moving all around us.

"Them being right bastards doesn't reflect a damn thing on you, precious. That's all on them," he murmurs as he bends his head slightly.

A loud laugh causes both of us to turn our heads and look at who's walking our way.

A couple comes toward us from the opposite direction. She's wearing a short veil on her head, and the man is wearing a top hat. They're just in jeans and t-shirts, but they're wrapped in each other's arms and they look blissfully happy and obviously just married—and drunk, very, *very* drunk.

Henrik looks from the couple to me and I watch as a wicked smile crosses his face. I know exactly what he's thinking, because my drunk brain is *stupidly* thinking the exact same thing.

It's stupid, it's immature, it's reckless.

It's going to be a blast.

"Marry me, Caitriona," he whispers.

Henrik

How could this woman in front of me never have known love? Her friend loves her, but that isn't the same as a parent's love or one from a lover. The depths of hurt in her eyes when she said that her parents didn't love her, that she just wanted to be loved for her—it spoke to me.

She speaks to me.

It's dangerous, the question I've just asked her. Not only for me, but for her as well. I'm supposed to marry that *Ice Bitch*. Maybe I'm sabotaging it all on purpose, maybe I just want to have a little fun before I'm tied down, or maybe I want to show this woman in front of me that she's worthy of more in life.

I'm so pissed that I don't even make sense inside of my own head. But I don't care.

I'm marrying this girl. Right here and right now.

Then, I'm going to fuck her over and over again. I'm going to watch her cry out, as she comes undone around me.

I can't fucking wait.

CHAPTER
Four

Caitriona

"WHAT DO YOU SAY, PRECIOUS? WANT TO MAKE AN honest man of me?" he asks, holding out his hand to hail a cab.

"We haven't done anything but kiss, Henrik. You *are* honest," I counter back with a small smile.

"In a few hours, I'll be filthy dirty, and so will you—at least this way it'll be legit," he shrugs before he places a sweet kiss on my lips as the cab pulls up next to us.

Together, we climb in as he asks us where we're going. This is foolish, *so foolish*, but looking into his eyes, I want to be reckless with him. It feels good, and it feels safe. Like I know that even when tomorrow comes, even when we get this annulled, that I'll still feel good, that he'll make this all easy and fun and just—*nice*.

"The nearest wedding chapel that's open," Henrik announces, his eyes never leaving mine.

"You're gonna regret this in the mornin'," the cabby mutters as he pulls into traffic.

"Never," Henrik and I murmur simultaneously.

The cabbie drops us off at *Little White Chapel.* I feel like I'm in a movie; like I'm not inside of my own body, but instead watching all of this from afar.

Why I'm doing what I'm doing, I have not a single clue. But with Henrik's arm wrapped around me and the big smile on his soft lips, I'll do whatever he wants.

I'm that gone for him.

I'm that drunk off of him.

The chapel is busy, so much busier than I had anticipated. There are couples like us in party attire, waiting for their turn. But there are also couples dressed up in actual wedding gowns and tuxedos.

We stumble past all of the other drunken couples to write our names on the list and fill out our paperwork so that we can join the rest of the people here and say *I Do.*

"We're really doing this," he announces as we sit down in the back and wait for our names to be called.

"We are," I nod with a big goofy grin.

"I can't wait to fuck my wife," he murmurs as he bends down and presses his lips just below my ear.

I turn to face him, and it's as if we're pulled into each other—like we can't be stopped, and it can't be helped. Our lips touch as though we've just ignited a fire between them.

When Henrik's tongue slips between my parted lips, I whimper. That somehow breaks the control he's been holding onto, and he goes wild. He nips and tugs on my lips, his tongue invading my mouth as he consumes me.

Then, when he needs to catch his breath, his mouth travels down my neck and begins to explore, lick, kiss, and nip the tops of my breasts.

"I can't wait to have these in my mouth," he groans against my chest as his fingertips dance along my shoulder.

I can't wait for his mouth to be on every inch of my body. To hear his whispered words in that sexy accent in a quiet room.

I'm ready, right now.

We both jump when we hear our names and stand before hurrying to our spots at the front of the chapel, both in fits of laughter. There are no flowers, I don't have a bouquet, there's no wedding march, and, honestly, I could care less.

This is Vegas, and I'm marrying the sexiest man I have ever seen in my life, even if it's only for the night.

All I can think about and all that I want is Henrik's body pressing against mine. I want him inside of me as soon as physically possible.

There aren't rings, but Henrik whispers that he'll buy me whatever I want in the morning when the jewelers open. It's just the two of us in this little chapel, along with the officiant. There's nobody else, and nothing has ever felt so *right* in my entire life.

We do decide to say our own vows. I don't know why, but it seems important that we do.

"I, Caitriona Geneva Grace, take you, Henrik…" I pause, realizing that I don't even know his full name.

"Henrik George William Richard Stuart," he interjects.

I gape at him, too drunk to remember *all* of the names he's just spouted off. I decide immediately to use his first and last name. I cannot repeat the rest in the correct order, so I'm not even going to try.

"I take you, Henrik Stuart, to be my lawfully wedded husband. I promise to be loyal and faithful. I will be barefoot and pregnant as often as you request. I will cook for you and clean for you. I will never deny you. I will take my wifely duties completely and totally seriously, and I vow that I will give you blowjobs for more than just your birthdays.

"I promise to take care of you, and to care for you in sickness and in health, to always stand at your side and give you support."

Henrik clears his throat and, in his beautiful British accent, he makes his own vows to me.

"I, Henrik George William Richard Stuart, take you, Caitriona Geneva, to be my lawfully wedded wife. I vow to be faithful to only you. I will take care of you from this day forward. You will want for nothing and I will give you everything.

"I promise to shag you as often as you'll let me without reservation. I vow to give you at least four sons and one daughter, because every duchess deserves her own princess to dote upon. I also vow to keep you safe and away from all dangers, physical or otherwise. I will honor and protect you, all the days of my life."

Immediately, tears stream down my cheeks at his beautiful words. Not one ounce of funny, except for the shagging part, and completely and totally beautiful from start to finish.

I wish this were real. I wish that this were the man I was meant to spend the rest of my life with. Falling for him would be exceptionally easy to do, especially with the words he's just said.

The minister, I use that term loosely because he's wearing an *Elvis* one-piece bedazzled suit, announces us man and wife, and even includes a hip swivel.

Henrik pulls me into his body and kisses me, indecently deep, his tongue filling my mouth and his hand grabbing a handful of my ass, taking me and tasting me. I moan as I wrap my arms around his neck and open my mouth even wider for him.

The minister clears his throat and we quickly break apart.

My face flushes red and Henrik chuckles before he thanks him and wraps his hand around mine, pulling me toward the exit. There's a cab waiting for us outside, and I tell him to take us to the *Aria*.

"We can go to my suite," he murmurs against my ear as he nibbles on my lobe.

"No, Madison would worry if I don't make it back to my room," I breathe, trying my hardest not to throw my leg over his and grind against him.

I've wanted him all night long, and *it's almost time*. My palms start to sweat with nervous anticipation, but he doesn't notice. He's too busy nibbling, kissing, and running his hands all over my body. When the cab stops, I watch as Henrik takes out some money and tosses it up at the driver in the front seat before he's out of the car and pulling me behind him.

"We've *got* to hurry," he mutters, practically running through the hotel's lobby.

"Henny, I'm going to fall," I warn with a giggle.

Less than a second later, I'm scooped into his arms, and he's swiftly walking toward the elevator. I squeak and try to put my hand under my ass so that the entire hotel doesn't see my bared center.

"I'm not going to show anybody your goodies. Well, *my* goodies—now," he chuckles as he continues with his hurried pace toward the elevator.

Once we're in the elevator car, I expect him to put me down, but he doesn't. He doesn't release me from his hold until we're in my bedroom and he's locked the door behind us.

"Why'd you carry me the whole way?" I ask as he deposits me on the bed.

"Two thresholds to carry my new bride over. How could I not take advantage? I like it when you call me Henny, by the way," he murmurs as he begins to unbutton his shirt.

I lose all thought as he exposes his chest to me. He's even sexier with his shirt unbuttoned, standing in front of me, than he was at the pool. Maybe because he's technically *mine* now. *My* husband. It's silly to think of him as that really, when in reality, we'll have this silliness annulled tomorrow, but for now, he's *mine*—nobody else's but *mine*.

"I want to see my wife," he murmurs, his voice dipping lower than before.

The mischief in his eyes is gone, replaced with a much more serious look of desire and heat.

I try to gracefully peel Madison's tight dress from my body, but I'm afraid it isn't very graceful at all. It feels much more like I'm fighting with it as I shimmy the tight fabric down my hips, and finally, my thighs and legs, leaving it in a pile at my feet.

"*Fuck*, you didn't wear knickers *at all* tonight?" Henrik asks, his voice ratcheting up a bit higher with surprise.

I shake my head as I bite my bottom lip, trying not to

laugh at the word *knickers*. It's adorable slipping from his lips in a still drunken slur. I suck in a breath as he reaches out and, with just the pads of his fingers, traces down my collar bone to the swells of my breasts before he swirls around my nipples. He's doing this too slowly, too lightly, and too far away from where I want him to really touch me.

"Henny," I whine.

"Yeah?" he murmurs.

I watch as he takes a step back and strips himself of the rest of his clothes. He's muscular and chiseled, like he works out every single day.

I lick my lips at the sight of his cock jutting out from between his legs. He's long and thick, but not overly so, and he's hard. He's hard—*for me.*

He grunts before he's in front of me again, and his hands are wrapped around my thighs, picking me up. He tosses me onto the center of the bed, as though I only weigh ten pounds, and not like I'm five-foot-eight and well over ten pounds. He then divests me of Madison's high heels, dropping them to the floor one by one.

"My wife," he murmurs against my lips.

"My husband," I say back.

His lips crash against mine in a rough, brutal, wonderful kiss. I feel his hand between my legs and whimper as he eases two fingers inside of me.

"You're wet," he grunts as he slides in and out of my ready and waiting body, slowly a few times before he thrusts them inside of me with a grunt.

"I've been waiting all night for you," I sigh.

My eyes roll in the back of my head as his movements become a bit rougher.

"Fuck, *yes*," he murmurs as he pulls his hand from between my legs and replaces it with the tip of his cock.

"Please," I whisper.

"I'm all yours, precious," he groans as he slams inside of me with one swift thrust of his hips.

Henrik's hands slide under my knees and he spreads my legs wider as he sinks deeper inside of me, his eyes fixed on mine and never moving. *We don't speak.* No words are needed as our eyes stay locked onto each other, and we give and take what the other person is offering.

It's the most connected I've felt to a person in my entire life, and he's a stranger—a one-night stand I married that I'll probably never see again after the annulment.

I try to not let that fact sadden me. I push it out of my mind as I force myself to cherish every second Henrik's arms are around me and his cock is inside of me.

Henrik

I try to open an eye, but holy shit, the pain in my head will not quit. Then there's some god awful noise happening right next to my head. I finally crack one eye open and reach in the direction of the offending sound for my phone.

"'lo," I croak.

"Henrik, what in the fuck?" I hear my brother yell.

Fuck, but my older brother is a pain in my arse. He's perfect, everybody thinks and says so. I know the truth. He's pigeonholed into a stereotype, and he just stays there and does exactly what's expected of him because he doesn't want to rock the boat.

I, however, want that boat swaying and rolling over, rocking and rolling like a fucking hurricane. I may agree to my families wishes, verbally agreeing to their requests, but I find my chances to do as I wish. It's all about knowing when the right time and place are.

"*Shhh*, my head is about to pop off. What's the problem?" I mutter.

I'm sure there are photos floating around of that sexy minx and me dancing it up at the club. Fuck me, but Riona is delicious.

"Well, it was brought to my attention that my dear little brother was partying in *Las Vegas* last night with a sable haired tart," he announces.

I shoot straight up. How dare he call sweet Riona a *tart*. She is anything but. I look over and see her beautiful mass of curls splayed all around her, her face down in the pillow, her back bare.

The sheet is pulled up to her delicious arse, covering more than I would prefer in the moment. *Fuck, but she is perfectly delectable.*

I want to take her again. Last night is fairly fuzzy, so I want a coherent memory of how it feels to be inside of her. Something I can tuck away for the days when I know I will have to be wed to some cold, frigid, crotchety bitch from *good breeding.*

"She's not a tart. Fuck, Philip, you know how these things happen," I explain quietly as I stand and grab my jeans, pulling them up my legs and hips.

I don't bother buttoning them before I bend down to grab the rest of my things, walking out of the room so I won't wake up sweet Riona.

"I have already sent security to gather you and bring you home," Philip explains, as if his order is law and I have zero say so in the matter.

"Hugh's somewhere around here, so absolutely not. I'm enjoying my holiday," I say, sounding like a child. Since Philip is going to treat me like one, it seems almost necessary.

"Hen, come on, my hands are tied. Grandfather saw the photos; he is beside himself. The plane leaves in an hour. Don't make this difficult, please," Philip explains.

I let out a puff of air. The last thing I mean to be is a pain in Philip's arse. I love the bastard, but I want to have fun. I want to do everything I can before I'm forced into settling down. Philip took to settling with his fiancé with ease, but I don't want to.

I want to live.

I want to have fun.

I want to shag Riona at least a dozen more times.

"All right," I finally agree.

I turn to walk back to Riona's room.

"Don't bother," Madison says, her body leaning against the door to Riona's room, her eyes focused directly on me. They're assessing.

"What?" I ask, turning to look at the little beauty.

"Don't go in there and make promises to Cait that you can't, and won't, keep. You should just slip out now. She's never had a one-night stand. She'll be feeling shitty enough about herself without your empty promises," Madison announces. The little Sprite is a damn cutthroat.

I vaguely remember Riona telling me that she's an attorney. I couldn't picture it before, but now, I most definitely can. She's kind of scary.

"I do want to see her again…" I start to say. I'm promptly interrupted by Madison.

"But you won't. She's had a hard enough life, Henrik. I think you're a really nice guy, and I can tell you mean well, but let's be honest. If you could, how would you stay with her? Would she be this dirty little secret, hidden away, and visited a few times a year? Would she have this nice, modest home and plenty of money direct deposited in her checking account monthly?"

I close my eyes and think about her words, her questions. She knows who I am. But Riona didn't seem to know. Was it all a ruse?

"You know who I am?"

"I do. Should I bow, *Prince Henrik*?" she asks as her lips tip at the corner.

"Does she know who I am?"

"No. She doesn't have television, and she doesn't pay attention to tabloids and gossip. It's not her thing. She has no clue," she says.

"That was my brother. Apparently, Riona and I have made the paps. The family isn't happy," I explain. "I really do like her," I whisper, sliding my shirt on and buttoning it.

"I'll tell her as best I can that you didn't *choose* to leave her," Madison says with a sad smile.

I can't even muster a partial grin. Everything inside of me is screaming to crawl back in bed and make love to the woman I want. Never have I felt so free, so connected to a woman in my entire life. She doesn't know who I am, and if she does, she truly does not care. I've never felt so carefree before. I want that again. I want it every single day.

I don't say anything else, though. Instead, I wave at Madison before I walk out of the hotel suite. My whole body aches with each step that I take away from the closed door.

I close my eyes whilst on the lift and imagine her face, how utterly devastated she's going to be when she wakes up and realizes that I'm gone. Madison kept saying it was a one-night stand, and though it started out that way, it doesn't feel like one now.

It feels like so much—*more*.

I step out of the lift and make my way toward my own suite. I can shower and change on the plane after a quick stop to my room to grab my luggage. I have a feeling that this will be my last weekend of debauchery—for the rest of my *life*.

I know my grandfather and father will surely tighten the reigns after this; but not my mother. At least my mother will always be at my side. She believes that I should be allowed my freedoms. The freedom to choose any woman I wish as a wife, to fall in love and be married.

Unfortunately, my grandfather and father will always win any arguments, or *discussions,* as they would deem them.

Fourteen hours later I am proven correct in my thinking.

My party days are now over. The *ice bitch* is ready to announce our engagement, and plan a wedding. It's also time to focus a bit harder on my duties as a prince. I detest the entire idea.

As the second son, the odds of me being in control of anything are almost laughable. So why should it matter who the fuck I marry?

Once Philip produces an heir, it is fairly impossible. Beyond all of that, I don't want it. I enjoy my work as a venture capitalist, and I have no desire to do anything else, career wise. Philip is great at his duties. I, however, don't give much of a flip about them.

"Don't be too upset, Henrik," my mother says after my grandfather and father storm out of the room, once they've of course waved the paps in my face, and they've delivered their demands.

"I'm sure I'll be fine. Father gave me a dossier, to look over, she's who've I've chosen," I murmur, looking down at my shoes.

"I'm sure she was a lovely girl, but we all have our duties," my mother, Helena, murmurs before placing a kiss on my cheek and walking out of the room.

Caitriona Geneva Grace wasn't just a *lovely girl.* She was sexy and beautiful, fun and sweet, all rolled into one. I fucking hate the fact that I can't remember the entirety of the evening. I can only remember bits and pieces, and that's the fucker of it all.

I can't remember every detail of the best night of my life.

CHAPTER
Five

Caitriona

THE WHOLE FLIGHT HOME, I'M BUSY STARING OUT THE window, wondering what happened to make Henrik leave the way he did. I didn't expect him to be my new boyfriend, but I thought that what we had, the short time we had it, was fantastic, and that he'd at least stay in my bed until morning.

I'm so consumed in my own thoughts that I don't even realize I've been ignoring Madison the entire flight home.

"You're allowed to sulk over him on this plane only," Madison announces as the plane begins to descend back into Portland.

"What?" I ask in confusion.

"There isn't any reason to dwell on someone like him. One-night stands are meant to be full of regret the next morning," she exclaims.

I really want to regret it, but I don't. Not a single part of it.

I don't remember every single second of the night, and I regret *that*—the fact that I got too drunk to keep the memories fresh.

I do remember the way I felt when his fingers danced across my flesh. I remember the way he held me when we walked together, or when we danced.

I remember the way his beautiful green eyes danced when I acted silly. I also couldn't forget, even if I tried, the way my body felt when I came with him inside of me. I'll never forget any of that.

"What exactly happened between you two?" she asks as the plane touches down.

I shake my head, unwilling to answer her. That night with him is my secret, my very own piece of rebellion. And our wedding? I remember we were married. I highly doubt it is all legal, but it's still ours. We were in Vegas, and we were married at three-thirty in the morning, by an Elvis impersonator.

I'll never forget the pieces that are bright and burned into my mind. I just wish the entire night was bright and unforgettable.

Walking into work on Monday morning has me feeling nauseous. I'm tired, hungover, and just plain depressed. The last people I want to see are my coworkers, especially Natasha, who is sitting behind the receptionist desk with a cat that ate the canary type of grin on her lips.

"Have a good weekend?" she asks.

"I did," I shrug, not getting into any details with her.

"I'll just bet you did," she chuckles.

"Caitriona, can we see you in the office, please?" Teri, my manager, calls out.

I ignore Natasha and make my way toward the office to find not only Teri, but Stephanie, the owner, sitting at the consultation table. I sit down in the plush chair across from them, which is usually reserved for clients, and look from Teri back over to Stephanie, back over to Teri again, waiting for whatever is coming my way.

"You have to know why you're here?" Stephanie asks.

I shake my head. I have zero clue why I'm in their office. They're looking at me like they expect me to say something, but I have no clue what they want from me.

"This," Teri says, tossing a magazine at me.

My eyes widen and I look down, shocked at what is splayed out in front of me.

I'm on the cover of a gossip magazine.

The. Cover.

I'm on the cover of this gossip magazine, wrapped in Henrik's arms, wearing Madison's skimpy dress while dancing in Vegas. I look slutty and awful. The angle is terrible, too. Henrik, of course, looks as handsome as ever. Then my eyes catch a glimpse of the headline.

Badboy Prince Henrik's sexy night in Vegas with mystery woman.

"What the hell is this?" I ask in a whisper.

"This is going to give us business like you wouldn't believe," Stephanie chuckles.

"I don't want anyone to know it's me, are you crazy?" I shout.

"Oh, they're going to know, and it'll boost sales like mad. Imagine, the woman who spent a night with a prince checking you into the MediSpa. People will book appointments just to meet you, just to try and get you to talk," Teri says, her voice going up an octave with excitement.

"No, no way," I say, shaking my head and pushing the magazine away from me.

I don't want to look at everything I had on display, everything that the world can now see.

"Too late. We've already sold that little piece of information," Teri snickers.

"What?" I breathe.

"It's probably already online, but we sold your name to the paparazzi—and your place of work. You can't think that we'd sit on something so juicy, could you?" Stephanie asks with a grin.

I want to slap the grin off of her face, but this is my job and I need it. I don't know what I'm going to do. This is insanity. Complete and total insanity. I want to scream and cry and bitch slap my bosses all at once. Then I want to curl into a ball and eat a vat of chocolate and drink wine by the gallon to try and forget that this is now my life.

"I'll give you ten minutes to collect yourself, then it's back to work. This is going to be a great thing, Caitriona. Don't make it ugly. You never know the opportunities publicity on this level can bring you," Stephanie says, squeezing my hand before she and Teri stand and walk away.

I ignore them completely and pull my phone out of my purse before I find Madison's number and press send.

"You are *not* going to cry," Madison practically shouts in my ear.

"You've seen?" I ask in surprise.

"I get *TMZ* updates on my phone by the minute, Cait, you know that. Who the fuck leaked your name this morning?"

"Wait a minute, when did you know about all of this?" I ask in confusion.

"I knew when he picked you up on the date. I didn't know the *world* knew until a little later. The morning after your date, he was on the phone in the living area with his brother. News had leaked about his weekend with you, and he was being forced to leave. He looked conflicted, like he didn't want to go, but he knew he couldn't stay. I told him to go. I thought it would be easier than if he woke you up and made empty promises," she explains.

"How could you not tell me?" I breathe.

"I didn't think anybody would find out it was you. I figured, a few days from Saturday, something new would hit the gossip news and nobody would care about the mystery girl anymore. I knew you didn't realize who he was, and I knew you liked him and you had fun. Why spoil any of it?"

"You should have told me," I mutter, resting my head in my hand.

"It's the first time you've ever thrown caution to the wind, Cait. You met a beautiful stranger and had an awesome night. I didn't want anything to mar that," she explains.

"Well, I'm fucked now. My bosses are the ones who leaked my name—*for money*," I groan.

"Those fucking bitches," she screeches.

"Agreed."

"Come over for dinner tonight. James is making salmon;

you love salmon," she begs.

"I need tonight alone. How about tomorrow?"

"No backing out on us."

"No, I'll be there. I promise. I just need to freak out tonight alone," I say with a strained laugh.

"I'm sorry. I should have told you so you'd be prepared," she murmurs.

"It's okay, Mads. I understand why you didn't."

We end the conversation, me swearing to call her as soon as I get home to ensure that I'm not a complete basket case and can make it through the night without hugs, chocolate, and wine with my best friend. I take a deep breath before I decide to face what is surely going to be a circus shit show of a day.

"You should have done the *CoolSculpting* when I suggested it. Bet you're sorry now," Natasha giggles as I sit down behind my computer.

I ignore her snide remark and go about my business. The day is filled with walk-ins and busy bodies whispering and pointing at me. Only a handful of women actually have the nerve to ask me about Henrik.

As much as I want to be a bitch and ignore them, this is my job and I need it, so I give them the vaguest answers I can and then excuse myself.

I've never been so happy to clock out as I am by the end of the day. I drive home, in my shitty, royal blue Chevy Cavalier, on auto-pilot, unaware of anything but the road and the cars in front of me. That is, until I step out of my car in my apartment's parking lot and I see the dozens of people surrounding my doorway.

"Oh, shit," I breathe.

I take a deep breath and decide to be as brave as possible and make my way toward my door. With my head down and my eyes trained on the ground, I climb my staircase. I know when I've been spotted because it's like the air has been sucked from around me.

The crowd of reporter's circle around me and start screaming questions at me, all of them talking over each other. I do my best to get through their bodies and make my way to my door without saying a single word.

I refuse to speak, not about Henrik or my time with him. That was for us.

I hate that the world has seen even a glimpse of it.

I don't bother eating dinner. Instead, I make my way toward my bed, strip my clothes, and slide between my scratchy, cheap sheets.

Sitting straight up in bed what feels like minutes later, my heart beating out of control against my ribcage. My eyes dart around my darkened room, wondering what startled me awake, and then I hear it. My front door rattles.

I live in a studio. I don't have a bedroom, so I grab my phone and run into the bathroom, closing the door and locking it before I dive into my bathtub and call 9-1-1.

The dispatch stays on the phone with me until the police arrive. Then, as they're checking out my apartment and door, I call James.

"I'll be there in two seconds," he grunts, his voice gravelly from sleep.

I stay completely out of the two officer's way as they look around, check my door, and look somewhat bored by the whole scene. I have to admit, it's not very exciting. Nothing really happened, and nothing was taken.

"It looks like your lock was picked. It's easy to do with these cheap ones," one of the officers informs me.

"What happens now?"

"Anything taken?" he asks.

"No, I don't know if he even came in. I was hiding in the bathroom," I say.

"Do you have any idea who it could be?" he asks, pulling out a small notepad.

Instead of verbally answering, I shake my head.

"Old boyfriend, anybody like that?"

Again, I shake my head. I haven't dated in forever.

"There were some reporters outside my door when I got home. Do you think it could have been one of them?" I ask.

"What were they doing here?" the other officer asks, furrowing his brows.

"I was seen with someone famous over the weekend and my bosses sold my name to the paparazzi," I mutter.

"You're the girl who partied with the prince?" one of them asks.

My face heats with embarrassment at his question. I whisper an almost inaudible *yes* before James bursts through my door.

"Holy shit, Cait. Are you all right?" he asks, running over to me and pulling me into an embrace.

"I'm fine, James. Nothing happened. It just scared me is all," I admit before taking a step back.

"And you are?" one of the officers asks.

"This is my friend, James Beck," I introduce.

"Who was it? Did you catch the bastard?" James rattles off, demanding to know.

The officer explains about the paparazzi at the door, the

fact that they don't see any damage or stolen items, and that they have no real leads. James insists they write up a report anyway, and it takes another thirty minutes of questions to gather their information for the report.

"You're coming back to our house," James announces.

"James…" I start to say. He glares at me and the look instantly shuts me up.

I pack a small overnight bag with just a few days' worth of clothes and together we lock my front door and leave my shitty little apartment.

"Why didn't you call me when those reporters were swarming around you?" James asks once we're settled into his pickup truck.

"I honestly just wanted to go to bed. Did Mads tell you what happened?"

"She did," he nods.

"I just wanted to be alone," I mutter, staring out the passenger window.

"Yeah, you wanted to wallow and feel sorry for yourself," James announces.

"I can't have one day to feel sorry for myself?" I ask defensively.

"Madison and I are your family. We're here for you, Cait. You don't have to do anything alone, and that means braving those fucking vultures who were at your door."

"I didn't think anything like this would happen. I just wanted to forget about it all and put off dealing with it," I sigh.

"No more, Cait. That right there scared the shit out of me," he grunts as we pull into the driveway of his and Madison's house.

I love their place. James owns his own custom home building company, and he completely remodeled the main house and the pool house as soon as they purchased the property a few years ago. The details he added and the love and care they both put into the project pours out of the house itself.

We don't say a word as we walk inside of the living room, and that's when I see Madison sitting on the sofa in her robe. Her hair is in a messy bun and she's makeup-less, a sight nobody on earth has probably ever seen aside from James and me.

"You are going to move into the pool house. We'll clear it out this weekend. You'll give notice to your landlord, and you'll live rent free for *forever* and be right in my backyard, just as you should have always been," Madison announces, her eyes staring straight at me and her voice never wavering.

"Madison, I can't mooch off of you and James. I wouldn't feel right."

"I don't give a fuck what you *feel*, Cait. Tonight was the scariest night of my life. Not to be a bitch, but your apartment is shit, the neighborhood is worse than shit, and it terrifies me on a regular day. If you're in the pool house, then James and I are close enough to help if you need us and vice versa. You can help out with cooking, laundry, housework, and yard work if it makes you feel any better. But you're staying. You need us, and God knows I always need you, Cait. I won't take no for an answer and neither will James," she states.

I don't know how to respond to that.

What is there to say to her?

"I want my best girls close by," James mutters, finally

speaking.

He hasn't called us his best girls since high school. I turn to look at him and see that he's obviously concerned. This move wouldn't just be for my benefit, but it would make the two people I love most in the world feel and sleep better.

"You guys are crazy and too much," I whisper as my eyes fill with tears.

"We're having a packing party tomorrow after work, and some of James' guys can help you move on Saturday," she grins.

I nod, unable to say anything else. I can already feel the tears falling from my eyes.

Once we've loaded up one pickup full of my things, I look around my apartment and realize I own nothing decent. Madison and James have fully furnished their pool house, so the only things I need to really bring are my personal items.

Originally, I thought about putting everything in storage, but as my eyes scan the space, I realize it's all worthless.

"I think I'm just going to have a donation place pick up everything else," I announce.

"Really?" James asks.

"Oh, thank god," Madison sighs.

"Yeah, it's not really worth storing," I shrug.

"Cait, I love you, but it's crap," Madison announces. If I didn't love her, I'd probably strangle her.

She's right, though. All my stuff is second hand, and the things she and James have given me were all used as well. The few things I've bought were because I needed them, not because they were pretty and I wanted to make my house a home.

As we carry boxes up and down my staircase, I'm thankful that the paparazzi aren't hanging around today, and I'm hopeful that they've moved onto someone else.

Though, the clients at my work haven't. We were busier today than we have ever been, and I seemed to be the resident side show. Stares, giggles, and silly questions one right after the other all day long were aimed toward me.

Driving my crappy blue car, following behind James' pickup, I can't believe that I'm moving. I can't believe that I just packed everything I wanted, donated the rest, and now I'm going to be living in James and Madison's pool house.

It's crazy to me.

Completely and totally crazy.

Before we can pull into the driveway, I let out a gasp. The paparazzi weren't at my place because they're gathered at James and Madison's.

"Get the fuck off of my front lawn," I hear Madison screaming as I open the front door of my car.

"Go around the back, don't let them see you," James whispers loudly toward me.

I glance over to where Madison is. She's keeping them busy by ranting and raving about her marigolds. I hurry as fast as I can toward the back fence, and slip into the backyard, latching the gate behind me. I close my eyes and let out a breath as I let my head fall against the back of the closed gate.

I can't believe the nightmare isn't over. It's here, and it's in my face, and now I've brought it to my friends' home—their beautiful home.

"Don't even stress about it," Madison says, her voice cutting through my thoughts.

"On *your* yard, at *your* home, Mads," I mutter.

"I hate marigolds. Fucking did me a favor," she chuckles.

"Mads," I whisper.

"You're home now. It's fine. I wouldn't be able to sleep if I didn't know you were going to be safe. There's too many weirdos in the world."

Madison wraps her hand around mine, giving it a squeeze before she leads me toward the newly remodeled pool house. I've never actually been inside, not since James re-did it, finishing construction only a couple of weeks ago. I saw it in its original state, which was pretty sad. It was just a big empty room they used for storage that happened to have a bathroom inside.

"Now it's only one-bedroom, but it's all yours, Cait," Madison announces as she opens the door and steps inside.

My mouth gapes at the sight in front of me. It's the nicest place I've ever lived in my life. I turn to my left and see the small kitchen with granite countertops and top of the line stainless steel appliances. The granite is a deep blue with white and gold swirls throughout. The cabinets are white with gold glass pulls on the drawers.

The floors are a deep mahogany, rich and beautiful throughout the entire house. There is a dove grey sofa, and a deep blue chair and ottoman, with a white coffee table to tie in the kitchen cabinet colors. There's even a small dining room that has a tall, dark blue table with four chairs.

Madison takes my hand and pulls me toward the room that's to be my bedroom. It has a queen sized bed with two nightstands and a matching dresser, with a flat screen television that is mounted to the wall right above it. The bed's comforter is a deep purple with turquoise and gold throw pillows.

"You are too much," I whisper as tears steam down my cheeks. "This is all too much."

"You should have moved in as soon as it was finished. It's yours. You're our family," James murmurs, walking into the bedroom.

"We love you, so much," Madison whispers as she wraps her arms around my shoulders and pulls me in for a hug. James follows suit, pressing his front to Madison's back and wrapping his arms around us. This is my family.

When James and Madison go into the main house for the evening, that's when I climb into bed and my mind drifts toward Henrik.

I close my eyes, imagining his smile, his messy hair, and if I concentrate really hard, I can still imagine his smell. I've never had a man be as nice to me as Henny was.

I just wish that it could have all been real.

I wish that we could have had more, even if it was just one more day.

Henrik

I flip a coin in my hand while my friend Rueben talks about a new car he's just bought himself. Apparently, it's fantastic. I don't care about it, though; I don't care about much.

"Hen, what is your deal?" he asks.

"Huh?"

"Is it the black-haired Vegas girl? Is that what's got you all twisted up?" he asks. I lift my eyes to look at him and he's grinning like a fool. "She was quite the piece."

"Shut up, you arsehole," I growl.

"You ready to marry, Eugenie?" he asks, changing topics.

"And have my cock freeze off and break into a million shards?" I ask, arching a brow. He shivers at my words and shakes his head.

"Right."

"Yeah, *right*," I grunt.

"You're really going through with it, then?" he asks.

"I am," I shrug. "Family, country, and all that shit."

"You've been lost since Vegas. In all seriousness, the girl?"

"She's gone. It doesn't matter," I shrug.

"The look on your face says she does. You sure you can't try and make a go with her?" he asks, sounding almost hopeful.

"She's sweet, yeah. She's soft and warm, and nothing like the acceptable women I'm allowed to consider. She's also *American*, which makes her so far from acceptable it's ridiculous. So, yeah, I'm sure I can't try and make a go with her."

"Fuck. I used to want to be you, you know?" he admits. "Now, the older we get, the more shit responsibilities that get thrown at you, I don't envy you at all. Does that make me a shit friend?" he asks with a grin.

"That makes you smart. You see past all the smoke into the truth of it all. I don't have control over anything in my life, and that is the fucking worst."

I close my eyes for a second, seeing Riona when I do—wishing I didn't, but glad at the same time that I still remember every single curve of her soft body. *Fuck*. I want her again, and again, once more wouldn't be enough.

"What would happen if you just, took control?" he asks.

I think about his words. What *would* happen?

I honestly don't know. But I kind of wish I had enough fortitude to find out.

CHAPTER
Six

Caitriona

It's been four weeks since I moved into James and Madison's pool house. The paparazzi still haven't left me alone, though it's died down a bit. They're sticking to bothering me while I'm at work, or walking to and from my car in public, not so much James and Madison's house anymore—which I'm extremely thankful for.

Tonight, we're eating together around James and Madison's dining room, a family dinner of pasta from James' favorite restaurant. While I'm loving it, I can tell that there's something up with Madison. She's bouncing all over her chair and can't sit still.

"Mads, what is going on with you?" James finally asks, taking a sip of wine.

"I'm pregnant!" she blurts.

I stand as quickly as I can and run over to my friend, enveloping her in a giant hug. It takes us a minute to realize that James hasn't said anything. Both of us stop and look over at him. He's sitting across the table, a wine glass in his hand and his mouth hanging wide open.

"Go be with your husband. I'm going home," I murmur, giving her one last hug.

"No, stay and celebrate," she urges.

"Absolutely not. We'll celebrate soon with loads of chocolate and ice cream. Tonight, be with your husband." I turn and take my plate of food and fork, placing my hand on James' shoulder, giving it a squeeze. "Go to your wife, James."

I don't turn around to even catch a glimpse of their happiness on my way out of the house. This is a private moment between them. I'm so happy for my friends, but they need to be alone and relish in their joyous news. They've been trying so hard and have been stressing out so much about this, they deserve to relish in the happiness *together*, without a third-wheel.

Once I'm back in my own home, I turn on the television and, like a train wreck, I can't look away. There, in bright colors, is Henrik. He's standing with his brother and his brothers fiancée.

How had I not recognized him? I feel so foolish now, looking back. The security, the VIP treatment at the club, and the surprise in his eyes when he told me where he was from—it all makes sense now.

I turn up the volume and listen to the news on the royal family.

They're announcing his brother Philip's wedding date

and, at the same time, Henrik's engagement. The camera pans over to a woman standing at Henrik's side.

She's absolutely stunning.

The announcer says that she's tamed the badboy of the castle.

She's blonde and petite, dressed in a skirt suit with perfectly styled hair and makeup. She's everything I'm not, including from a royal family herself.

I can't comprehend anything else the reporters are saying. My focus is solely on Henrik. He's standing next to his brother and his new fiancée, *in a sweater*, with not a hint of the fun loving man I met just over a month ago in Vegas. My heart aches at the news and the sight of him.

I turn off the television, unable to hear anything else, unable to look at him a second longer—it hurts too badly.

One night shouldn't hurt this bad.

To see him with someone else shouldn't affect me the way that it does.

We had a connection.

I fell for him instantly.

As I chew on my bottom lip, the truth slaps me in the face—he wasn't single. I am the other woman. He cheated on her with me; he *had* to have.

I decide to change into my pajamas and go to bed. Today is a happy occasion for Madison and James, I don't need this dark cloud above our home. That's what thinking of Henrik does; it brings this dark cloud of doom over me. I can't have him, and I shouldn't even think about him.

Henrik

Standing next to my brother, in the hot as fuck sunshine, and trying to smile for the television cameras, in a fucking *sweater,* is my version of *hell.* Luckily, I like Philip's fiancée, Bee, so I'll endure this paraded shit show, just for her. I do not, however, like the woman at my right.

"You know now all attention will be on you, don't you?" Philip murmurs out of the side of his mouth.

"Yeah," I shrug.

"You should try and pick your own woman," Philip urges, trying to keep his voice down so the icicle standing next to me doesn't hear him.

"It doesn't matter."

"Henrik." He sighs but then, thankfully, drops the topic.

What I neglect to tell him is that it doesn't matter because I can't have the only girl I have ever wanted. Caitriona would never be accepted by my father and grandfather. I wouldn't be allowed to marry her, and though it's been five weeks since I have seen her, I've wanted nobody else since I had her. She's the only woman I desire. I've gone over the possible scenario in my head a million times and there's just no way in fuck my family would accept her.

I can't forget her—her infectious smile, her thick dark hair, or her gorgeous full body. She's nothing like I've ever had before, and yet she's *everything* I desire now.

Nobody else will do.

Nobody else is even appealing. And isn't that the fucker? I don't even *know* her. She was supposed to be my one last hurrah before settling down with the ice bitch, my one last shot of fun.

I'm not supposed to crave her the way that I do, and yet, I can't get her off of my mind. I was just Henrik to her, *just me*, and not a prince. A breath of fresh air that breathed life into me, that's how I describe Caitriona.

Once my public appearance is finished, I strip off the bullshit sweater, ditch the bitch at my side, and go to my car. I need some fresh air and a long drive to clear my head. I need to get into the right state of mind.

I can't obsess over a woman I can't have.

I need to let her go—if only it were so easy.

Caitriona

I wake up feeling terrible, the news of Henrik's engagement hitting me harder than it should—harder than I have any right for it to. I don't love him; I don't know him well enough to love him, but that doesn't take away my want of him. That doesn't take away the fact that once he marries this woman, there will be zero chance of us ever being together again. Not that we had much of a chance anyway.

I hear a knock on my door and I grab my robe, throwing it over my pajamas before opening the door. There, standing and looking sadder than they should for people who just found out they're about to have a baby, are James and Madison.

"Can we come in?" Madison asks.

I already know what they're going to say, based on their hesitancy.

"What's going on?" I ask.

"I didn't want to tell you this, but I know you'll find out sooner or later," James begins.

I look over at Madison who has suddenly become very interested in the throw pillow on the sofa.

"Just tell me, Jimmy," I urge.

"He got engaged yesterday. It was announced. Some Duchess or Lady or something or other. I don't get their monarchy system," he rambles.

I close my eyes as the pain slices right through my entire body, again. Hearing the words repeated doesn't dull the pain.

"I know. I saw the news last night," I murmur. "I suppose he can't stay single forever."

"It's only been a few weeks. That guy is such an asshole," Madison says.

"It doesn't matter, Mads. He's who he is, and I'm *nobody*. I knew I was never going to see him again, not after all the paparazzi and everything. I just hope that now they'll leave me the hell alone."

"That's the other thing," James mutters.

"What?"

"They're everywhere. There's more this time. I think you should sleep in the house for a while, until it all goes away," James suggests.

I don't bother responding verbally. I nod at both of them and then go to my room and pack a small bag with my necessities. When we step outside, I can hear them at the front of the house.

If it wasn't already bad enough that I watched on television as the only man I have ever felt an electric connection to announce his engagement, now I have reporters and paparazzi all over my best friends' front lawn, hoping to get a picture and a statement from me about the engagement.

I want to scream and act crazy.

I don't.

Instead, I go inside, shower and change, thankful that it's Sunday and I don't have to leave the house. Then, Madison and I spend the entire day vegging in her bed, eating junk, and watching sappy girl movies, and talking babies in between.

It's the most relaxing and stress-free day I've had since returning from Las Vegas. Henrik isn't brought up once, and eventually the parade of people leave. I know that it's only a brief moment of silence, but I'll take it. I hope that this is all over with soon, and that I'll be able to move on.

If I can move on.

The next day, I drag myself to work, only to find that the swarm of paparazzi that were at James and Madison's the day before are now in front of my building's entrance. I decide that enough is enough. I'll be silent no more. Madison and James have both told them to go away. But maybe if I tell them, they finally will.

"How do you feel about Prince Henrik's engagement?" one woman shouts out.

"I'm happy for him," I say with as much of a genuine smile as I can muster.

"Was it a surprise to you that he moved on so quickly?" a man asks.

"We had one weekend together. It was wonderful, but that's all it was. He's engaged now, and I'm glad that he's found happiness."

"Did you spend the night with the Prince? What was he like in bed," a woman shouts.

My face heats in embarrassment, but I ignore her. What we shared was so much more than I could describe in words. I may not remember every detail about the night we shared, but I sure as hell remember how he made me feel.

"Saw your boy got engaged," Natasha says with a fake pout on her lips.

I ignore her too.

By the end of the day, I feel like if I hear the word *engagement* one more time, I'll scream. It's all everybody could talk about. They all wanted to know if Prince Henrik called me personally to tell me about his upcoming nuptials. I wanted to yell that he didn't have my number so he couldn't call me; and even if he did, why *would* he call me?

My only freaking one-night stand, ever, and it's bound to haunt me—not only in my mind, but also in my everyday life—*forever*.

I slump into the sofa in James and Madison's living room with a heavy sigh, ready to be finished for the day. No, the *year*. Maybe by next year, none of these people will remember or care who the hell I am anymore.

"What's up?" Madison asks as she shovels cereal in her mouth.

"Why are you eating Lucky Charms?"

"I'm fucking starving," she shrugs as she pulls her legs into the oversized chair's seat.

"I want to disappear for a year," I admit.

"It'll die down," she says sympathetically.

"It's been over a month, Mads. He's engaged to somebody else and that freaking sucks, but you know what else sucks? Having to hear about it all day fucking long," I grind out.

"Robert Dayton begged me to go out on a double date with us and you," she blurts out.

"Do not tell me you said yes," I demand, narrowing my eyes on her.

"He's a partner, I couldn't say no. I need to make partner, and the sooner the better," she mutters.

"That guy is a creep, Mads."

"I know, I know, but James and I will be with you. It'll be fun. A free meal, if nothing else," she shrugs.

"When?"

"Friday night," she says, chewing on her bottom lip.

"Might as well end my week off with a bang," I sigh.

"I'm sorry. I can come up with an excuse to cancel. I shouldn't have said yes. I know how he is, and how he is with you."

"No, I'll do it. Maybe he isn't such an asshole when he's away from the office," I offer with a fake smile.

"He probably is," she mutters.

"I know," I agree.

The rest of the week goes by in a blur. The paparazzi haven't left me alone, and it seems as though they've actually gotten worse since I spoke to them. I thought that by now, by Friday, everything would have died down and they'd be onto something else. Henrik is engaged to another woman, why aren't they leaving me alone and bothering *her*?

I groan as soon as I walk through my front door. Tonight, I have to go on a double date with James and Mads, with Robert Dayton. I shiver in disgust. I really hope that he can tone down his douche-like personality for the evening, just one evening.

I flip through my clothes, trying to find something that is nice, but not overly sexy. I don't want to give the wrong impression. I'm not going home with him tonight.

In fact, I have no desire to have sex again anytime soon, with anybody. Being with Henrik was amazing, but the re-percussions of just one night have been a nightmare.

I decide on a black skirt and blouse; the skirt is a pen-cil shape that skims my knees with a small kick pleat in the back. The blouse has a V-neck front, showing off a little more cleavage than I would like, but it's classic and nice, with a matching back that makes it sexy without being *too* sexy.

I grab my nude high heels and slip those on before I touch up my make-up and hair. With just a few brushes of mascara, a darker shade of lipstick, and a refresh of my face powder, I fluff my curly hair and I'm ready.

Just as I'm taking my clutch from off of the bed, there's a knock at the door. I take the few steps toward the peephole and look out to see Robert waiting. He's dressed much like he is for work—dark blue suit pants, matching jacket, a black button-up shirt, sans tie, and he's opened a few buttons to show off his tanned chest. I close my eyes and take a deep breath, trying not to snarl my lips at the unbuttoned shirt and the slicked back blond hair.

"Robert," I greet as I open the door, a fake smile plas-tered on my lips.

"You look delectable this evening, Caitriona," he says as his eyes narrow in on my cleavage.

This is going to be a *long* night. Madison owes me big. *Huge.* I suppress my shiver of disgust at his words and his wandering gaze. Tonight, I have to suck it up. I'm doing this to try and move on and forget about Henrik, but I'm also doing this for Madison and her career. I know Robert's a prick. If I can have grace for just one dinner, then I'll have done my part and maybe all of this will help me move on with my life.

Once I've locked the pool house, Robert slides his hand along my lower back before it settles on my hip. I repeat to myself, over and over again, that this is just one evening. James and Madison will be there for support.

I can do this.

I will do this.

It's just dinner, how bad can it really be?

CHAPTER
Seven

Henrik

"WE HAVE AN EMERGENCY MEETING WITH HEAD OF security," Philip announces as he walks into my office.

"About what?" I ask, not looking up from my computer screen.

Today I'm working on my crown duties, instead of my venture capitalist company. I'm looking at a contract proposal for new tactical gear for our military. It's all very advanced, and very expensive, but this company is amazing. I think investing in them will really be a wise decision.

"Doesn't matter what it's about, it's now," Philip rambles.

I close and lock my computer before standing up and following my brother. I don't know what this meeting is about, I sure as fuck don't care, and neither do I want to go. I hate all this pomp bullshit.

I just want to spend my days alone, hiding from my new fiancée, Eugenie. She's a pain in my royal arse. Aside from being a general spoiled brat, she's a complete and total icicle. I always joked that I'd end up with one, now I've gone and done it. *Reality is a fucking cunt.*

Together, we enter the office, and I notice that my father is sitting in one of the two chairs that faces the head of security's obscene wooden desk; my mother is in the other chair. I'm surprised to see my mother in attendance, as she has never been in on anything that has to do with business matters in the past.

Mother does her own thing; she has her own business to attend to. She enjoys her charity work around the world, something my father rolls his eyes at. Father doesn't like how her work takes her away from his side. He's just as spoiled as Eugenie.

Philip and I sit down on the sofa, and I stretch my long legs out in front of me, crossing them at the ankle. I'm ready to be done for the day. It's past tea time, and all I can think about is going home and drinking a few glasses of scotch before going to sleep, so that I can get up and repeat this mundane day all over again.

"What's this about, Malcom?" I ask, prompting the head of security, who is sitting behind his desk.

Malcom is short and round, smokes heavily, and drinks like a fish. He's normally loud and funny, but today there's no smile on his face, and he looks a bit perturbed.

"Well, Henrik, I was getting all of your wedding documents in order, readying them so that when the date is closer, the process will be speedier. Except, I've hit a snag," he mutters.

I watch as my mother's eyes grow wide and her lips purse together. I have a feeling she's hoping something is amiss with Eugenie's background. She adores her as much as I do— as in, *not at all*.

"Snag?" I question.

"Seems you will be committing bigamy if you wed Eugenie in six months," he announces.

Several emotions cross over my mother and father's faces, but I can't focus on them. I'm in my own state of shock. Is he really saying that I'm already married? And if he is, then how can that be? I think I would fucking remember getting *fucking married*.

"What's this?" I whisper.

"It seems one, Henrik Stuart, married a one, Caitriona Geneva Grace, almost two months ago, in Las Vegas, Nevada U.S.A.," he says.

In the distance, I hear my mother gasp, my brother groan, and my father growl.

Riona.

I haven't stopped thinking about the wild, dark haired beauty every single day since I left her passed out in bed. She was gorgeous, and fun, and sweet, but there was no way I *married* her, is there? I wouldn't do that to my family, to my grandfather—to *her*.

If I did, I married her and left her. What kind of piece of shit am I?

"Wouldn't the paps have gotten ahold of all this?" I ask, dumbfounded. "This must be a mistake. Yes, I was with her, but I don't recall *marrying* her."

"We've been trying to keep it a secret, but the paparazzi have discovered her name—not your marriage, but her name. She's been all over social media," Malcom admits.

"Why am I just hearing this now? What the hell?" I demand.

"You've been staying focused on work, on your duties. I felt it best we not derail you, especially with some little American tart you spent all of one night with," my father announces.

"I should have been informed," I grind out, refusing to look my father in the eye. The controlling fucking bastard.

Malcom stands and waddles toward me before shoving a piece of paper at my chest. I take it and look down, a certificate of marriage, complete with my signature. The only girl that has ever plagued my mind day-in and day-out is my *wife*.

We're married.

I notice there's another piece of paper behind the certificate, and I bring that to the front. It blows my mind. There, in color, is a photograph of the two of us.

I'm in my jeans and button-up shirt that I wore on our date, my hair is a mess, my eyes rimmed red from alcohol, and there, standing next to me, is Riona.

She's wearing that ridiculous scrap of fabric she insinuated was a dress. It's too short and too small, but there she is, plastered to my side with a gigantic smile on her face.

I look from her back to me and see that I, too, am smiling a wide grin. I look ecstatic. I feel a presence at my side and see that my mother has stood and is now sitting down next to me on the sofa. I watch as she reaches down and takes the photograph from my grasp.

"This is her, Henrik?" she asks, already knowing the answer. "In all the photographs I've seen, I've never actually been able to see her face."

The only person I've confided in is my mother. She understands me. She knows how I think and how I feel. I told her that I met Riona, that I fell hard for her instantly. She knows that I wish to marry for love and not for status or for the good of the country. She also knows that because of who I am, those things are not possible. She suggested that I date within my circle, and hopefully one day I would find a woman that I could love. My desire to date and love isn't there. All there is, is Riona, in the back of my mind, filling my thoughts with—*what if.*

"Yes, mum, that's my Riona," I murmur, unable to take my eyes off of her face.

"This tart, this *girl*, you *married her*?" my father roars, snatching the photo from my mother's grasp.

I do not react; I only nod my affirmation.

"You'll get it annulled. You'll pay her off, if you have to. This will not reach the media," he announces before he storms out of the room, dropping the photo onto the floor.

Philip reaches down and picks it up. I watch as his eyes scan the image of Riona and me. Then he nods once and looks up.

"She's beautiful, Henrik. Now I know why it was so hard for you to leave her be," he murmurs.

My brother has a much softer heart these days. He's about to be married, in only a few weeks, and he and his fiancée have been talking about children. He loves his wife with his whole heart. He's been against my engagement with Eugenie from the start. He, like my mother, wants me to marry for love.

"You will go to her, you will tell her everything, and she

will sign the papers. You will have this marriage annulled, but you will do it gently," my mother informs me as she wipes her eyes and practically runs out of the office.

The hesitancy in her voice tells me that she didn't want to say the words out loud. I know her well enough to assume that she wanted to tell me to go, get my girl, and come home; but she would not, could not, ever verbalize such a thing. She would never go against my father—*ever*.

"I have her address in America right here," Malcolm says, handing me another piece of paper.

"Do you know anything else about her life?" I ask, hoping for any piece of her.

"Sorry, Henrik, just her address. I can dig up more, but you'll be leaving within the hour for America. Philip, I think you should accompany him," Malcom suggests.

Philip nods as we both stand. I don't question why he wants Philip at my side. I already know. He wants him to hold me accountable. He wants to ensure that I'll do what I'm supposed to do.

Philip has always been the responsible brother.

I've always been the screw up.

This whole thing proves that, once again, I'm the fuck up.

"You'll bring Bee?" I ask him as we make our way toward our living quarters.

He nods, never verbalizing his answer. We make plans to meet in twenty minutes and then separate.

As I pack my bags, the only thought that runs through my head is the fact that I'm married. I'm married to the only girl I have ever *felt* anything for. I've been married to her for weeks, and I don't remember a goddamn thing about it—nothing other than the club and the morning I left her alone, thinking I would never see her again.

I close my eyes after zipping up my suitcase. I think about what Malcom said. How the paps know who she is, that they've been hounding her.

I curse aloud.

How could I have been so careless, so stupid and self-ish? She's probably been living in a nightmare, a nightmare I created for her. I should have never taken her out in public. I should have been more careful. I should have been more aware, and I shouldn't have only been thinking with my fucking cock.

One hour later, we're all in the jet and taking off toward Portland, Oregon. Philip, Bee, a team of security, and me. There's a hotel with several suites already booked and waiting for us, along with a few rented cars.

Philip suggested that we arrive at Riona's home without security at our sides, so he rented a car for us to take there. Our security will be there, of course—they're always there—but they'll be hidden.

I agree. The less attention we can draw to ourselves, the better. I don't know what awaits me when I am reunited with Riona.

Will she remember me at all?

Will she be angry toward me?

I have no clue what to expect. Although she's technically my wife, I don't really know her.

I *lust* for her, I *desire* her, but I don't *know* much about her.

"Are you okay?" Bee asks.

Her voice is soft, interrupting my racing mind. She's so very kindhearted and soft spoken, much like my mother. I completely understand why Philip adores her and is happily marrying her. She's lovely inside and out.

Philip dated within the circle of acceptable women, always with the family's wishes, the crown's wishes in mind, from the time he was a teenager.

He's never been rebellious, and when he met Beatrice at a party, he immediately found her attractive; but Philip didn't approach her, not until he researched exactly who she was.

I made fun of him for it, laughed at him even. He just said to me very plainly—*just because I find her pretty doesn't mean I need to take it any further than gazing upon her, Hen. Not until I know that she is an option. What good would it be to hurt her that way, if we liked each other but knew it could go no further?*

Now, I understand exactly what my brother meant.

"No, I'm not okay," I sigh, answering her question. "I swear I didn't know we were married. I don't know if *she* knows or not. I just left her the next morning. She probably hates me," I murmur.

Although, Riona hating me is the least of my worries. If the media finds out about this, it's going to be catastrophic for both her and me.

"I'm sure she doesn't hate you. Though, she may not be thrilled that you left her the morning after your nuptials," she says. "Do you really not remember anything?"

"No, Bee, I really don't remember. I remember dancing with her at the club, and drinking, I remember getting into a cab. I remember some *adult* activities," I say clearing my throat before I continue, "lastly, I remember waking up with a raging hangover, Philip ringing me up, and her lying next to me looking like a fucking dream."

"Fuck, Henrik, you've got yourself in a right tough spot," my brother mutters.

"No, shit," I chuckle.

I lay my head back against my seat and close my eyes. I need to try and rest. I have a feeling that the next few days are going to be an emotionally taxing hell for me.

I have no idea what I'm going to be walking in to. Will she laugh at the whole scenario and just sign the papers? Will she make a scene and alert the media?

The fact is, as much as I think about her and want her, I truly do not *know* a damn thing about her. I don't know what she's capable of and what she isn't.

I awake as the plane is landing. We're at a small airport, desolate except for two cars waiting for us. I watch as security unloads their bags and equipment into one car and then Philip and I follow suit, loading our luggage into the other.

Once I've entered the hotel's information into the car's GPS system, and remind myself that American's drive on the wrong side of the road—not the correct side, like we do—I point the car toward the hotel to drop our bags off and freshen up a bit.

The hotel is nice; as nice as Portland has to offer, I'm sure. It could be a rat infested shit-hole and I wouldn't care at this point. The only thing I want to do is lay my own eyes on Riona. I want to see her, in person, talk with her, perhaps even hold her.

What kind of fucking torture am I trying to inflict upon myself? *Hold her?*

I run my hands through my hair, tugging on the strands in frustration.

"It's late, Henrik. How about we rest tonight and then go

over first thing in the morning?" Philip asks as we ride the lift toward our room.

I'm so caught up in my own mind, I hadn't even realized that he and Bee were still standing with me.

"No, I want to see her tonight," I demand. "I'm leaving in twenty minutes, with or without the two of you."

I don't give them an opportunity to speak. The lift doors open and I march toward the direction of my room, opening my door and slipping inside. I need space. I need to breathe, alone, for at least five minutes. I walk toward the bedroom, noticing my bag has already been placed on the luggage rack. I grab a change of clothes and rush to the bathroom to take a shower.

Fifteen minutes later, I'm downstairs, waiting at valet, when Philip joins me at my side.

"Bee?" I ask.

"Resting. She will want to meet your Caitriona. Tomorrow, though," he mutters.

I nod my agreement as the car pulls up. I quickly hand the valet a tip and slide into the driver's seat of the car before typing in the address that Malcom gave me.

The car ride is silent the entire way to Caitriona's home. I think Philip is afraid to talk. If I were him, I would probably be afraid to talk to me, too. I'm feeling a mix of so many different emotions, as though I'm about to explode. I'm excited, angry, nervous, and fucking sad.

Anger, I can handle; sadness, I cannot. I despise feeling sad. It's an emotion I don't allow myself to feel. Though, right now, it's the biggest one running through me.

I pull up to the address and note that it's a nice, quiet neighborhood. It looks like a family home, though. It's a big two-story with brick and rock on the front, a large front yard, and a three car garage.

This home does not say *single-woman*; this home says *family woman*. I wonder if she lied to me. Perhaps she has a man and I was just a night of fun. She is doing quite well for herself, for a girl who had never consumed champagne before.

"This is a nice neighborhood. Perhaps she lives with her dad and mum," Philip remarks as my hands tighten around the steering wheel.

I look over at him and notice that he's grinning at me. He's already read my mind, the smug-bastard. I hadn't thought about Riona living with her parents. The dread I felt just moments ago quickly leaves my body and I grin back at him.

"Let's go, then," I grunt, opening the car door and swinging my legs out.

We walk up the front pathway to the porch. I'm too nervous to knock, so Philip rings the buzzer for me. I feel that dread and anger instantly cover me like a heavy wool cloak as soon as the door opens. A man stands there, a man around my own age, definitely *not* a father.

Rage sweeps through my veins.

I want to kill the bastard.

I clinch my jaw and my fists simultaneously. Words are not coming to me. All I can see is red hot rage.

"We are looking for Caitriona Grace; do we have the proper address?" Philip asks, noticing that I am incapacitated.

"Cait? Uh yeah, can I tell her who is asking?" he asks.

The man is tall, but he's thin and has light hair. Caitriona shouldn't be with a guy like him. She should be with a man who can handle her curvy body. I know for a fact that this prick can't possibly know how to handle her. Not like I can—like I *have*.

"I am Philip, this is my brother, Henrik. Our late visit is somewhat of a personal matter," Philip, ever the diplomat, explains.

I watch as the man's eyes grow five times their size. Shit, he recognizes us.

"Holy fucking shit. Umm, Cait's out back. But right now really isn't a good time," he mutters.

"It's the perfect time," I grunt before I push past him and walk through his house.

Vaguely, I hear both his voice and that of Philip's behind me, but I'm on a mission to get to my Riona. I walk through the kitchen and open the door that leads to what I assume is the backyard.

As soon as I step out of the house and into the cool Oregon air, I see her. I stop abruptly. She's standing with her back to me and another man's hands are around her waist. I can't hear what she's saying, but it doesn't matter.

I march toward her, *my* precious girl.

CHAPTER
Eight

Caitriona

"THANK YOU FOR TONIGHT, ROBERT," I MURMUR.

I don't tell him that I had a good time, because that would be a down right lie. I don't lie, and I'm not about to inflate his already gigantic ego. He takes my thanks as an invitation and wraps his arms around me, his fingertips pressing against my waist.

Lifting my hands, I press them against his chest. Pressing firmly, I try to get away, to get him off of me.

"You can thank me properly—without words," he murmurs as his face starts to dip closer to mine.

I wrench my head back and try to escape his obvious intentions.

"Take your hands off of my wife," a low accented voice booms.

My entire body freezes, and I feel a tingle run down my spine. I know that voice. I may have only heard it for one night, but I could never forget it. Not in a million years.

Henrik.

"Your *wife*? I think you're mistaken, buddy," Robert says, his voice challenging.

"I think I know my own wife," Henrik says, his voice a bit closer this time.

"Please, Robert, let me go," I whisper.

Not only do I want his hands off of me, I want to see Henrik. It's been almost two months since I've laid eyes on him in person. I need to see him. It's not a want, and it's not a desire, it's a *need* that's rooted so deep inside of me that I don't think anything could stand in my way, except Robert's obnoxious iron grip on my waist.

"No, you went out with me tonight, this guy can fuck off," Robert growls.

"If you don't take your prick hands off of my *wife*, we're going to have a serious fucking problem," Henrik shouts.

Luckily, Robert decides to release me. As quickly as I can, I turn to face the man I've been dreaming about. The man who left me the morning after the best night of my life. The man I had no clue was a royal *prince*.

The man I never thought I would see again.

"Henny," I whisper, looking up into his green eyes.

He doesn't say a word as he takes the few strides he needs to be directly in front of me.

"The fuck?" Robert says from behind me.

I imagine him stomping like a toddler, but I'm too mesmerized by Henrik to bother turning around to see.

"Piss off," Henrik mutters.

There's movement behind me. When the door into the house slams closed, I know that Robert has left. We're alone now.

"Let's go inside, Riona," Henrik mutters.

I nod and take my key with a shaky hand, turning the lock and opening my door. Once we both step inside, Henrik closes and locks the door behind him before he leans his back against the closed door.

His eyes are glued to mine and have me pinned to my spot in the entryway. If I reach out, I could touch him; but he's not looking at me with lust in his eyes. He's not looking at me with any expression at all.

"Who was that prick?" he asks, finally speaking.

"Robert Dayton, a partner at the firm Madison works for," I state.

"And you're shagging him?" he asks, arching a brow.

"Not that it's really your business, but, no. I went on a double date with him, James, and Madison. I didn't really want to go. I did it as a favor to Madison," I explain.

"So your friend is pimping you out?" he asks.

I reach out and slap him across the face before I gasp in surprise at my actions. I've never hit anybody, *ever*. I've also never had a man insinuate I whored myself out for any reason. His head shifts to the side and then he brings it back. His eyes find mine again, instantly.

"He touched you," Henrik whispers.

"I didn't ask him to."

Henrik doesn't say another word. Instead, he closes the distance between us, and his lips crash against mine without a word spoken.

I moan as soon as his hands wrap around my waist and

glide down to cup my ass. Henrik's tongue takes that opportunity to invade my mouth, owning me as if it were always meant just for me.

"Riona, my sweet precious Riona," he murmurs against my lips.

"We can't do this," I warn as his lips kiss down the column of my neck.

"Why? We're married," he whispers against my flesh as he works his way down to the swells of my breasts.

"No, no we're not; not really. And you're engaged," I state, placing my hands on his shoulders and shoving him slightly.

Henrik ignores my protest and smashes his lips to mine, his hand lifting to twist in the back of my curls and his hips pushing against me, his hard length pressing against my stomach.

I whimper and he takes that as an invitation. I lift my hands to push him away but end up wrapping them around his neck and pressing myself closer to his chest.

He unzips my skirt, pushing it down my hips, and it pools at my feet. Then he picks me up by my thighs and walks me over to the front of the couch. I lift my face from his and gasp at the fact that he can actually carry me. He doesn't respond to my reaction; rather, he wraps his fingers around the hem of my shirt and wrenches it over my head, throwing it somewhere behind him.

"Fucking hell," he whispers as he looks at me, standing in my bra and panties.

"Henrik," I murmur.

"You're fucking gorgeous. My hazing memory did not serve any justice at all," he rasps.

"We shouldn't do this," I whisper.

"No, this is exactly what we should do, Riona," he grunts as he unhooks my bra and pulls the straps down my arms, exposing my breasts. "*Fuck*, yeah—exactly what we should be doing."

I watch as he quickly removes his own clothes before he wraps his fingers in my panties and yanks them down my legs, then his hand is shoved between my thighs. He fills me in an instant with his fingers, and I whimper.

"So wet," he whispers against my breast, sucking a nipple into his mouth.

"Henny," I sigh as I roll my hips.

"Are you going to take your husband's cock?" he mumbles against my nipple.

"Oh, god," I moan, letting my head drop as I ride his hand.

I'm on the verge, so close that I can practically taste my orgasm, then he pulls his fingers from my center, wraps his hands around the backs of my knees and bends them so that I fall on my ass, on the couch.

"*Henny*," I hiss before I gasp as he fills me with one quick thrust.

My legs wrap around his hips, my high heels digging into the flesh of his hard ass, and he fucks me. His thrusts are hard and fast. His knees are propped on the edge of the sofa for his body's support, his hands next to my head on the back. His green eyes focus completely on me, and his top teeth sink into his bottom lip.

"This cunt, *fuck*, you feel so good," he rasps as he moves in and out of me.

"Oh, my god," I murmur as my body shakes.

"Come all over me, precious. Be a good girl, now, and

come," he urges.

His soft demand, mixed with the praise, is too damn much.

His strokes come faster, harder, and more erratic when his hand slips from the back of the couch and wraps around the back of my hair, tangling in the strands before he tightens his grasp and yanks back—hard.

"Come. Make it happen," he grunts, his eyes wild.

I slip one of my hands between us and stroke my clit with a whimper that turns into a long moan. His fingers tighten again in my hair as soon as I gasp and my entire body stills as I come around him.

He doesn't stop his movements, doesn't stop the way he pounds inside of me, not until I feel his cock twitch inside of me as he stretches me even more, filling me with his release. Henrik's eyes widen, almost in surprise before he lets out a long groan.

"We really are married, Caitriona," he murmurs, against my neck.

"How is that possible?" I ask trying to get my wits about me and catch my breath. "It was Vegas and it was, like, three in the morning *with* an *Elvis* impersonator," I ramble.

"You remember it?"

"You don't?" I whisper, as he pulls out of me.

Henrik's brows are furrowed and I watch as he pulls on his jeans and then hands me my clothes. My mind is racing, wondering what the hell he's thinking as I put my clothes back on quickly, not wanting to be so vulnerable for this conversation.

He doesn't remember *anything*, not even marrying me.

"I'm sorry, Riona. I don't remember anything from the

time we left the bar until the time we were in your room," he mutters pulling his shirt on.

"At least you remember *that* part."

"Burned into my memory banks for eternity, precious," he rumbles, cupping my cheek with his palm.

"So we're really married?" I gasp. "You're engaged *and* we just had sex."

"I know," he nods with a slight grin.

"I'm the other woman, *again*. Oh, my god," I say as I stand up and then fall back down to the sofa in disbelief, the reality of the news finally hitting me.

"Technically, *she's* the other woman. We were married before Eugenie and I ever really met," he says with a grin.

"Oh, my god—*oh, my god*," I repeat, still in complete shock.

"You look ill. Are you okay?" he asks, walking toward me and crouching down in front of me.

I look up and am face to face with him. He's beautiful; classically handsome with a chiseled strong jaw, and stubble that my fingers itch to feel.

"We're married and you're engaged, and oh, my god," I say, repeating the scenario, unable to look away from his face—afraid that if I do, I might forget what he looks like. This could very well be the last time I see him this close.

"I don't love her. Hell, I don't even *like* her, Riona," he mutters.

"It doesn't matter. You're engaged and the media—*oh, holy shit*—the media," I say as my stomach drops.

"They won't come near you again," he says, lifting his hand to rest against the side of my neck.

"They haven't left me alone since they found out who I

was. *I had to move, Henrik,*" I shout as I narrow my eyes on him.

"Move?" he asks in confusion.

"Do you think I've always lived in Madison's pool house? I used to live in a studio apartment on my own. Someone broke into my apartment in the middle of the night when I was asleep in bed. The police and James came. He refused to let me live alone another night."

"Holy fuck, precious," he breathes as he sinks to his knees and moves his free hand to cup my cheek. I don't realize that I'm crying until his thumb wipes one of my tears away.

"Never again," he murmurs.

"How are you going to stop it? Once they find out, once they find out it's going to be an even bigger nightmare," I blubber.

"I don't know yet, but I will figure it out," he states.

A knock at the door interrupts our discussion, and I watch as he stands and greets whoever is standing at the other side.

"It's my brother," Henrik announces, opening the door.

I watch as a lighter haired version of Henrik walks into the small pool house. He's cleaner shaven, and a bit thinner than Henrik, but there's no denying that they're siblings. His brother eyes me up and down from my seated position on the sofa before giving me a sad smile.

I must look like a disaster from the shock and the tears that I've just cried, plus the round of unbelievable sex we had. I cringe to myself hoping it's not obvious we've just screwed.

"We need to let these people rest for the evening, Henrik. We'll schedule an appointment tomorrow and get all of the necessary paperwork handled then," he murmurs.

"Paperwork?" I ask as my eyes dart from Henrik to his brother.

"The annulment," his brother answers with a nod.

"If, if that's what needs to be done, of course, Henny," I mutter, more to myself than anybody else, feeling as though a knife has stabbed me in the chest.

"Henny?" his brother questions.

"We'll discuss everything tomorrow," Henrik murmurs. "Let's go, Philip."

Henrik doesn't look at me before he leaves. He turns and walks away without a backward glance, a move he seems to have perfected since he did it weeks ago in Vegas.

I stay seated on the sofa, unable to move, unsure of how I'm actually breathing. I'm just staring at the closed door, wishing for him to walk back through. Wanting nothing more than for something to change, for him to declare *something* for me.

I'm not naïve to believe that I'm in love with him, or that he could be in love with me, but there is something between us. At least, to me—there's something between us.

The door swings open and instead of Henrik filling my doorway, it's Madison. We don't speak. One look at me, and she knows all she needs to. She rushes to my side and wraps her arms around me. Burying my face in her neck, I cry.

I wail because the fantasy has disappeared, and reality has set in. He's marrying another woman and I'm a stain. A stain he wishes to rid from his past, to brush away and pretend never happened. He wanted one last taste of me, and I gave in, just like I did in Vegas.

At least I won't have to wonder *what-if* anymore. I know the answer now. He found me. He knows who I am, and he doesn't want me. I was fun—for the night. I was never meant to be anything but that. I built us up too much in my own mind, like a silly little girl—like my mother.

Madison holds me until I fall asleep in her arms. I can hear James' voice in the background as she moves around and places a pillow under my head before she covers me up with a throw blanket. My best friends in the world, my only family, the only people that I can count on to love me and to care for me.

Tomorrow, I'll have to be strong; but for tonight, I need to be broken. I'll break again when he leaves me to go back to his regular life. I'll pick up the pieces and I'll move on. Maybe not right away; no, I think I need to feel this.

I've been broken so many times that I should be used to it. My mother hasn't wanted me, and no man has ever stayed, yet the fantasy that Henrik might come for me one day, that's shattered.

It's silly.

It's completely and totally silly, yet it hurts so much more than any other shattered dreams I've had in the past.

Henrik

"I don't want to talk," I interrupt Philip before he can even get a word out.

"She's lovely in person," he murmurs.

"I told you that I didn't want to talk," I bark.

"You like her, truly you do," he says with a nod.

"It doesn't matter if I do."

"Oh, I don't know. You *are* legally married," he points out.

"Let me point out just a couple reasons why it doesn't matter. One, she's not royal. Two, grandfather, and three, father. Anything else that you can think of just adds to the dramatics of why it doesn't fucking matter," I grind out through a clenched jaw.

I do like her. I like her a fuck of a lot, and leaving her tonight was even harder than leaving her in Las Vegas all those weeks ago. Seeing that prick's hands on her, knowing that when the papers I have are signed, she'll have other men's hands on her, and she'll even marry another man one day, that makes me rage filled. Then, being inside of her again, it was like fucking fireworks. She was absolutely everything I'd remembered and even more.

"Mother would back you."

"Mother would be steamrolled and you know it," I huff.

"You don't give her enough credit, Henrik."

"It doesn't matter. I've come out publicly and it's been announced that Eugenie and I are engaged. What a cluster fuck of a scandal would bringing Riona home cause?" I point out.

"Eugenie is an ice-cold bitch. When the day is done and you're lying in bed next to your wife, the rest of the world doesn't matter. All that will matter is the woman you hold and make love to, the woman you want to carry your heirs. That's what matters. Politics and the crown are rubbish and you know it."

"You're a fucking rebel underneath it all, Philip. Why am I just discovering this?" I ask with a chuckle.

"I'm far from a rebel. But I saw the way she looked at you, Henrik. She looks at you the way Bee looked at me when we were first together. It's not love yet, but that girl, she adores you. Eugenie only wants a title and status. Caitriona, she only wants *you*. Take tonight and think it over. Choosing her will cause a rift and it will cause dramatics, but are you prepared to live a life without her? Without at least finding out if there's something more there?"

Philip pulls the car to the valet at the hotel and faces me as he turns the engine off, giving me one last piece of his wisdom for the night.

"I know my brother. I know you, and I know that although you are impulsive and reckless, you are not *that* impulsive and reckless. You may have been drunk, but you knew what you were doing when you married her. It wasn't for nothing. It's up to you to decide if there was a real reason behind it. Nobody can make that call but you."

Without allowing me to speak, I watch as he steps out of the car and walks into the hotel. I sit for a few moments before I follow suit and make my way up to my room. My mind and heart are heavy tonight.

The decision I have to make affects so many people; my family, Caitriona, her family, and to some extent, the rest of the world. Though the impact on the world will not be great, it will go down in history books.

It will be a scandal, and Eugenie will not receive it well. Not in the slightest. These are all factors I must weigh, and I only have a few hours left to weigh them. Then, I must decide, if I give a flying fuck how Eugenie feels about anything—which I don't. She's a spoiled, entitled, ice cold cunt and the only thing about this situation, that would piss her off, would be the fact that she won't be made a princess in a few months' time.

I'll be heading back over to James and Madison's home tomorrow to either take Caitriona home with me as my wife, or ask her to dissolve our union with her signature on the annulment papers.

CHAPTER
Nine

Caitriona

LOOK OUTSIDE MY WINDOW AND WONDER IF I HAVE enough time to take a swim before Henrik returns. I don't know what time he's returning, and swimming would give me a way to release the nervous, anxious energy I have flowing through my body. Without another thought, I hurry and change into my swimsuit. It isn't sexy, just a black one piece that has the sides cut out.

I dive into the pool and start to swim laps, thankful that James turned it into a heated pool when he renovated the entire home and pool house. The talent on that man is astounding to me. It never ceases to amaze me the beautiful things he can accomplish with the combination of his mind and hands. I wish I could find a man like him for myself. Robert Dayton is certainly *not* that man, and unfortunately,

Henrik isn't either.

Once I'm physically exhausted, I step out of the pool and dry off. A throat clears behind me and I jump with a screech before I turn around to see Henrik standing just a few feet from me, his hands in his pockets, and a smirk tipping his lips.

"How long have you been there?" I ask bringing the towel up to cover myself.

"Don't," he murmurs, stepping close to me.

I don't move.

I'm frozen as he lifts his hand and traces my breast where my swimsuit's edge is. Just along my skin, just enough to send goosebumps over my entire body—as if he hadn't fucked me so hard last night that I still feel him between my legs today.

"Henrik," I whisper.

"Henny."

"What?"

"You—*you* call me Henny," he murmurs.

I open my mouth to ask him what on earth he's talking about when I feel his lips brush against mine. His kiss, though soft, sweet, and brief, renders me speechless. I lift my arms and bury my fingers in his velvety hair as he deepens the kiss. His tongue fills my mouth as his hands roam down my bare sides.

Last night was hurried and frantic, this kiss is luscious, slow and sweet, making me melt a little closer to him.

"We can't," I whisper against his lips, refusing to open my closed eyes.

"We can't *not*, Riona," he murmurs. "I'm supposed to be married in less than six months to a cold, bitter, spoiled bitch. Most of my family will probably never accept you, and we're sure to be a scandal. You'll be splashed all over the paps, more than you currently are as it is," he says.

I finally open my eyes and look into his serious gaze. I'm not sure why he's explaining these things to me. These are things that I already know, aside from the news of his fiancée being a spoiled bitch—though I could have probably guessed that if I were to judge her at a glance. Let's be honest, I did judge her, a long time ago, out of nothing but pure jealousy.

"What are you trying to say to me right now?" I ask, needing clarification from his rambling.

"Precious, you're my wife. You're mine and I made you that way for a reason. I didn't sleep last night. I couldn't, because all I could do was think. All I could think about was *you*. If I left you, then another man could and would claim you one day. Another man would put his child inside of you, and that isn't something I can accept."

"We don't even know each other, and you're engaged," I point out.

"I don't care. *You're mine*. You were meant to be mine, and I'm keeping you," he whispers as his head dips and he places kisses against my neck.

"Henny—," I breathe.

"Don't. Don't say anything. You're not signing the annulment or the non-disclosure. You're coming home with me, as my wife and by my side. We'll face the shit storm together. I don't know what's going to happen with us, but I do know that it isn't going to be easy, luv. I also know that we met and married for a reason, so we're going to find that reason out." I start to protest, but his lips touch mine again.

I melt into him, I melt for him, just like I did the first time he kissed me; just like I've done for every kiss after.

Henrik picks me up and carries me inside of the pool house, locking the door behind him before he takes me into my bedroom. He sets me down on my feet and slips his fingers beneath the straps of my suit before he gently slides it down my body, stripping me completely bare, just as I'd done for him weeks ago.

I hold my breath as he lifts his hand again and takes the tie out of my unruly hair before running his fingers through my wet locks.

Henrik then takes a step back and undresses himself, never saying a word—never taking his eyes off of mine.

"You're beautiful," I murmur, my eyes drifting from his messy dark hair to his wide broad chest, skirting over his lean muscular frame, and then landing on his cock, hard and waiting.

"No, precious. I am just a man. You are completely spectacular."

I don't respond, knowing that I'm not what he says I am, but enjoying the words nonetheless. I gasp when his strong hands wrap around my waist and he lifts me slightly before laying me down on the bed. I spread my thighs to accommodate his hips between them. With his eyes still completely focused on mine, Henrik skims his fingers up my body to my breast, squeezing my flesh with a moan.

"*Fuck*, these tits, Riona," he murmurs.

I moan when he pinches my nipple and tugs, sending desire through my body immediately. I wrap my fingers around his shoulders and tip my hips in an invitation. This is so different from last night. He's taking his time, and it's absolutely wonderful.

"Does your cunt need me, mmm?" he asks as his fingers

leave my breast only to caress my center.

"*Henrik*," I whisper as he slides one finger inside of me.

I moan as he pulls out and swirls his finger around my clit before he plunges back inside of me, two fingers, filling and stretching me.

"Do you want me, Riona? Do you want your husband?"

"Yes," I moan as my hips search for more of him.

I watch in fascination as a smile reaches his lips before he moves his other hand from the bed, where it had been propping him up, to twist in my hair at the nape of my neck. The other hand leaves my core, and without warning, he's inside of me.

One thrust, and his cock is fully seated to the root, causing a gasp to escape me.

"Wrap your legs around me, precious, and take me in," he growls.

I lift my legs and wrap them as high as I can around his waist. He shivers above me, but I need him to move, to take and to own. I move my hands from his shoulders to twist in his hair lifting my hips slightly as my eyes stay on his. He's completely focused on me, his eyes roaming my face.

"Fuck me, Riona," he groans.

I do, I squeeze my thighs around him and hold onto his body, lifting my hips until he murmurs for me to stop.

Then, with a grin, he begins to pump in and out of me with long, lazy strokes.

"I didn't want to leave you that morning, Riona. You have to believe me," he explains as he continues with his never breaking rhythm.

"Henny," I gasp, unable to concentrate on his words; hearing them, but unable to respond as my body climbs higher and closer toward my release.

"Fuck, you feel so good, precious," he whispers as a sheen of sweat appears on his forehead.

"Let go, Henrik, let go," I urge.

He is holding back, and I don't want him to. I want him all, every single piece of him. I want that rough man from last night to take and take, and demand from me.

"Come back with me, make this dream a reality," he murmurs into my ear as he starts to thrust harder and faster inside of me.

I don't answer, I can't. All I can do is cry out as my orgasm rips through me with an intensity I have never felt before in my life. Henrik roars as his own takes over, and he comes inside of me.

"What about Eugenie?" I ask after my breathing has come back to a semblance of normal.

"What about her?" he grunts.

"If I come back with you as your wife, what happens to her?" I ask as I run my fingers up and down his spine.

"I'll tell her before we even touch down on British soil. There's no love lost there, Riona. I've never even shagged her," he murmurs as he sucks on my neck.

"What?" I ask in surprise.

He chuckles as he rolls to the side, gathering me in his arms. I press my cheek against the warmth of his chest and wait for him to speak.

"A marriage of status, not love. We don't even like each other, Riona. I didn't even propose properly. It was all arranged for us through our PR people and our parents," he shrugs, as if its no big deal.

"But you were going to marry her, have children with her

and everything?"

"Yes, I was prepared to do that," he says, nodding.

"*Forever*?"

"Forever. But then you came along, or at least you reappeared," he murmurs as his fingers comb my still damp hair.

"Are you doing all of this just to get out of your engagement?" I ask, chewing on my bottom lip nervously.

"I thought all night long. Naturally, I'm more of an impulsive person than the other members of my family, but I'm not *that* impulsive. I married you, even if I was completely pissed. I did it and I don't think I should question it.

"I can't discount the fact that not for one day since I left Las Vegas have I not thought about you, dreamt of you, and regretted the way I walked away. Then to find out we're married? It's too much to simply be a coincidence. I know the repercussions are bound to be grave and uncomfortable, but when I fall asleep at night, I want to do it with you at my side, nobody else."

"Henny," I choke as tears fall from my eyes.

"Let's get this news over with and tell our families," he mutters.

"Can you kiss me one more time before all hell breaks loose?" I practically beg.

"I'll kiss you every day for the rest of your life, if you'll allow it," he murmurs as his lips crash against mine and he takes me in a hard, wet kiss. "Even if you don't, I'll kiss you anyway."

We break apart and I hurry to the shower to rinse off the pool water and wash my hair. I don't bother styling my hair. Instead, I just braid it down one shoulder before I get dressed. I throw on a pair of cuffed black shorts and a loose, yellow sleeveless top before slipping into a pair of flat sandals.

"Ready?" Henrik asks.

I look over at him, lounging, his back against the headboard of my bed and his legs stretched out. He looks nothing like the prince that he is. He looks like just a regular man around my age. It's then that I realize I don't know how old he is. There are so many things that I don't know about him; his age is just one of the many things.

"How old are you?" I ask.

"You don't know?"

I shake my head and wait for his answer.

"C'mere," he murmurs.

I walk over to him as he swings his legs around and plants them on the floor, widening his thighs before he wraps his hands around my waist and pulls me between them. I don't speak, waiting for his answer, enjoying his hands as they wrap around the outside of my thighs and move up to my hips.

"You really don't know anything about me, do you?" his voice rumbles deeply.

"No. I only know what little you've told me, and I saw on television that you were engaged. But no, I don't know anything else," I admit.

"Do you know how absolutely refreshing it is to meet a woman who has zero clue who I am? Who isn't looking at me and thinking of all the things she could gain from knowing me? This, this is one of the many reasons why I truly believe you were brought to me, Caitriona," he murmurs as he looks up at me. "I'm thirty-one years old. I'm much too old to have behaved the way I did by getting pissed and marrying a stranger, but I'm glad that I did."

"We're crazy. *This* is crazy," I whisper.

"Right. It's insanity; but do you want to wonder about us for the rest of your life?"

"Not one single minute more," I admit.

"Then let's tell everybody. Let's tell them our decision and then tell them to fuck off when they try to change our minds," he grins.

I don't speak. I nod as my response and he stands, moving his hands up my spine until one is wrapped around the back of my neck and the other is pressing against the middle of my back. Then he kisses me again. It's another, hard, wet kiss that sends my brain and body into a tailspin of want and lust.

"Let's get this over and done, precious," he murmurs against my lips.

"Yeah," I sigh.

Together, we start to walk toward the door, then Henrik grasps my hand and pulls me into his chest.

"This is going to be all right, Riona. This is going to work out, I swear to you," he says with conviction.

"Are you trying to convince me or yourself, Henny?" I ask, watching as he closes his eyes and his grip on me tightens for a second.

He nods once, not answering me at all, and I know his answer. He's trying to convince himself, and that's okay. It really is. This whole situation is scary, and I can't imagine what he's feeling. This doesn't just affect us and our families, this is an impact that we can't really estimate. I watch as he closes his eyes for a second, inhaling a deep breath as his grasp on me tightens. We walk hand-in-hand toward the main house, toward our families—or at least part of his.

The scene inside of James and Madison's house is almost comical. *Almost.* James and Madison are sitting on one side of the table while Phillip and his fiancée, are at the other.

James and Beatrice are looking everywhere but at the people across from them, and Phillip and Madison are staring straight into each other's eyes. Madison is looking challengingly at him, and he's just smirking at her.

"Everything is all sorted, then?" Phillip asks as I close the sliding back door behind me.

"It is," Henrik announces, without offering any more information.

"Well, somebody fucking tell me *something,* dammit," Madison growls.

"Madison—," I warn and am cut off by Henrik.

"Apparently, our weekend in Las Vegas was very fruitful, Madison, as we're married," Henrik announces.

I watch as she gasps and her eyes bug out of her head. James' eyes are now focused on the table top, and I can tell he's extremely uncomfortable. He likely knows that Madison is about to freak the hell out.

"*What?*" she whispers.

"It's true. I didn't think it was a legal marriage, though I remember it all. Henrik doesn't remember any of it. The palace's security team discovered it while they were gathering documents for Henrik's marriage to Eugenie," I explain, knowing that if I don't tell her everything, she won't let me even think before she finds out every detail.

"What do you mean, you didn't think it was *legal*?" Madison asks with a narrowed eye. "You've known this whole time and you never said anything to me? You do realize I'm an attorney. I could have found out if it was legal or not," she scolds, shouts, and glares all at once.

"It was a ceremony given by a terrible Elvis impersonator after three in the morning, and we were completely plastered," I say in my defense.

"Never mind the details, what's done is done," Henrik interrupts.

"Yes, and now that that's sorted, I have the annulment papers and the non-disclosure agreement that Caitriona can sign so that we can all be on our way," Philip announces.

I feel Henrik tense beside me, squeezing my hand tightly again.

"That will not be happening, Philip. Caitriona and I are married. I'll not be abandoning her," Henrik says as he releases my hand and slides his arm around my shoulders, bringing me closer to his side.

"Bloody hell," Philip mutters; but instead of a frown, I watch as a smile tips his lips. "The family is going to completely come unglued at this news."

"Yes, I realize this; but there are more important things in life than how grandfather and father *feel*," he mutters.

"Damn right, there are," Philip chuckles.

"Philip, I don't understand," Beatrice whispers loudly.

"My brother has taken some rather fantastic advice, and he's going to end the engagement he has with that horrible woman by keeping his wife—his wife," Philip says.

"This is going to be a mess," Madison mutters. "I fucking love it. But you listen here, mister—Caitriona is my best friend, and I will hunt you down if you hurt her."

"Understood," Henrik chuckles.

"So you're leaving me?" Madison says, turning to face me with tears in her eyes.

I don't speak. I can't. All I can do is nod. I am leaving her. She's finally pregnant, and I'm going to be an aunt, and I'm leaving her. It's all too much. Madison stands and hurries over to me, wrapping me in her arms.

"I want you to be so fucking happy," she whispers through her quiet sobs. "But why do you have to be happy so far away from me?"

Together we cry softly and hold one another. Everybody else in the room melts away, and it's just my best friend and me. Then, I feel another's arms around me, and I realize it's James.

"This is bullshit," he rasps.

"I love you, James," I sigh.

"Let's all take a few hours to regroup, rest, and then we'll have a dinner here. A family dinner," Madison says, clearing her throat as we break away from our hug.

We all go our separate ways. Henrik informs me that he has several phone calls to make and that he'll be back later in the evening with Philip and Beatrice for dinner. He leaves me with a soft kiss that, of course, leaves me wanting so much more from him.

CHAPTER
Ten

Caitriona

"**Y**OU'RE A DIRTY LITTLE SLUT, CAIT," MADISON announces as I begin chopping up vegetables for our salad.

"How so?" I ask.

"You fucking *married* him and didn't tell me? Plus, you fucked him today, didn't you?" she says with a wide smile. How she knows about that, I have zero clue.

"I didn't know we were married, Mads; I swear. I told you that I thought it wasn't legal," I answer, evading her second question as best I can.

"Okay, I can possibly believe that crap, but you fucked him today, right?"

"I did. I'm his wife. How can I hold out on him?" I ask, taking a gulp from my glass of wine with a giggle.

"How was it?" Madison asks while filling a pot full of water to boil noodles for spaghetti.

It's the only thing she knows how to make, and since my brain isn't functioning, I just let her make it for tonight. I'm not in the mood to cook a fancy meal for everybody, and James is hiding out, afraid to get in the middle of girl-talk.

"Dare I say, *amazing*?" I watch as her eyes shoot up and her smile turns into a knowing grin.

"Good. Good that's good, Cait, you deserve amazing sex," she nods like she's agreeing with herself.

I do deserve amazing sex, especially since I haven't ever *had* amazing sex with anybody. I'm not a timid virgin by any means, but the partners I've had have all lacked in the bedroom department.

Henrik lacks in nothing, not a single aspect of the bedroom, and this morning proved it. We were both completely sober and it was still absolutely outstanding.

"I'm scared," I whisper as I walk over to a barstool and sit down.

"Yeah, I would be fucking terrified. You don't even know what kind of shit storm awaits you. He's going to have to publicly break off his engagement to Eugenie, and then, publicly announce your marriage all at once. Then, as if that isn't bad enough, there is the major detail of his family. I highly doubt they're going to be welcoming you into their waiting, loving arms."

I wince. She's totally right. I am so fucked. Completely and totally fucked.

"You aren't making this any better, Mads."

"I wish I could, but *newsflash*: this situation is about to go public, and viral, and there isn't any way around that shit.

Your whole life is about to change. Plus, you'll be moving to a new country. Shit is going to go down, sweet cheeks, and there's nothin' anybody can do about it. So, you better just put on your big girl panties, strap those huge titties down, and roll with the punches, 'cause I'm betting those punches are going to be heavyweight champion shit."

I gape at her, my mouth wide open. She's right on all accounts. Even if her analogies are a bit odd, she's right. This whole thing is going to be a media circus. I feel like hiding in the fetal position under a table just thinking about it.

"What time are they supposed to be here?" James asks from the kitchen's entrance.

I open my mouth to tell him, but the doorbell rings instead. He chuckles and waves it off before he turns and walks away to answer the door.

"I'm freaking out," I admit.

"Well, yeah," Madison shrugs.

"You're supposed to help me," I say, giving her a small glare.

"I can't help with this one. This is way over even *my* head."

Our conversation quickly comes to an end as Henrik walks into the kitchen. The air is thick with tension. We're all stressed out about the unknown that awaits us.

"You need to relax, precious," he whispers in my ear as he wraps is arms around my waist from behind.

"Hhmmmm," it's all I can say back.

I need to relax. Sure, I'll relax—when I'm not thinking about the media circus, or my face being plastered everywhere, or the fact that I'm his *wife*, or his family and, I'm sure, my eminent public humiliation.

"It will be just fine, Riona," he whispers. As if on cue, his cellphone rings.

I chance a glance and it says *Eugenie Ice Bitch* calling. I feel dread fill the room and my entire being. Henrik doesn't leave the room to talk to her. He answers the phone as he's standing right next to me.

"Hello," he says into the phone.

Henrik

Of course, Eugenie chooses this exact moment to return my phone call from earlier. I cringe before answering, knowing that this conversation is going to be extremely unpleasant, and that her voice will become even louder than normal and probably shrill enough to break glass.

"Henrik," I hear her cold shrewd voice bark.

"Eugenie," I greet.

"I just tried to go to your place and *your* security detail wasn't there. The doorman wouldn't let me in and told me that you'd gathered your things and left for the airport," she says.

The woman could work for British Intelligence. She's like a fucking spy.

"Yes, Eugenie, I'm in America. It's why I rang you earlier. I need to have a somewhat delicate conversation with you and, unfortunately, I'm afraid it must happen now and over the phone. I had no intention of speaking with you about it like this, however, I'm afraid you'll hear from the paps first. I would hate for that to happen."

"Does it have anything to do with that Trollip that's been plastered all over the media for weeks, with a connection to your little last hurrah in Las Vegas a few weeks ago?" she asks.

I almost laugh at her words; she's really *should* be an investigator. I look up and see that both Madison and Caitriona are staring at me. Madison has a smirk on her lips, as if she can't wait to see what I'm going to say next, hoping it's going to be some juicy tidbit of information; and Caitriona looks as though she's going to be sick all over the kitchen floor.

"Caitriona and I are married, Eugenie. We were married weeks ago in Las Vegas. We just didn't recall it, and Malcom found out only a few days ago," I explain.

"*What*?" she screams.

"It's true. Our engagement must be over. I've already approved a proper press release that my team will issue tomorrow morning bright and early. It will in no way implicate that you were the other woman, but it will announce Caitriona as my wife," I explain as I turn to meet my Riona's beautiful blue eyes.

"How *dare* you, Henrik. How am I supposed to come off as unscathed? I *will* be the other woman because I was, if you're telling me that you were married in Las Vegas *weeks* ago," she growls.

"Eugenie, the press release tells the truth. I fell deeply in love at first sight with Caitriona Geneva Grace in Las Vegas. However, I had to leave the next morning, unaware that we were, indeed, legally united in marriage. Then, during the time my security was filling out the proper paperwork and preparing to file it for our union, it was discovered that I was already married.

"Once I came to the states, I discovered that the marriage would suit me. We're not going to be dissolving our union. I am sorry that you have been caught up in the scandal, but there it is, and there you go. I will not be offering any other information on the matter as of late, so accept my deepest apologies. I am sure I will see you around," I explain.

"Well, just wait until your grandfather and father hear of this. She's an *American*, Henrik, a *title*-less American," she spews. I can practically feel her hatred.

"We aren't in love, Eugenie. We've never even been to-gether. The titles and the pomp bullshit don't mean anything to me," I explain.

"They could strip you, and then what?" she challenges.

"I will think about that if it ever happens. For today, I'm not going to think about it. Now, I must be going. I will see you assuredly at some party or another. I wish you all the luck in the world," I murmur before I end the call.

"Henrik," Caitriona whispers next to me.

I don't know if she's angry or what she is. The look on her face is indescribable to me. I know that she was unaware of the press release. I'd done it as soon as I left her this morning. Perhaps she's upset about it, but it is something that cannot be avoided.

"Riona," I murmur back, afraid to say anything else.

"You fell in love with me at first sight?" she asks, tears shining in her beautiful eyes.

"Any man would, Riona; and any man who couldn't is a fool."

"I fell for you, too," she announces before she wraps her arms around my neck and presses her lips to mine.

My Riona.

My wife.

"Alrighty, now let's eat," Madison announces after clearing her throat.

The six of us gather at James and Madison's large dinner table, and after we load our plates with food, there's silence in the room. The tension is so thick you could cut it with a knife.

"Caitriona, tell Philip and I about yourself. This has all happened so quickly. I would love to know more about my future sister-in-law," Beatrice asks Riona very sweetly.

"There isn't much to tell; not really," she shrugs.

"What about your family, your work, hobbies?" Beatrice offers.

"Ummm," Caitriona mutters.

I can feel her leg next to me as it begins to shake. I place my hand on her knee before taking a bite of salad.

"My, umm, James and Madison are my family. I work at a Medical Spa as a receptionist, and it was my boss who called the paparazzi and told them that I was the *mystery woman* in the tabloids, in hopes of drumming up more business. It's been a nightmare, and I've hated every second of it. I don't have hobbies, because I don't have time to really, and even if I did, I've never had money for them."

Caitriona rambles before she stands and rushes off, leaving us to stare after her pathway in surprise. I didn't know any of this; though, how could I? We don't really know each other, and that's never been more apparent.

"What does she mean that you're her family? She must have blood relatives," I mutter.

"That's Cait's story to tell. Maybe you should go and ask her," Madison suggests.

I excuse myself from the group, hearing Bee's apology vaguely in the background and Madison's assurance that all will be well. My focus is not on them, though, it's on Riona and her obvious distress. I don't know how to handle it—how to handle *her*.

I've never been in a relationship before. I've fucked, and I've played at dating, but a true relationship, where you discuss backgrounds, pasts, and futures? I'm a complete novice, and this scenario is making me feel uneasy.

I walk into the backyard and see her standing at the swimming pool's edge, just staring into the distance as the sun sets. She's gorgeous, as always, her dark hair still set in the braid she put it in earlier. She's like a vision before me, an untamed, untrained vision, and it's the most frightening thing I've ever encountered. With a woman of breeding, I know what to expect. With a woman like Riona, I have no idea what will happen, what she will say, or what she will do—she's beholden to no one.

"Talk to me," I murmur as I wrap my fingers around her hips from behind, pressing my lips to the side of her bared neck.

"I come from trash, Henrik. My mother has hopped from man, to man, to man my entire life. I left the day after I graduated high school, and I followed James and Madison here to Portland. They had been accepted to college; and even though that wasn't my future, I came here with them anyway. I had to get away from my life. I've been working at the MediSpa for over five years, and I'm just a receptionist, Henrik. I'm nobody, and I'm nothing. *This cannot work*," her last few words end on a choke, and I know that she's crying.

Unable to stand not looking into her eyes a moment

longer, I turn her around so that she's facing me. Pulling her in close, I shake her slightly until she lifts her tear stained face to meet mine.

"One look at you, reading your book by the pool, not paying attention to anybody else around you, and I just knew you were *somebody*. When you spoke, I instantly knew that you were *something*. You, Caitriona, you are not *nothing*. Philip asked me if I was prepared to spend the rest of my life not waking up beside you, if I could live without knowing what could have been between us. I can't live without knowing more of you, Riona. I couldn't in Vegas, and I surely cannot now. You're not nobody. You are a princess, *my* princess." I declare.

"Henny—," she begins to object.

I shut her up by placing my mouth on hers in a firm kiss that quickly deepens, as it seems to always do when my lips touch hers.

Nothing else matters. Nothing except her and me.

Together, we'll face what needs to be faced. Philip was one hundred percent correct. When the sun has set and I'm lying in bed with my wife, who do I want at my side? The answer is crystal clear—my Caitriona Geneva.

CHAPTER
Eleven

Caitriona

THE REST OF DINNER WASN'T AS AWKWARD AS I HAD anticipated it to be. Philip and Beatrice are much kinder than I could have ever imagined. I truly hope that Beatrice and I can become friends of some sort, because she seems extremely sweet.

Once dinner was complete and we cleaned up before dessert, we visited with each other for a few hours. The conversations weren't anything deep or meaningful, everything was completely on the surface, but it still felt nice and even calm.

As the evening grew late, Philip and Bee excused themselves to retire to their hotel, James and Mads also excused themselves to go to bed, and now Henrik and I are in the pool house, alone.

"We leave tomorrow. Shouldn't you be packing your things?" Henrik asks as he flops down on the sofa.

"Leaving? *Tomorrow*?" I ask, unaware of travel plans.

"Well, of course. I need to get back," he announces as though it's common sense and he cannot fathom that I'm shocked at all.

"Henrik, this is too much, too quickly. I don't think I can just up and leave like this. You didn't even ask me or talk to me about it," I murmur, thinking about what leaving truly means—to James and Madison, and my job.

"You *are* moving with me, and you'll be doing it tomorrow," he states, his green eyes holding me hostage with their stare.

"This is crazy. *You're* crazy. I can't just leave everything and everybody," I try to explain. It falls on deaf ears.

Henrik stands and stomps toward me, his jaw set and clenched, his eyes narrowed as he makes his way to me. I gasp when his fingers find the buttons of my shorts. Before I realize what's happening, he's pulled them and my panties down simultaneously.

I'm too shocked to react to his bold move. I'm frozen until he moves my body and positions me the way he wants me—bent at the waist over the arm of the sofa.

"Henny," I whisper.

"*Quiet*," he mutters as his hand slides up the inside of my thigh to my center, cupping me.

The room is completely silent, until I hear the rustling of his clothes behind me; the clanking of his belt opening, the teeth of his zipper as he pulls it down, and then the thump of his heavy jeans as they hit the floor in one big whoosh.

I gasp when I feel his cock at my entrance. He pushes in

just the tip and holds his body completely still behind me. I feel his hand slide up my spine and fist my hair before he pulls back my head and twists my neck so that I can see his face.

"You're my *wife*. You come with me, wherever that may be. This is us now, Caitriona. You're at my side, not in a completely different country where I can't protect you, hold you, and *fuck* you," he grunts as he pushes further inside of me, centimeter by centimeter.

"I'm scared," I confess.

"Right, of course you are. Let me protect you, Riona. Give us a real chance," he murmurs as he seats himself completely inside of me.

He doesn't move, his green eyes completely focused on mine, his jaw still clenched, and his face like stone.

"Move, Henny, please," I beg, needing him to move inside of me before I cry out of frustration.

"You're coming with me tomorrow?" he asks. I can hear a smile in his voice.

I don't verbally answer him. Instead, I move back as much as I can before I slip my hand between my body and the sofa. I reach down, grazing my fingernails against his tight balls before I move my hand to my clit. I need relief, and I aim to have it, even if I have to give it to myself.

"You play dirty, precious," he groans.

Without another word spoken, he pulls out of me and slams back inside, hard, causing my breath to hitch. He doesn't slow, doesn't stop, and doesn't lose his forcefulness as he fucks me against the arm of the sofa. He's relentless in the way he's taking my body. My scalp screams as he keeps ahold of my hair and seemingly tightens his grip with each thrust of his hips.

"Make yourself come all over me, Riona," he groans.

I move my fingers against my clit, chasing my climax. When it hits, I don't even try to hold back the sob that escapes me.

"Fucking hell, precious," Henrik calls out before he stills inside of me.

He sounds so far away, muffled and in the distance as I try to focus on the simple act of just breathing.

I feel his chest press against my back before his lips touch my neck and he releases my hair.

"I know it's scary. The future is terrifying, but if we're to make a true go of things, we need to be together," he murmurs against the shell of my ear, his lips brushing my skin with each word spoken.

"Okay, Henny, all right," I sigh.

"I'm your husband, just as you're my wife. We're united."

"My prince," I murmur.

"Fuck yes, I am, precious," he chuckles before he releases me and slips from my body.

"There's something else we need to discuss," I announce. He freezes, midway through pulling his jeans up.

I continue to pull my own shorts up before I speak. Not wishing to have this conversation that makes me feel extremely vulnerable sans pants.

"Each time we've been together, it's been unprotected," I announce.

I watch as Henrik blinks slowly and then grins before shaking his head.

"I thought it was something serious, precious," he chuckles.

"I think no protection is very serious."

"Right, well, you've been my wife since the first time we were together. There's been none other than you. I have physicals regularly, and you're the only woman I've ever shagged without protection. I'm clean and safe," he shrugs.

"Eugenie?" I ask, arching a brow in question.

"I think my dick would probably get fucking frost bite if it came within ten feet of her. I've never touched her, not like that. Only you, Riona," he shivers in disgust as he finishes pulling his jeans up. He zips them, but doesn't bother buttoning the top.

"Okay, but what about children?" I ask.

Henrik's face pales as he sits down on the sofa.

"Could you be?"

I shake my head, afraid to let him imagine children for another moment longer.

"After Vegas, it was a possibility, but I'm not. As soon as I was certain, I went to the doctor, and I'm on the pill," I explain.

"We don't need children yet. One day, but not yet," he mutters.

"No, we certainly do not."

"One day, when we're past all of this newness, when we're ready, I'm going to give you those four boys and a princess, just as I promised you," he murmurs, wrapping his hand around my waist and pulling me closer to him, between his spread thighs on the sofa.

"You remember?" I choke.

"I don't remember everything, but there are bits and pieces, and I recall that vow very clearly," he admits, looking up at me.

"Henny—."

"Pack, precious. Let's go home and build this life we both desire," he sighs.

"Okay," I agree with a nod.

How can I deny him? There's no way I can't give him everything he wants, not when his green eyes are looking at me and focused completely on me. Not when he's promising to take care of me and protect me as we prepare to wade into unknown waters, together.

We're taking a complete leap of faith, *together*, eyes open and running directly into the pitch black future. I've never been more scared or more excited all at the same time. If there's anybody I want to do this with, it's Henrik.

I spend the next few hours packing my largest suitcase. I don't have much that is solely mine here, aside from clothes and shoes. Henrik falls asleep in bed before I finish, and it's hard to concentrate on what to bring and what to donate when he's sleeping in my bed.

He looks younger, more at peace as he falls deeper into sleep. The stress and worry from his face fades away, and he looks more like the carefree man I met in Vegas. I wish there was a way to keep his face this way always, like in Vegas, like in sleep. I sigh, knowing it's probably not possible, and continue to pack, trying to decide what to take and what to leave here, knowing that I'll have to ask Madison to donate it to charity for me.

Once I'm finished, I change into a pair of sleep shorts and a tank before crawling into bed and curling into Henrik's side. He moans out a sigh and wraps his arms around me, pulling me deeper onto his side before he throws his bare leg over my thigh.

I wait for his eyes to open, or for him to speak, but neither happens. He's lost in dreamland, and I smile as I close my own eyes, happy to be wrapped in his arms.

The first night of the rest of our lives.

It's going to be a total roller coaster, but if the good times are as wonderful as I imagine, every headache will be worth it in the end.

Henrik

I wake before the sun rises, and I look to the woman curled into my side. *Caitriona*. She'll be right here from now on. The thought doesn't scare me or fill me with panicked dread, like it did when I imagined waking up next to Eugenie, or anybody else for that matter. Instead, it excites me. I can't wait to see what our journey will bring. I just wish that the gloom and doom of the paparazzi and my family were already over.

My phone rings and I reach over to answer it.

"The press release is live, and Eugenie is talking," Philip murmurs in my ear. I can tell he's probably been awake as long as I have.

"What's the cow saying?"

"She's saying it's all come as a surprise to her. That you lied to her, you played her for a fool. That you cheated on her with Caitriona. Poor pitiful Eugenie," Philip mutters.

"Of course she is," I exhale. "I don't even care. She can say what she wants."

"The plane leaves in three hours. We need to get back and try to do damage control. Father has already called me five times."

"Nobody has tried me," I say, confused as to why he's been calling Philip and not me.

"He's angry; probably wants to save his screaming for in person, when he can scream at you to your face," Philip chuckles.

"Oh, grand."

"Bee and I will be round to pick you up in two hours. Be ready," he says before he hangs up the phone.

I gently wake Caitriona up and urge her to start to prepare to leave. Groggily, she makes her way toward the bathroom. Once the shower has started, I get up and head outside for some fresh air.

"You're leaving and taking her, aren't you?" Madison's voice cuts through the crisp morning breeze.

"We leave in three hours," I admit.

"I figured you'd be heading out today. I want to tell you to take care of her, and that if you don't, I'll chop your dick off; but I have a feeling you've been handed enough shit, and there's only more that will be flung your way before this whole ordeal settles. So I won't say those things, but…"

"You've been reading the gossip rags," I chuckle.

"I have a feeling you'll have a whole fan club awaiting your return. Let that bitch have it, though. Calling Cait the *other woman*. I'm glad she lives in England and not here," she practically growls.

"Go inside and talk to her. I'll stay here until you're done," I say, jerking my head toward the pool house.

I don't watch Madison run toward the little house. I keep my gaze directed at the man who is watching us, *James*. The other man in Riona's life; a man she has known for years, whom she adores and loves. He's looking at me like he might feel great satisfaction from dismembering me at any moment. I ignore his evil glares and make my way toward him.

"You're taking her away. I should beat the shit out of you right here and now," James announces.

"You and Madison are always welcome at mine. Any day and anytime—*always*," I offer.

"You'll be taking care of her, of all her needs?" James asks.

"Any single whim she could dream up, it's hers and I'll give it to her."

"Good. She deserves everything and more."

"Thank you for taking such great care of her all these years," I say, holding my hand out to shake his.

James shakes my hand, but we don't speak to each other. We separate, an understanding now between us. I'll take care of her. He cared over Riona like a sister for so long, it must be hard to let her go, especially since I am taking her so far away. I can only hope that I'll be able to make her blissfully happy—the happiest woman on earth. I hope I don't fuck this up completely.

CHAPTER
Twelve

Caitriona

MORNING COMES TOO EARLY. WHEN I STEP OUT OF the bathroom, Madison is sitting on my bed with tears in her eyes. There's nothing to be said. My bags are packed and ready to go; it's obvious, and she knows that I'm leaving. I wish I weren't.

I wish I could stay here in Portland forever, with her and James, but I can't. I have a whole new life waiting for me, and it just happens to be across an ocean. I wish it weren't, I wish we could be closer; but it's Henny, and I can't deny that I'm drawn to him. I have to know what lies in store for us.

"I want baby updates, *daily*. I want *FaceTime* every Thursday during lunch, I don't care what time of day or night it is for me, and I want you to swear you'll be coming to visit, regularly," I demand as tears stream down my cheeks.

"Yes to all. Fucking yes," Madison sobs as she pulls me in for a hug. We clutch onto each other.

A few minutes later, James is here, and he joins our hug. The three of us, best friends from five years old, inseparable and yet, here we are, doing just that—separating.

It seems surreal, completely and totally surreal that it's happening. I'm leaving, and it hasn't fully hit me yet. I have a feeling that when it does, it will hit like a freight train.

"Stay strong, Cait. Seriously, don't let those snooty, up-tight, ice crotch Brits get you down," Madison whispers in my ear.

"I won't," I chuckle.

James and Madison leave me, and a few minutes later, Henrik walks through the door. He brushes his lips against mine before he makes his way to the bathroom to shower, wordlessly.

I take one last, long look around my tiny home. I haven't lived here long, but it felt more like a home than anywhere else I've lived. What I'll miss most isn't the pool house. It will be James and Mads. The past twenty years have been the three of us, living life, making mistakes, and loving each other.

"Philip will be round soon to get us. Are you ready?" Henrik asks gently as he walks out of the bathroom.

"Yes. No. I don't know," I admit truthfully.

"Riona, you're going to be all right. I swear to you that I'll take care of you," he murmurs, cupping my cheeks with his palms.

"I hope so," I whisper.

I hear a car pulling up in front of the house, interrupting my insecurities, and I know it's time. I feel like someone should be playing the bugle in the background, or there should be a lone drummer boy beating his drum or something. This, all of this, feels so final.

I know where I'm going. I will have no friends and no confidants. I am going to be lost and very alone. I'm not sure how I'll be able to handle it all. I'm so anxious and nervous about the entire thing. I honestly just want to run away with Henrik, just the two of us, and never look back.

"Come on, precious, it's time for us to head out," I hear Henrik's soft voice call out faintly.

I walk out of the pool house, following behind him toward the main house, where I see both James and Madison holding hands waiting for us. Henrik is pulling my luggage and leaves it at the front door. James, Madison, and I envelop each other in another group hug, not knowing when we'll be able to do this again in person. The weight of me leaving is settling on me, and I'm feeling like I should stay. I don't want to leave them.

"The paparazzi's out there. Philip just phoned. They can't get out of the car to come to the door," Henrik announces, breaking up our hug.

"How are we going to get out?"

"Security is making their way to the door and they're going to escort us," he murmurs.

"Security?" Madison asks.

"I travel with security always. They've been here the whole time, just in the shadows," he shrugs.

"You're going to have a security detail now. *Fuck,* that is so awesome," Madison says with a grin as a knock sounds at the door.

"Shall we?" Henrik asks.

I look back at James and Madison one last time. *This is it.* This is the moment that my life changes forever. The second I step out that door, nothing will ever be the same again.

Though meeting Henrik changed everything once my name was released, my day-to-day life didn't change. Not really. I still woke up and went to work every single day; I still had lunch with Madison on Thursdays.

But now? *Now,* I'm going blindly into the unknown. *It's scary as hell.* I feel a warm hand grip mine, and I look up into Henrik's sparkling green eyes. He smiles with a nod, and together we walk out of my old life and into my new one.

The security guard is gigantic and helps to make a pathway for us to walk toward the car; after, of course, he takes my bag from Henrik. The cameras' flashing lights and the reporters' loud voices echo in my ears, but I keep my head down and my hand gripping tightly onto Henrik's.

It feels as though it takes an hour just to make it from the front door to the car waiting at the curb. Once we're inside and Henrik slams the backseat car door closed, the noise finally drowns out from around us.

"You did great, Riona," Henrik murmurs, wrapping his arm around my shoulders as the car eases onto the street.

I look up to the front seat, surprised to find Philip driving and Beatrice sitting next to him.

"Where is the security now?" I ask, ignoring his praise.

"They're in the car behind us. They'll be travelling back home with us on the plane. I'll introduce you then," Henrik murmurs.

"That was awful. Are you all right?" Beatrice asks, turning around slighting in her seat to look me in the eye.

I take her in, poised to perfection, as she has been the

few times I've seen her. Her dark auburn hair is pulled up into a flawless bun on top of her head, and her makeup is outstandingly perfect, including her deep burgundy lipstick.

I need to ask her for help, I decide. She's wearing a navy blue blazer over what looks to be a silk, cream blouse, and one glance at her dark wash skinny jeans let's me know she definitely has it all together.

I find myself cursing my own wardrobe choice of a pair of mint colored skinny jeans, a plain white tank top, and gold ballet flats. My hair is down and wild, my makeup is minimal, and there's no lip stain, only gloss, on my light pink lips.

"Precious, are you okay?" Henrik asks, pulling my attention away from Beatrice.

I blink, not realizing that they've both asked me if I'm doing all right. I feel so lost and stupid and out of my element.

"I'm sorry," I apologize, "that was just a lot at once. I've had them bombard me before, but nothing like that."

"I would like to tell you that you'll get used to it, or that it will calm down, but you won't and they don't calm down, ever. It's part of your life now, Caitriona. It's a burden we will all carry, as will our children and our grandchildren." Beatrice explains.

"How do you accept it?" I ask as the car pulls into the airport hangar.

She smiles but doesn't answer me right away as she opens the door and steps out of the car. Henrik does the same and I follow suit; then Bee is right next to me, and she links her arm through mine. My breath hitches in surprise, and she smiles kindly before she leans her head in to whisper to me.

"I'll tell you what Philip and Henrik's mother shared with me when we were newly dating and the paparazzi were everywhere. She told me that the media would always be around, no matter what, but that it was up to us to decide what to do with the power they give us. We could ignore them, be annoyed by them, or we could use them to do good in this world. Use them as a platform to help others and to spread love and kindness in a cruel world," she murmurs.

"I would like that. I would like that very much," I admit.

"I thought that you might. You remind me very much of myself when I first came into this family. Scared and unsure, not looking to be in the limelight, and definitely not wishing to become the center of attention. However, those things are going to happen, no matter what, so it's up to us to give them the proper voice."

"Use our powers for good," I laugh as we approach the airplane steps.

"Exactly," she winks before she releases my arm and begins to climb the stairway onto the airplane.

"You're good?" Henrik asks, pressing his palm to my lower back.

"I am. She was giving me advice on the media," I shrug.

"You'd do well to take it from Bee. She's loved by all, and for good reason. She's *lovely* all of the time," Henrik states.

"I can see that," I murmur, feeling very self-conscious and aware that I am not lovely all of the time.

In fact, right now, I look like a disaster, especially compared to her.

"Riona?" Henrik asks. I turn to face him.

"Her personality is lovely all of the time. I meant nothing else, precious."

"I'm just scared, and nervous, and very aware that I am nothing like her," I whisper.

I'm afraid to speak the words too loudly; afraid that if I do, he'll discover what a mistake he's made by not going through with the annulment.

"You're gorgeous, and I'm the luckiest man on earth. Now, let's climb up in this airplane so I can take you home and show you off—my wife," he murmurs as he cups my cheeks and brushes his lips against mine before he releases me. I sigh, wishing there were time for more of his wonderful kisses.

I climb up the airplane stairway and walk inside of the plane. It's the most luxurious thing I have ever seen. Plush leather seats and legroom for days, it's like something I've only ever seen on television. Philip and Beatrice's chairs are turned around and facing the empty seats that Henrik guides me toward. I sit down and settle in my chair, still a complete ball of nerves at what awaits me when we land overseas.

"Oh, I forgot," Beatrice says as she hands Henrik a small box.

Henrik smiles at her as he takes the box and then thrusts it toward me.

"Open," Henrik murmurs in a gruff voice.

I open the box slowly and gasp when I see what is inside.

It's a ring—though, to call it that seems ridiculous, since it's so much more than just a *ring*.

There is a red ruby, emerald cut stone that's at least ten carats in the center, with diamonds surrounding it. There are also diamonds around the entire band. One of the wedding bands is a row of red stones and another is a row of diamonds—three rings in total. I look up to Henrik with question in my eyes.

"The red diamonds are rare; it signifies everything beautiful and rare that you are to me. The red diamond wedding band and the diamond wedding band are because Bee declared you had to have them, that one ring was simply not enough," he says with a slight chuckle.

"It's the most beautiful thing I've ever seen," I whisper in awe.

"You'll wear them, then?" he asks with a grin.

"Forever," I agree and wait with a shaky hand as he slips the three rings onto my finger.

I look down at my finger and am unable to hide the gigantic smile that crosses my lips. I never imagined that I would own anything so beautiful, that I would have a man so handsome at my side. Yet, here I am, living in a dream—a dream I never want to wake from.

"I think they're lovely," Beatrice says as she takes my hand to inspect it.

I look at her finger and notice that her ring is a colored stone as well—amethyst, by the look of it, oval cut, and surrounded by diamonds. I touch her ring with my free hand and she smiles widely.

"No matter what is said, they do pick lovely jewelry," she murmurs.

"My mother picked that, and you know it. I have atrocious taste in jewels," Philip chuckles.

"Well, it's lovely," I say.

"I picked yours, so you may thank me thoroughly *later*," Henrik whispers in my ear.

My eyes widen and I cough, trying to hide my surprise at his words. The man is simply devilish, my Las Vegas poolside husband. The man that is now to be at my side for the rest of my life. I hope that I always feel this excited for the anticipation of the future with him.

Henrik

I glance down at her as she sleeps. My precious, Caitriona. She's not as polished and poised as Beatrice, but she's still the most beautiful woman I've ever known. I could be making a huge mistake, and the repercussions from my family could mean a stripped title. Though I hope that it won't come down to that, I have to be prepared for whatever my grandfather decides. I know that this is not what he desires, that he wanted me with Eugenie—a woman who has all of the training and the title he wishes to have in the family. Too bad she's an ice-cold shrew.

He'll see this marriage to Caitriona as a disgrace, as a stain on our family. Weeks ago, I would have done as he wished. I would have given Riona the annulment papers to sign and turned my back on her, walked away from her without a backward glance.

I would have endured a life of misery.

However, Philip is correct. When the sun has set and you're in bed with your wife, what does it matter her title, her breeding, or her background? All that matters is happiness, mine and hers.

We're not truly hurting anybody by being together. Eugenie never loved me, she never even felt affection for me, so while this is public, personally, I've not hurt her.

"You look like you may be sick," Philip murmurs quietly, as Bee is also asleep at his side.

"Just ready to get this initial shit over with; ready to get the lecture from grandfather and father done."

"I truly like her for you. She's calm and sweet, though I have a feeling there is fire underneath it all. She compliments you well, brother," Philip says.

"She does compliment me, and there's fire, definitely. I don't know even close to anything about her, but I can't wait to find every detail out that there is to know," I admit.

"That's good. I don't know everything about Beatrice. I learn something new about her daily, and I find that I adore it. Truly, I love learning about her and how she thinks."

"I only hope that the family doesn't make this too difficult. There's already so much pressure with the media," I mutter, voicing my concerns.

"Whatever happens, you'll brave it together, and you'll be stronger for it."

CHAPTER
Thirteen

Caitriona

I WAKE WITH HENRIK'S LIPS KISSING DOWN MY NECK, HIS deep voice softly murmuring that the plane is about to touch down. Slowly, I open my eyes as I let out a sigh. I don't want to wake, not really. I want to stay here forever, with Henrik, not exposed to the rest of the world and the unknown.

"Wakey, wakey," Philip calls out through a chuckle.

"That is awful. Never say it again," I grumble.

Everybody laughs and he rolls his eyes at me. Beatrice offers to come to the bathroom with me so that we can freshen up, since there could be a circus waiting for us when we arrive. I'm thankful that she helps me tame my hair a bit, and even shows me where the airplane houses extra toothbrushes.

"Everything is going to be okay, Caitriona," she says in

her soft, sweet voice.

"I've never done anything like this before. I don't know what I'm doing," I confess.

She smiles and nods. She knows I've never done anything like this before. Why I felt the need to tell her, I don't know. I'm rambling nervously, and I just want it all over with. Beatrice takes both of my hands in hers and smiles warmly before she speaks.

"You're going to get it together, Caitriona. You are a strong woman, and you are going to take your husband's side and do so with a smile. Let him do all of the talking, as you don't need to. They'll be asking questions about your union, and about Eugenie, all things that he can answer. He's been trained in how to properly speak to the media in a way where they're less likely to cut and chop his words up to evoke a different meaning and a backlash."

"Okay," I whisper.

"Let me see your beautiful smile," she coos.

I smile but it feels awkward, and she laughs at me.

"No, give me the smile you get when you think about Henrik. When you think about the fact that you'll be spending the rest of your days with that beautiful man," she murmurs.

I smile again, but this time it's genuine, and Beatrice responds with a smile of her own.

"Now, we should be landing any minute. Let's join our men."

We walk together the short distance back to our seats. I look over to the other two men on the plane, both poised and ready for what's next. Jasper and Hugh are our detail. Jasper is assigned to Philip and Hugh to Henrik. They're both built like tanks, and they're quiet—so quiet, in fact, that I've not heard them speak once, not even when we were introduced to each other.

I close my eyes as the wheels of the plane adjust and we begin to land. Takeoff and landing always make me nervous, and this time is no exception. When the plane has finally landed, we go about gathering our things, and I decide to lift the window shade and look out at the tarmac.

I shouldn't have looked.

There are swarms and hordes of photographers that line both sides of the steps and the pathway that leads to a waiting car. I gasp at the sight and Henrik places his warm palm on my thigh, squeezing it to garner my attention.

"There's so many," I mutter, turning away from the window to look into his green eyes.

"There are, and you're going to be just fine," he assures, giving me a soft smile.

"Beatrice told me to let you do all of the talking. I think that's a great plan," I announce.

Philip chuckles as does Henrik.

"It is a smashing plan. Now, wife, shall we?" he asks as he stands and holds out his palm for me.

I take his offered hand and pull myself out of my seat, thankful that he's going to do all of the talking and the only things I need to worry about are smiling and not falling on my face. Usually, those are simple tasks. Today, however, I'm not so confident.

I watch as Jasper leads the way for both Philip and Beatrice to exit the plane. Hugh is waiting at the door for us, and when his dark brown eyes meet mine, I feel a little more at ease. Though he's not spoken, his eyes look soft, warm, and kind. Then he grins before he dips his chin and Henrik tugs on my arm as he follows him.

I smile as naturally as possible, my grip unyielding as I hold onto Henrik's hand, assuredly cutting off the flow of blood to his fingers. We take a few steps down the plane and stop at the bottom, my side plastered against his arm as the camera's lights flash with the millions of photographs that are being taken.

Henrik moves his head, and I lift mine to look up at him. He smiles, and his green eyes twinkle, making me relax just a little bit more. He's so charismatic and handsome. I'm in awe of the fact that he's chosen me, especially since he can have anybody.

"I'm willing to answer five questions," he announces.

It surprises me that he's willing to answer anything at all.

"Is this your American bride?" one reporter asks.

"This is my wife, Caitriona, that is correct," Henrik confirms.

"Is this the woman from the night club in Las Vegas that you were reported dancing with, several weeks ago?" another reporter asks.

"Yes; can you not recognize her beautiful hair?" he chuckles "That was the evening we were married," Henrik finishes, placing a chaste kiss on my cheek, causing the camera flashes to go insane. I stay smiling, afraid to even attempt to speak.

"Will you be having an official marriage ceremony?" someone yells out from behind.

"If that is what my Riona would like then, yes, we will; but we've not discussed it as of yet." I hear a buzz of voices when he says my nickname, and I can't help but bite my lip as my smile grows.

"Two more," Henrik calls out.

"Is your family upset about your secret affair?" a woman asks from the right of me.

"We never had an affair, and there's been no secrets. We simply made a decision that neither of us remembered the next morning," he chuckles, as do many of the reporters. "However, I'm not quite sure how my family feels, as I've not spoken to them yet."

"How does Eugenie feel about being dumped?"

"I don't know how Eugenie feels about the situation, but I have spoken with her. None of this has to do with her; she's a lovely woman, and she'll make whomever she chooses as a partner an extremely happy man," he gushes.

The guilt over the publicity of his break-up eats away at me with every word spoken. I understand that he said he doesn't care for her, and that he's happy to be rid of her as a fiancée, but it doesn't change the fact that this must be a painful thing to have shoved in her face from every direction.

Henrik and I begin to walk toward the car, his five questions now finished. Hugh stands with the door open and waiting for us. I'm just about to climb inside when I hear someone call out my name.

"Show us your ring," I hear several reporters chant.

Without thinking, proud of the gorgeous piece of jewelry Henrik gave me, I hold my hand up so that they can take photos of the beautiful ring. I can't wipe the smile off of my lips as the reporters gush and snap pictures of my hand.

Then, after about thirty seconds, Henrik presses his hand to my lower back and we slide inside of the car, Hugh closing the door behind us before the car whisks us away.

"Are you ready for what awaits with grandfather and father?" Philip asks as we drive toward our destination, someplace that I'm unsure of at this moment.

"Never," Henrik chuckles.

What seems like only a few moments later, we pull up to a gorgeous, all brick, red building with white balconies. It looks like a palace, but I know it's not *the* palace. There are no gates or guards, but it's the largest building I have ever seen. It looks so old, so grandiose, so spectacular, it is just plain beautiful.

"You'll be joining us for dinner then, at father and mum's?" Philip asks as the car comes to a stop.

I watch as Henrik offers a chin lift as his response. My door opens, and the driver is standing at the curb, offering me his hand. *Is this where we are to live?* I am completely shocked.

"Hop out, precious," Henrik whispers.

My legs finally move as I grasp the hand of the driver and step to the side. Henrik joins me a moment later, taking my hand in his.

I should have guessed they would be here, too. I should have seen it coming, but I was semi-relaxed, and extremely tired, therefore I didn't realize that there were even more photographers waiting for us, or that it would even be a possibility, I figured they were all at the airport.

Henrik wraps his arm around my waist as he guides me toward the security of the building's doors. I watch as he slides a card and the doors open. We slink inside before they close and lock tightly behind us. Henrik doesn't utter a word as he walks us to the front deskman.

"William, I need to introduce you to my wife, Caitriona.

She'll be living here permanently, so I need to add her to my apartment list and get her keys, full access," Henrik announces with his arm still firmly wrapped around my waist.

William's eyes widen, his face in a look of complete shock at Henrik's words. He's portly and round, with just a few gray wisps of hair on his shiny head. When his eyes cut to mine, I notice that they're a pretty pale blue, and they gaze kindly on me.

I feel a warmth fill my body, and immediately a connection is formed. He seems like a fatherly type, and I've never had one of those. I look at him, and *to* him, hoping that I've found a friendly face so soon in this country.

"Of course, Sir," he says, dipping his head. "I will have some keys sent up as soon as possible," he winks.

Henrik then thanks him and we walk toward the elevator.

"I hope you like the apartment. Whatever you don't care for decoration wise, you have full liberty to change. I hired a decorator to make it presentable; nothing really means anything to me when it comes to that stuff," Henrik says with a wave of his hand as the car climbs toward our destination.

"I'm sure it's wonderful. This building is absolutely stunning," I murmur.

"I want you to feel comfortable. I want you to feel as though it's your home, Riona, because it is," he explains, making me fall a little harder for him.

As soon as the elevator door opens, Henrik steps out and holds his palm out for me. Together, we walk into the apartment. My mouth practically drops to the floor; in fact, I think I feel some drool sliding down my face at the sight before me.

The apartment isn't like any apartment I have ever seen.

It is huge, and modern, and beautiful. The floors are a wide plank, dark, rich, hardwood, and one whole wall of the living area is nothing but windows, huge wide windows that overlook a park. The rest of the walls are painted a light gray with white crown molding and baseboards.

I follow behind Henrik as we walk straight into a sitting room, where there are cream colored tufted sofas adorned with chocolate brown pillows, a total contrast to the modern feel of the walls and windows. I immediately imagine turquoise pillows on the cream sofa, instead, for an added pop of color.

The coffee table is silver footed with a large mirrored top, another contrast to the seemingly modern feel of the room. There's a large flat screen television on one wall, and I smile. James, too, loves his televisions—*it must be a man thing*.

"Come, let me show you your new home," Henrik murmurs against my ear, making me shiver with anticipation.

We walk through the huge apartment, Henrik showing me the place, a guided tour of each room. The kitchen is beautiful—huge, dark, black square tiled flooring with white cabinets and black granite countertops.

The appliances are sleek, stainless, and so top of the line that I have never seen anything like it in my entire life, which is saying a lot, because James and Madison's kitchen is gorgeous.

There's a small breakfast table for four off of the kitchen as well. It's black and so very modern, exactly how it should be. I can't wait to cook in here.

Henrik walks me into the formal dining room, which has a table for *twelve*—it's massive. The chairs are covered in a corduroy black fabric, with rounded tops, and thickly padded seats. They look extremely plush and comfortable.

The table itself is also black. It has me wondering if he really loves black, because everything is just *black*. It needs some color. I decide my first wifely duty will be to add a bit of color to this house.

Then, he leads me to a media room, which has a huge projection screen and black leather recliners. It's a mini *movie theater*. I've heard of famous people having these in their homes, but I never in a million years imagined I would live anywhere that had one.

"This is beyond anything I have ever seen before," I whisper in awe as I look around the room.

"It's yours now, Riona. The sky's the limit," Henrik murmurs, wrapping his arms around my waist from behind and placing a kiss to my neck.

"It feels like a dream," I mutter.

"This may seem like a dream to you, but *you* are my dream."

I turn around in Henrik's arms and cup his cheeks in my palms.

"You're cheesy as hell, Henny, and I love it," I giggle before I rise to my toes and press my lips to his.

"I can't wait to fuck you in here with a movie playing in the background," he murmurs against my lips.

"You're dirty, Prince Henrik," I practically moan.

"Filthy," he chuckles before his tongue dives into my mouth.

Before he consumes me, he takes a step back and informs me that we must carry on with our tour. I don't want to. I want him to take me right here and right now, but I reluctantly follow behind him as he continues to show me *our home*.

There's a large room with a whole wall of bookshelves and a beautifully carved wooden desk; Henrik informs me that it's his office.

Then we come across a room with a full bar and a poker table, his *entertaining* room. Then, of course, he has his own mini-gym, complete with a weight room that has a mirrored wall and everything. It is insanity, and my head is spinning that this is where I'll be living.

Finally, he takes me on a tour of the bedrooms. There are four in total. All of the bedrooms are furnished, some more feminine stylings, and others more masculine.

"We don't need to have all of the bedrooms furnished. If you want to empty out a couple of them for your personal space, that's perfectly fine," he explains. I just nod, unable to speak.

Space of my own?

What would I do with it?

I'm unable to think any further as we walk inside of our master bedroom. I immediately want to wrap my arms and legs around him and take him down. It is perfect, better than I could have imagined or dreamed up for myself.

The flooring is the same deep, rich, dark hardwood that is laid throughout the rest of the house. There are French doors that lead to a balcony on one side, and a complete wall of windows on either side of the doors, floor-to-ceiling.

The bed is a black sleigh bed, and it is huge, the biggest bed I have ever seen. The comforter is a bright, dove grey, and I love it. The pillows are black, of course, as are the night stands and dresser. It suits the space, though; the walls are a medium gray color, bringing it all together and keeping it light with the dark floor and furniture color.

Then he leads me into the biggest walk-in closet I have ever seen. All of his suits are spaced perfectly, along with shoes, ties, belts, and then his regular clothes. It's like a show-room for an expensive department store. I'm in awe just looking around.

"This is my dressing room," Henrik explains.

I then watch as he opens the door next to it, and my mouth drops. The room is twice the size of Henrik's closet, and lit in glorious bright lights. There's a center dresser with drawers, rows and rows of shelving, cubby holes, and tons of space to hang clothes.

Never in my life would I have enough clothes to fill this space. It's all white and crisp, and waiting for hundreds of clothes to fill it up.

"This is your dressing room, precious," Henrik whispers, wrapping his arms around my waist and pulling me into his back.

"I'll never fill this place," I murmur.

"You will, luv," he assures me as he places a kiss on my neck. "I'll be right back. I have to check my messages."

Just when I think I can't be in anymore shock and awe, I make my way into the bathroom. I almost faint. It is about the size of the entire pool house at Madison and James'. The flooring is black, naturally, the cabinets black, and the counter tops, are a shock of white.

There is a huge, old fashioned, claw foot tub in the center of the room, separate vanities, a bench at one, with an area lit for perfect makeup application, I assume.

I look over to the shower that is off to the side. I count four shower heads—*four*. I want to laugh and cry at the same time. It is all so ridiculous and gorgeous.

I glance at myself in the mirror and my eyes grow wide.

Oh, no. We're supposed to meet his family for dinner tonight. I have absolutely nothing to wear—not to mention I don't even know what would be appropriate to wear.

Henrik walks back into the room and my eyes catch his in the mirror before I turn around and speak.

"What about clothes to wear tonight, Henny? What are we going to do? I didn't bring anything appropriate to meet your family," I panic, trying to ignore the way I want him.

"How about you and I rest a bit?" Henrik murmurs.

I watch as he stalks up to me, his long, lean body making its way toward mine. My belly clenches at the sight of him, the way his eyes are focused on mine, and the intent I can read on his face. I want him, I want him right here and right now, but my mind is so busy.

A million different thoughts are running through it all at once. He wraps his hand around mine and gently tugs me into the bedroom.

"I'll call Sarah right now, have her go and get you some things. What's your size?" he asks, pulling out his phone and punching a couple of buttons.

"I think the sizing is different here…" I began.

"Sarah, my wife is here and we will be going to my father and mum's for a family dinner tonight. We have just arrived and she doesn't have anything appropriate to wear. Will you pop over to a shop and grab her some clothes and shoes?" he looks over to me, and I tell him my American size. He assures me that Sarah will figure out everything and be at the apartment in the next few hours.

"Now, back to you and I and our—*resting*," Henrik murmurs.

I watch as he takes the hem of my shirt, lifting it up my body slowly, and then over my head before throwing it behind him somewhere. With his hands wrapped around my waist, he drags me over to the bed, sitting down as he spreads his thighs and situates me standing between them.

"Fuck, I can't believe you're really here," he whispers as his hands slide up my back and unhook my bra.

I sigh when his mouth closes around my breast and his tongue swirls around my nipple.

My hands automatically dive into his messy hair, holding him to my breast, arching my back and enjoying the feel of his warm mouth on my skin.

"Henny," I whisper.

"Come on, Riona, let's take a rest," he murmurs.

"A rest?" I practically whimper, wanting more of his mouth on my body.

He chuckles as he yanks my pants off, along with my panties.

Henrik stands and he sheds his clothes before he wraps his hands around my waist and tosses me onto the bed, watching me from the side as I bounce once. Then, he crawls up from the bottom of the bed and looks at me, resting back on his knees.

My eyes glide down his body until they land on his hard cock. Wetting my lips, I sit up before I crawl over to him on my hands and knees, and open my mouth, taking him inside. His hands fly to the side of my head as I look at him beneath my lashes.

"Fucking hell, precious," he groans as he thrusts his hips slightly.

I take as much of him as I can down my throat. He's long

and thick, and I'm unable to swallow all of him, so I wrap my hand around his base and squeeze as I bob up and down on his length.

"Just like that," he rumbles as he moves his hips.

I relax as much as I can, allowing him to go deeper down my throat. Then he suddenly pulls out of me and his eyes gaze down at me, a smirk on his lips.

"My cum is going to fill that sweet cunt, not your throat. Turn around," he grunts.

I do as ordered and turn around, but stay on my knees. I moan when I feel his hands slide up the backs of my thighs to my ass, up my spine, and then both of them tangle in my hair before he yanks my neck toward him.

"Henny," I gasp.

He looms over me from behind, his lips brushing mine upside down before he grins.

"Widen you knees," he rasps. I do as he asks, widening my legs. "Good girl, bend over a little."

He guides me by my hair to bending over slightly, I tip my ass back and my eyes flutter closed when he fills me from behind. He moves roughly, his cock pounding inside of me. When he stops, my eyes fly open. My neck aches from the way he's holding me, but he looks down at me and grins.

"You have no idea how spectacular you are right now. Your body arched for me, taking everything I give you. It's truly a vision, Riona. I'm happy you're mine," he whispers as his lips touch the tip of my nose.

I feel one of his hands leave my hair as it travels around my waist and down to my pussy, his fingers touching my clit.

"I need to move," I whimper

"No, you need to stay right where you are. Just like this, I

148

want that cunt on edge," he grunts.

"Henny," I cry out as his fingers start to stroke me harder and faster.

It's so intense, and I feel the urge to move so badly that it almost hurts. Tears fill my eyes, but he just looks down at me.

"Mmm, I'm ready for that cunt to squeeze me tight, like only yours can," he breathes against my lips before he brushes them with his own.

My whole body starts to shake, my legs unable to hold me upright anymore. The only way I'm staying where I am is because of his hold in my hair. Tears fall down my cheeks, I'm unable to hold them back as my body jerks with my climax.

"Fucking right," he growls as he releases my hair and wraps his hands around my hips.

My entire body falls forward while he thrusts in and out of me with strength I didn't know he possessed. *I'm going to ache for days,* I think as my pussy pulses with each thrust of his hips.

My orgasm is long and hard, my breathing as erratic as Henrik's thrusts, and then he plants himself deep with a grunt. I feel his cock twitch, along with his climax filling me.

"Christ," he sighs before he falls forward, pressing me flat into the mattress. "Heaven every time, precious," he rasps as his lips touch the side of my neck.

"Nowhere else I'd rather be, Henny," I whisper.

"Damn fucking right," he grunts as he pulls out of me and yanks my back to his front.

Wrapped in his arms, I know that this is exactly where I want to be. I don't know if it's where I'm meant to be, or where life will take me from here; but right now, here is exactly where I want to be, and that is all that matters.

CHAPTER
Fourteen

Caitriona

AFTER WHAT SEEMS LIKE FIVE MINUTES, I FEEL Henrik's lips grazing my shoulder before they touch the side of my neck while his hand cups my breast and gently squeezes my flesh. I whimper, feeling more turned on with every single second. I try to roll my body in his arms, but he holds me tight against his chest, and I'm unable to move.

"Henny," I practically whine.

"When you say my name like that, fresh from sleep, I want nothing more than to fuck that sweet cunt of yours," he rumbles against my neck.

I sigh when his tongue snakes out and he licks my skin.

"Can you please do that?" I ask unabashedly.

"Again? *Riona*," he warns.

I pout, though it does no good because I'm facing the wall and he can't see me. Then, as if he's read my mind completely, his hand drifts from my breast, down my stomach, and between my legs.

My belly quivers when his finger presses against my clit. Henrik slides his leg between my knees and lifts so that my leg is now draped over his, and my center is completely open.

I gasp when he slides two fingers inside of me. They go in with ease, as I'm already wet for him, drenched just at the thought of his touch. He groans into my neck, his chest vibrating against my back as his other arm readjusts and wraps around my breasts.

"You always feel so spectacular," he murmurs. It's all I can do to let out a hum as my response.

I shift my hips, searching for more of him, needing more than just his fingers filling me. Wanting, no *craving* him moving inside of me. His fingers across my breasts pinch and pluck my nipples, moving from one to the other, sending even more need throughout my body.

"Henny," I say with exasperation.

"Ssshh," he rumbles as he slides his fingers out of me and replaces them with his long, hard cock.

My breath leaves my lungs as we both freeze. Henrik's nose nuzzles my neck, and I pinch my eyes closed, trying to tamp down my desire to take control and move, knowing that it would not be well received.

"I want you to come around my cock," he whispers.

I gasp when his fingers begin to play with my clit, gently, yet firmly. I try to move, but he removes his fingers. A pattern I'm becoming to recognize as his, taking me hard and rough, and then the next time, being gentle and soft.

"I'm not going to move, and you're not going to move. You're going to stay perfectly still and come around my cock. I want to feel every flutter of your perfect pussy."

My answer is to whimper, afraid that if I speak, I'll sob or throw a tantrum. He's keeping himself from me, and asserting his dominance and control—I love it as much as I hate it right now.

Henrik's fingers move back to the space between my legs, and he begins to bring me closer toward my release, again. He starts gently petting me, swirling his fingers and pressing against my clit; then he switches tactics to pinching and every so often delivering a light tap against me.

"Oh, shit," I sob as I climb higher and higher toward my climax.

"I want you to scream my name when you come," he grinds out through a clenched jaw.

I don't wait another second. My orgasm rolls through me, and I scream out his name, the only name he wishes me to call him—*Henny*.

"Fuck," he clips as my pussy clenches around him, holding his hard length inside of me while the rest of my body shakes uncontrollably.

Then, he rolls me onto my stomach, never losing our connection, his hand leaving my breasts to tangle in the back of my hair.

My body is completely spent, and I'm unable to move, but he growls behind me, his legs shifting around until his knees are between my thighs. I grunt when his hands grasp my hips and he pulls them up; then finally—*finally*—he moves.

Henrik doesn't ease in and out of me. No, he slams inside

of me with rigorous, harsh, unrelenting power. My once completely exhausted body is ready and willing for more from him. I rear back against him, enjoying the groan that escapes him at the move.

"Fuck me, *Riona*, fuck my goddamn cock," he growls before his hand lands against my ass in a sharp slap.

I do as he's demanded. *I fuck his cock*, meeting his hard thrusts each and every time until I'm on the edge again, ready to topple over and succumb to another orgasm.

"Come, come all over me," he orders, slapping my ass again. As if on cue, I do as he's requested.

I scream out into the room, my arms unable to hold my shaking body up a moment longer. Henrik stills his own body as he roars with his release. Then, he collapses on top of me, his chest against my sweat soaked back, and his mouth against my neck.

"Spectacular," he whispers as he gently sucks on my skin.

"Wow," is all I can muster through my heavy breaths.

"Sarah will be here any moment. We should shower quickly," he murmurs as he stays unmoving, his cock still deep inside of me.

"You need to get off of me if you want me to shower," I say with a smile playing on my lips.

I really wish he could stay exactly where he is for as long as possible. Evading reality seems like the most splendid of ideas at the moment. However, he grunts and slides out of me before he rolls off of the bed and helps me up.

We hurry and shower, trying to avoid screwing against the warm, massive, shower wall. It's hard, especially when he makes extra sure that all of my two thousand body parts are the cleanest I think they've ever been in my entire life.

I return the favor, naturally; and when his length begins to grow in the palm of my hand, he bats me away from him with a smile and a wink.

Henrik hands me a robe to wear, assuring me that Sarah should be here within the half-hour to outfit me for the dinner this evening, and that getting dressed would be futile. I wrap myself in his black robe, which is plush on the inside but satin on the outside and extremely delicious.

Henrik emerges just a few moments later, dressed in a pair of light gray, which look as though they were made just for his body. If they weren't, I might be surprised. He's wearing a dark teal button-up shirt that is left open down to the second buttonhole at the top.

He's also wearing a dark gray belt that matches his dark gray loafers to perfection. His hair is still damp but combed and styled neatly, and he looks everything like the prince that he is, down to the big black watch that rests on his wrist.

"You look very handsome," I murmur.

"Thanks," he says distractedly as he looks at his phone. "Oh, Sarah's here."

I hold my breath as I follow him into the living area and toward the door. Once he swings open the apartment door, all I see are shiny, glossy department store bags and dress bags piled and hanging on a rack. Then I catch movement in the corner of my eye, and I gasp at the sight before me.

There is a short woman, round in every way a woman can be round, purple tinted hair, hot pink eye shadow and red lipstick. She's wearing a bright purple pencil skirt with a hot pink silk button up blouse, and a purple blazer that matches her skirt exactly. Her shoes are bright red kitten heels. She's so brightly colored; I feel as though I need my sunglasses just to look at her.

"I'm Sarah. Don't stare, duckie," she announces and admonishes as she walks through the door, pulling the cart behind her.

"Good evening, Sarah," Henrik chuckles before he leans down and presses his lips to her cheek.

"You go off now, I have to tend to your missus quickly so you're not late," she scolds.

I hear Henrik laugh and almost miss his wink in my direction before he closes the door and makes his way toward the direction of his office.

"I'm Caitriona," I say, smiling as best I can while holding out my hand to her. She shakes it as her gaze gives me a once over and then she grins.

"Okay, shall we get started then?" Sarah announces as we walk into the master bedroom.

I nod, unsure of what to do as she starts moving around. I watch as she opens two garment bags and holds up two dresses for me to look at. Neither are options I would ever consider wearing—*ever*. They are both so stuffy looking.

The first is a black, high neck, caped sleeved, straight cut to below the knee, boring-as-hell dress that looks like a giant rectangle.

Then there's an olive green, simple wrap dress that has a three quarter sleeve with a deep V cut up top. It looks as though it will fall to my knees, and, after a second glance, it looks pretty. I pick the bottom of the dress up and feel the fabric between my fingers. I like it; it's soft and feminine.

The shoes, on the other hand, are beautiful simple pale pink high heels. I love them. I take the wrap dress and try it on, then slip my feet inside of the shoes. I smile at my reflection in the full length mirror of my empty closet. It looks good on me, hugging my curves without being *too* much.

"They'll be expecting something like the black, but I saw your wedding photo, and I just knew this green was more you," Sarah announces, nodding her head in agreement to the choice I've made.

I cringe at the announcement of her viewing my wedding photo, the too short, too tight, dress of Madison's. I wish it would disappear. I look like I'm about to bust at the seams in the photograph. I shake the image away and decide to focus on the task ahead of me.

I quickly make my way into the bathroom and try to do my makeup, putting on a light foundation base with champagne eye shadow, a sweep of mascara and sheer lip gloss. It's more that I usually wear, since makeup isn't really my thing.

I notice, in the mirror, that my freckles are showing more than usual, but I just shrug that off. Perhaps it bothers some people, but I kind of like my freckles.

I run some curl enhancing elixir in my hair, and scrunch it up the way Madison has taught me how. I don't really have the time to try and straighten it; so it's going to have to be crazy and wild, per the usual.

One last look, and I can't believe it's really me. The new dress and the shoes really make a difference, making me look more polished than ever. Taking my new beautiful wedding rings and sliding them on my fingers as my only jewelry means that I'm ready to go.

I walk back into the bedroom area to find Sarah just finishing hanging up the rest of the clothes she's purchased, and her eyes meet mine. She smiles hesitantly, and I instantly start to panic.

"It's too low cut, isn't it?" I ask, looking into the full length mirror again.

The dress hugs me tightly from chest to waist, and then flares out at the hips. It shows a small amount of cleavage, but a massive amount of my bare upper chest.

"You look lovely. If those stuffy arses give you any grief, don't listen to them," she quips. "Now, I'll be round to pick you up at ten tomorrow morning so that we can outfit you with a proper wardrobe," Sarah murmurs before kissing each of my cheeks.

I stand in surprise, just watching as she waltzes out of the bedroom. I'm unsure of what she means by seeing me tomorrow morning, but I'm too baffled to question her.

I walk out into the living room to find Henrik with his eyes closed and his head leaning back against the sofa. I watch him for just a moment, wanting to remember his handsome face so relaxed. I hate to interrupt him, but I know that we need to get going. I do not want to be late for this dinner. I clear my throat and he sits straight up, his eyes popping open and then focusing on me before he smiles.

Henrik's lips part a bit once his eyes start to scan me; then they glaze over, and a lazy grin appears on his face, but he stays silent.

When he doesn't speak, I start to panic, *again*, wondering if I made the correct decision on the dress. I even contemplate running back to the bedroom and changing into the terrible black dress. Henrik begins walking toward me, all business, and ready to leave.

"Come, my beautiful girl, let's do this," he says, his voice hoarse and thick. "This dress is beautiful, precious. I'm going to be hard all night long," he whispers when he reaches me, his lips at my ear.

A shiver runs down my body, and he watches as he pulls away. I then notice a gleam in his gorgeous green eyes. I smile back at him and shake my head.

"Let's get this over with, so they can tell me how much they hate me, and we can come home and you can show me how much you *like* me," I murmur.

"They may not approve, Riona, but nobody could hate you. I don't want to hear anything contrary to that," he grunts.

Together, we walk hand in hand out of the apartment, into the elevator car, and then out to the front of the building. I'm thankful that there are no more reporters waiting with cameras, and I hope that leaving the apartment will forever be this quiet and calm.

We slide into the backseat of the waiting car, and I let the silent car relax me. I soak in the silence and just breathe. Henrik seems to know what I need, because he doesn't try to speak. He doesn't ask me if I'm all right, he just lets me be for a few moments, and I'm extremely grateful.

The car pulls up to a building. I'm too nervous to look at it, knowing that this is our destination. Henrik wraps his palm around the back of my neck and squeezes gently. I turn to face him, seeing his kind eyes on me—his kind and concerned eyes.

"All will be just fine, Riona," he assures.

"I want them to like me, and I know they won't—at least not right now, not after the way we've begun," I murmur.

"My mum will love you. No matter what, you have Philip, Bee, my mum, and me at your side."

I nod, not feeling any more confident after his pep talk. His lips brush mine as the driver opens the door.

Now is the time.

Now is when it all becomes a reality.

Everything up until now has been real, but it's felt like a dream. Right now, tonight, the dream ends and true reality sets in.

I'm not ready.

CHAPTER
Fifteen

Caitriona

STANDING OUTSIDE OF THE FRONT DOOR NEXT TO Henrik, I am more nervous in this very moment than I have been my entire life. There is a room full of people who will mostly likely hate me on sight, not to mention the fact that I'm also in a strange and new country; it all makes me uneasy. Nothing, not one thing, can prepare a person for meeting royalty who happen to be your new in-laws—*absolutely nothing*.

Henrik rings the bell and we wait. I twist my fingers around as his thumb gently massages my side, where his hand rests against my hip. The move is probably meant to be comforting, but all I can think about is how his hands felt on my bare body just hours ago.

When the door swings open, I blink, hard, *twice*. The

man standing before me is obviously a *servant*. He is dressed to a perfect science, and I feel frumpy just being around him, which means I am going to feel awful around Henrik's family.

Fantastic.

"Angus," Henrik says with a nod.

His hand moves to my lower back and he applies pressure to guide me through the door. I know I am trembling in fear, real *actual* fear.

Everything is so unknown, and I feel as though I'm walking into what could potentially be a complete and total disaster. Probably not even potentially. No, it's *going* to be a complete and total disaster.

Henrik's hand is wrapped around my waist, and I'm tucked in close to his side when we enter the formal living area. All eyes turn to us.

"Grandfather, father, mum, I would like you to meet my wife, Caitriona," Henrik announces.

I brace myself as I force my eyes from scanning the room to focus on each person, to face whatever music will be coming my way. I see several emotions as I make eye contact with each one. Disgust and hatred are the most common, but Henrik's mother looks at me with pure sympathy, and possibly even pity. I hate that.

Then I hear *her*.

"I couldn't believe it when I saw that awful tabloid photo of the two of you this morning, but it *is* true. She is just as fat in person as she is on the front of a magazine." Eugenie's voice floats through the air and cuts me like a sharpened butcher knife as she walks into the room from around the corner.

I know that it's her. I've not only seen her on television,

but I've also heard her shrill voice through Henrik's phone. My first reaction is to turn and cry, but then I feel Henrik's hand tighten around my waist, and I hear a low growl rise from his throat.

"Unacceptable, Eugenie," Henrik announces calmly. "Why are you even here?" he sighs.

"Edward invited me. I am almost family. I have a right to be here for this family discussion," she whines as she points to Henrik's parents.

"You are most certainly *not* almost family, that is what this is about. I told you we are not to be married," Henrik growls, turning to his father, who I now know is named Edward.

"You cannot be serious about sticking this farce out, Henrik. This is irresponsible and just plain stupid," Edward says. I watch as his eyes fill with anger.

"Everybody sit," Henrik's grandfather announces.

Everyone in the room freezes before they promptly sit, including Henrik and me. We walk over and sit next to Philip and Beatrice.

"I am most unhappy, Henrik," he begins. My eyes travel down to my shoes. I want to cry. "I am not only unhappy because of how you have behaved throughout your youth and up until just a few months ago, I am also unhappy with the careless choice you made to wed this girl. *Consciously* aware or not, you did something unheard of. It's a damned embarrassment and a stain on our family," he says.

I have never felt as ashamed, embarrassed, and downright *dirty* as I do right now. Henrik was a one-night stand, my one and only one-night stand, which ended in matrimony.

What we have isn't conventional, not for me and definitely not for him, but it isn't dirty either. It's a story for the books, and juicy gossip for the tabloids; but for us, between the two of us, it's so much more. I hate how his grandfather is making it something it's not, based off of perception alone—nothing else.

"This woman, if you wish to call her that, is not good enough for you. She is also not good enough for this country. She is overweight, to the point of complete disgust, her hair is absurd, and she dresses like common trash. I have seen the dossier on her, and I must say, I am not impressed. She is a bastard child who doesn't even know the name of her own father; her mother has been married more times than I could even count, and has lived with even more men than that.

"She lives in the pool house of a friend, and she has five hundred dollars in her checking account. She owns nothing, not even her *car*. This marriage cannot be accepted by me or the country. I will strip you of your future title, and any heirs you create with this *creature* if you choose to stay with her," he announces.

By the end of Henrik's grandfather's speech, I am in full blown tears, my body shaking with silent sobs. He is a horrible, awful, vile man, and he has hit on each and every negative aspect of my entire life in less than five minutes.

The mean old man stands and leaves before anyone can attempt to speak. Not once did he say that, though my life has not been easy, I've done well for myself. I have worked hard to provide what I can, to make my life better than the one my mother gave me.

Henrik wraps his arm around my shoulders and tucks me into his side, ever closer than I was before, as if he can shield me from the hurtful words that were just hurled in my direction. I should push him off and run away, go back to Oregon; but at the moment, I am too broken to move.

"Well, I think Father has said everything that needs to be said. Though, I will add something, a bit of a compromise," Edward says. My eyes lift to meet his wicked ones.

"Henrik, put her up in a modest apartment, give her an allowance, and divorce her. Wed Eugenie and make legitimate heirs with her," Edward offers with a smirk.

I look from Edward to Henrik, who I assume would be seething at the suggestion, but he isn't. He looks *contemplative*.

Panic enters my body, and I turn to look at Helena, Henrik's mother, who is watching me with even more pity in her expression than when I walked in just a few moments ago. My eyes swing to Beatrice, who is gazing at me the same way.

Then I look over to Eugenie, who has been silent this entire time, and she is smirking, looking very pleased with herself.

A few moments tick by and dread washes over me. Henrik is contemplating this. He brought me here, promised me a wonderful life, and now he is truly contemplating this. I can't take the silence or the stares any longer. I break away from Henrik and stand.

"I want to leave, *now*," I say quietly but firmly.

"Precious," Henrik warns.

I turn to look at him. He looks regretful. His decision has been made, and it makes me sick.

"Don't, Henny. Just don't. Fine—you all want me to go quietly, live in a modest apartment? To that I say, *hell no*. I'll go back to Oregon, to my real family." I take a step away from him when he reaches for my hand, and I wrench it away.

"Riona, I never said that was what I wanted," he says softly.

"You didn't have to, Henrik. I sat here in silence for five minutes while you contemplated. That is all the confirmation I need. You promised me things, you ripped me from my life and my only family with a big gesture of grandeur, but it was all bullshit, wasn't it?"

The room is silent, to the point where I think if a pin would drop, the sound it would make hitting the floor would be deafening. I look at Henrik one last time, take him in and feel nothing but sheer disappointment in him.

I'm disappointed in how easily he's letting me go, after he came all the way to Oregon and fed me line after line of promises. But I won't be around these people, not one more moment. My trust and faith in Henrik is in pieces.

I walk away from him, my heart completely shattered, the hopes I had now dashed away. I knew it would happen, but I didn't expect it to happen so quickly.

I wasn't meant to have a great love of my life, or to have an exciting, fantastic journey. It hasn't been in the cards for me since the moment I took my first breath. I hurry out of the house, following the exact path I took to get the hell out of the front door.

"Caitriona, wait," he calls out from behind me as I'm walking down the sidewalk, to where? I don't know.

"Please don't, Henrik," I say, tears streaming down my face.

I refuse to turn around and allow him to see me this way.

"Let's go home and we'll talk about this—we'll figure

everything out," he suggests on a sigh.

He wraps his hand around my bicep to halt me. I stop, still refusing to turn around. The defeat in his voice is blaring. He has given up on us.

"No, please just take me to a hotel. I'll stay there until I'm able to get back to Oregon," I grind out.

I don't want to be anywhere near him. I'm so disappointed, so fucking disappointed. I take a chance and look up into his eyes. They look dead. They've lost the sparkle they had just mere hours ago, and it makes my heart ache.

Maybe I'm being overly dramatic, but the hurt I feel right now, the hurt that his family's words caused me, and the way he just let them, not refusing to hide me away like his whore? It's all too much.

"Precious," he whispers, closing his eyes. "Let me insure your safety."

I nod, not because I want to go with him, but because I have no freaking clue where I am right now. The last thing I want to be is lost in a strange country and heartbroken all at the same time. Now I know where he stands. He wants to assure my safety, not anything else. My heart aches.

I watch as a car pulls up and the driver from earlier dips his chin as he opens the passenger car door for us. I silently slide into the car. Henrik follows directly behind me, and I hear him rattle off a name of a hotel.

I'm unable to listen, my heart is thumping too loudly in my ears, my blood rushing through me. I just want to be alone to cry. Not even twenty-four hours together, and my marriage is over.

We drive to the hotel in silence, separated as much as possible in the back of the car. I'm pressed against the door, praying that we arrive soon.

The travel time is minimal, and we pull up to a building that looks nothing like a hotel. It looks more like the apartment building that Henrik lives in. The driver opens my door and helps me out of the car, and I wait on the sidewalk for Henrik to join me. Wordlessly, he walks through the doors of the building, and I follow.

"Welcome to *41 Hotel,* how may I help you?" the woman at the front desk greets.

I ignore the exchange between her and Henrik, opting to look around the lobby instead. It looks like a club lounge, like somewhere you would see old, rich, British men lounging around drinking bourbon and smoking cigars while they talk about finance.

There are leather club chairs and small tables littered around on gorgeous patterned rugs. I catch a glimpse of a bar with seating tucked in the back. It's all very luxurious and high end, probably discreet too.

Henrik hands me my key and informs me which room I'll be staying in. I turn to walk away from him when I feel his hand wrap around my middle and bring my back into his front. Then his lips graze the shell of my ear and he inhales deeply before he speaks.

"Let me come up. Let's talk," he murmurs.

"There is nothing left to say, Henny."

"Bullshit, there is plenty," he growls.

I turn around and take a step back, needing to get away from his touch. That touch of his, it makes me do stupid shit—like go to a completely different country only to be left a few hours later.

"Are you going to defy your family and be with me?" I

ask. I already know the answer.

I also know that it is a lot to ask. It isn't black and white. I understand it isn't something simple, neither is it cut and dry. But I also don't want to be this second choice, this secret to be shoved away and forgotten about.

I want a man who is willing to do anything and everything to be at my side. It doesn't mean that I expect him to walk away from his family completely, but if push comes to shove, I want a man who loves me enough to do it anyway.

He pauses, and I watch as his brow furrows in concentration.

"I want to. You have to understand what my grandfather is threatening. I'll have to relinquish my title, and my heirs' titles. This isn't something to decide overnight. Let's get you settled in tonight, find you a place, and then we'll move on from there," he suggests as he reaches out for my hand.

"Is this where you suggest I become your mistress?" I ask.

"I wouldn't quite put it that way, Riona. I adore you, and I so very much want us to be together," he murmurs, his voice dipping down low.

I could blame his family for this, but I won't. Ultimately, it's his decision.

Apparently, keeping his title and his family's approval is more important than I am—than what *we* are. I shouldn't even be angry. I understand it. Rationally, I really do. Emotionally, I am still hurt.

My head comprehends why he can't just tell them to go to hell, but my heart hasn't quite caught up yet. I am angry that he promised me a life of togetherness, future love and happiness, and then ripped it all away from me when I had only a glimpse of all that we could be.

I wanted the fairytale to be true.

I wanted to be the star in my own *Cinderella* story. To make the lost, scared, hopeless little girl I once was realize that she is *allowed* to dream big, and she is allowed to throw caution to the wind, and it doesn't always have to end in disaster—that there is a man out there for her who will love only her and want only her.

Unfortunately, fairytales aren't real, and this is reality, and that little girl is used to being utterly disappointed in life.

So, I will go on, and I will be fine, and I will survive.

However, I will *not* do it as someone's mistress. Not even if that someone is Henrik.

"A few days a week, you mean? You want me when it is convenient for you, and then what? Go home to Eugenie and your adored heirs all with fancy titles? No, thank you. I don't want that for me. I respect myself a little more than that," I say quietly, as if it hurts to say the words aloud. In truth, it does.

"You don't mean that, Riona," he whispers.

I can't believe we are having this conversation in a hotel lobby, but I'll be damned if I let him up to my room, where he can try and charm my panties off—*again*. And why wouldn't he think that I mean it? Why *would* I want to be a man's mistress? I don't want to share my man with any other woman. *Hell* no.

"I do, Henrik. I need someone who follows through with his promises. I need someone who only desires me, and who is only *with* me at the same time," I say harshly.

I turn and walk away before he can react.

I don't need to hear anything else.

He didn't deny that he wanted me to be his mistress. It's exactly what he wants. To have his family's approval, but to still have his heart's desire. Maybe I'm being too harsh, maybe I'm expecting too much from him. I don't know.

I do know that I won't be a dirty secret, not to a man who is supposed to be my husband—*not even if he's a prince.*

CHAPTER
Sixteen

Henrik

WHAT IN THE FUCK AM I DOING?

I am the king of all arseholes.

I always envisioned that my father would rein that title for life, but here I am, swooping in to claim it myself.

I walk inside of my flat, completely alone, and I look around, listening to the hollow emptiness that surrounds me, wondering what in blazes is wrong with me? How could I let my family talk to my sweet Riona that way and do nothing—*say nothing*?

My grandfather, my father, and Eugenie all degraded her, and I said and did nothing about it.

And for what?

All because I was frightened that they would strip me of my title?

I did what I always do, and I took whatever they dished,

knowing that if I fought back, they would spew more venom at Riona.

Honestly, I could give two fucks about the title for *me*, but then grandfather had to throw in stripping titles from my heirs, and I fucking froze.

They have everything on her, and her *mother*. My poor Caitriona, living such a horrible life, struggling all of these years since childhood. She didn't deserve that, and it is obvious she wants so much more for her future.

My father handed me the dossier when Caitriona stormed out of the room. I tucked it into the back of my pants, not wanting her to see it. When we were in the car, I slid it between the seats. I wasn't going to look at it, I didn't want to know, but I find myself too curious to stop.

I sit down on the sofa and I open it, seeing a picture of Caitriona from what looks like her high school yearbook. She's stunning, even as a girl before adulthood, she's just as beautiful as she is now.

Caitriona hasn't had a boyfriend, or even been seen in the presence of any man other than James for years. She doesn't date, she works, and she works hard. She's obviously determined not to turn into her mother.

Her bank account is as my father had stated, sad. How has she survived all of these years on her own with the meager wages she earns? I look even deeper into the file, seeing photographs of the apartment she vacated when the paparazzi started harassing her. It was *indescribable*. I have never seen anything so small and so bare. I close my eyes before closing the actual file, unable to look for another minute.

I call my driver back. He's going to get an extra bonus this month just for dealing with me on this night alone. I hurry down to the lobby and am grateful to see him already at the curb.

"Take me back to the *41 Hotel*," I announce as I slip into the backseat.

I notice his lips twitch, even in the shadows of the front seat. It only takes a few minutes to drive to the hotel. I thank him and get out, slamming the door behind me. I palm the key in my pocket, knowing it's probably wrong that I had the front desk receptionist give me one while Riona was looking around the lobby.

I have one thought, and one thought only as the lift climbs toward her room's floor —*I will fix this.*

I will not lose my wife.

I refuse to lose her over my family problems, over their dramatics. I will earn back her trust in me. If I can't last hours without her, how am I to last the rest of my life?

I was stupid to think I could degrade her, even letting the suggestion hang in the air at her being my mistress. I feel dirty and disgusting for even entertaining the idea for the sake of simple convenience—for the sake of *avoidance*.

Madison warned me about hurting her. I have done it; in less than two days, I have hurt my sweet Riona, my precious, my *wife*.

I slip the key into the door and hesitate, not because I don't wish to see her, but because I'm truly afraid of what her reaction may be. She's angry and hurt. She may decide she doesn't want anything to do with me ever again.

I was a fucking pansy tonight whilst dealing with my family. I should have stood up. I should have happily relinquished my title. What does it matter when, in the end, I'm without the only person I want? There's no other woman that makes me feel the way *Caitriona Geneva Grace Stuart* makes me feel.

I want more of her. I want more of us. And if that means giving up a piece of my heritage, then I suppose I'll just have to do that. I'll do whatever it takes to make her smile, to fulfill the promises I made to her.

It's not as though I'll lose my daytime job. I'll still work in my field, but I'll probably be relieved of any of my duties as prince; which, to be honest, may be a relief. Perhaps one day my family will come around. Perhaps they'll accept us and reinstate my title, or at least adorn my children with titles. I refuse to lose her.

The room is dark, but the bed is bathed in moonlight, and there is Riona, curled into a ball. Her eyes are closed and I hear her whimper, knowing that she's obviously been crying. How could I have walked away from her? How could I have left her?

I quickly toe my shoes off and then strip down to my boxers before walking around the bed and sliding in behind her. I wrap my arm around her middle and pull her into my chest, needing to feel her warmth beside me.

She sighs before she turns in my arms, and then her eyes open and she looks straight through me, seeing all of me the way she has since day one. To her, I'm just her Henny, nobody else. Right now, in this bed, after everything this evening—that hasn't changed. I'm still just her Henny.

"We must make this work, Riona," I murmur as I rest my forehead against hers.

"It can't," she whimpers.

"There is no other choice. I'm not leaving you, and you are definitely not leaving me. I refuse to allow it," I grunt.

"I wanted this so much. I didn't think about the reality of any of it. I didn't think," she rambles before she closes her eyes.

I press my lips against hers before I slip my tongue inside of her mouth. Words won't convince my Riona that she's mine, only actions will. I'll show her that we're meant to be. I'll convince her with my body.

I quickly peel her dress down her torso, thankful that its stretchy and easily manipulated. Riona shimmies her dress the rest of the way down, before I remove her lingerie. I roll my body between her legs, breaking our kiss only to pull my own boxers down my legs.

Sliding my hands up her thighs and her stomach I caress her breasts, before delving my fingers into her mane of wild hair. Keeping my eyes connected with hers, as I slip between the folds of her center, sinking into her wet heat.

"You're not leaving me," I mutter as I thrust in and out of her body, claiming her and taking her as my own—*my wife.*

"Henny," she whimpers as tears slide down her temples, her hips lifting to meet mine.

"You're my fucking wife, and you are not leaving me," I say, slamming my cock inside of her, my pelvis crashing against her clit.

I feel her sweet cunt squeezing me, fluttering around me, and I know without a doubt that we are meant to be. She's mine. "Come," I rasp against her mouth.

Her body stiffens and she moans, arching her neck. When her tight body finally relaxes beneath mine, I know that I've won, *for now*. I thrust a bit harder a few more times before my own release fills her, and then I kiss her, my tongue invading her mouth.

Tomorrow will bring its own set of challenges, but for tonight, she's in my arms, welcoming me inside of her body, and it's all I need to feel like a fucking *king*.

Caitriona

In the harsh light of day, last night feels like it was a mistake. Maybe we just needed to have one last time together; maybe it was the finality we needed to end this sham, this charade.

But when I turn my head to the side and see Henrik sleeping next to me, I know that I'm full of it. There will never be closure or finality when it comes to us. We both feel that pull and tug with one another that is unexplainable.

I exhale a shaky breath and close my eyes. I don't know what today brings, and to be quite honest, I don't want to know. Every hour that has ticked by since Henrik came to Oregon is stressful—completely and totally *stressful*.

Last night just proved that we don't just come from different backgrounds and countries, we come from completely different universes.

"You're thinking too loudly. You've woken me," Henrik murmurs as he opens one eye and then the other.

"Our situation is unfixable, Henrik," I announce.

"Nothing is unfixable."

"They'll never accept me, and I can't live with myself if I force you to choose between me and them," I explain.

"What if we dated? Lived separately and got everybody used to the idea of you. We could lay low for a while in public, not give the paparazzi any more ammunition, and then my family could get to know *you*, not your file?" he suggests.

I think about his suggestion, knowing that it doesn't really make any of this better; it doesn't solve a single thing, and yet I want to say yes. I want to say yes just to have him anyway I can get him. I hate myself for contemplating the absurd agreement. He isn't changing anything, just his words. He essentially wants to keep me hidden as a mistress.

I can't allow that.

I can't *be* that.

No matter how badly I want him, no matter how he makes me feel.

"I'm sorry, Henny. Call me selfish if you must, but I want all of you. I came here to give us a chance at a real marriage, knowing there was something possibly very special between us. I can't step back and agree to something like that. Maybe that makes me more like your family than I care to think about. I'm willing to compromise on most things, but not this, not when it comes to our relationship and the way I want to be yours and have you be mine."

I watch as he closes his eyes, a pained expression crossing over his face.

"I won't allow you to leave me. I can't. So, we do this a different way. We do this together," he says.

"Your title?" I ask.

"We'll just have to cross that bridge when we get there. I don't know what tomorrow brings, but I know that I want you to be here next to me, to be at my side every step of the way. If that means relinquishing my title because my grandfather and father are being stubborn, then so be it," he announces with a slight nod before he shifts and rolls on top of me.

I sigh as his weight presses down against me, feeling him from chest to thigh, looking into his gorgeous green eyes. He's right in that this is where we are meant to be, with each other—nobody else.

His lips brush mine before he begins kissing down my cheek, then my neck, licking and biting his way down until his lips close around my nipple. I can hear him hum, and then he bites down on my hardened bud, causing me to cry out in delicious, pleasured pain. Then, he licks and kisses his way over to my other breast to repeat his ministrations.

Henrik's mouth makes its way down the center of my chest, to my belly button, swirling and dipping his tongue inside before he makes his way to my lower lips. He sucks one lip fully into his mouth before he licks and kisses my clit. I feel him flick it with his tongue before he sucks it between his teeth, gently scraping his teeth across as my back arches and I widen my legs even more to let him in.

"My precious Riona. My greedy little wife and her greedy little cunt," he growls.

I shiver at his words. They're usually words I wouldn't want to hear, but coming from him, with that sexy accent and with his mouth on me, they don't bother me one bit.

"Only for you, Henny," I whisper.

He grunts before his mouth is between my legs again, and he fills me with his tongue. I squeal with surprise and dive my fingers into his messy morning hair, holding onto the thick strands as he brings me closer toward my release.

When he slides two fingers inside of me, moving them in tandem with his tongue against my clit, I lose control. I topple over the edge and cry out in pleasure with my release.

Without another word, he rolls over and pulls me along

with him, so that I'm straddling his hips. I don't hesitate, taking his cock in my hand and lining it up with my center, slowly sinking down on his hard length. I moan when I'm fully seated, when his cock stretches me like only his can.

Henrik's hands slide up and cup my breasts before he pinches my nipples and firmly tugs, sending chills over my body. My eyes fly open to see his green ones completely focused on me, his brow furrowed in what looks like worry.

"Love your cunt, Riona," he murmurs. "Stay still."

His hands wrap around my waist and I gasp when he surges inside of me from the bed. His fingers tighten, holding me perfectly still. He slides almost completely out before he thrusts back inside. His pace remains slow and steady, his eyes never breaking mine, even as sweat begins to bead on his forehead.

"You're not leaving me," he murmurs.

I don't know if he's trying to convince me or himself, and I don't care. He's fiercely convinced, and it's beautiful.

After a few thrusts, he shifts us so that I'm on my back and he's on top of me. His pelvis grinds against my clit with every down stroke, and it makes my body shake. I'm sensitive as it is, and the extra friction is only pushing me closer toward a second climax.

"Henny," I gasp.

Henrik grunts before he wraps his hands around the backs of my knees and pulls my legs higher and apart. Then he looks down at our connection, watching as he takes me.

"Love watching my cock slide deep inside of you, my lover, my wife," he groans. "The way you take me is so fucking beautiful."

Then, without warning, he begins to wildly thrust into

me with abandon. One of his hands slides between us and begins to circle my clit. His focus is on *us* still, watching as he takes me, as he bites on his bottom lip in concentration. It's probably one of the sexiest looks I've seen on him.

"Come for me, my precious," he growls in between thrusts.

My legs begin to quiver as I close my eyes, and I let my body succumb to my climax. I come so hard that I see stars, and then I feel his warm release enter my body as he stills inside of me.

Henrik sags and presses his weight against me again as his face nuzzles my neck, his lips pressing against my sweat soaked skin, kissing me lightly.

"I will never make you feel unwanted again, my precious. We will stand together. We will stand united," he murmurs.

I want so badly to believe him, but I'm not sure that I can yet. He was so conflicted last night; and just not long ago, he wanted to live apart from each other.

I don't know what to expect anymore. I just know that whatever comes my way, I have to be strong. I have to put on a brave face and dig deep for strength.

I have a feeling this road we're about to embark on is going to be the roughest one I've encountered in my life.

CHAPTER
Seventeen

Caitriona

HENRIK AND I LEAVE THE *41 HOTEL* ONLY AFTER WE'VE enjoyed possibly *the* most delicious breakfast I have ever tasted. The weather is dreary on our way back to his apartment, and I groan at the sight that awaits us.

There is a group of about thirty paparazzi waiting outside of Henrik's building, and I'm wearing my dress from the evening before. I showered, but had no change of clothes, makeup, or hairbrush. My hair is in a braid that rests down my right shoulder, but the rest of me looks like a campaign for the *walk of shame*.

"This isn't good," I mutter.

"Why?"

"Look at me," I exclaim.

"I am looking at you. You look absolutely delectable," he

181

murmurs, pressing his lips against mine.

"I'm in last night's dress, I have zero makeup on my face, and I haven't even brushed my hair."

"Doesn't matter. You're still gorgeous," he states.

The door opens and the driver is standing on the curb with his hand out to help me. I place my palm in his and exhale a shaky breath, slowly exiting the car as Henrik follows suit behind me.

The driver disappears and the swarm of paparazzi surround us. Then, magically, Hugh appears at my side, holding his hand up and in the view of the cameras, completely ruining their shots of us.

Thankfully, the building's front doors aren't too far away, and we're able to get to them without incident.

"Thank you," I whisper, looking up to Hugh.

He smiles and shakes his head but doesn't respond verbally, then he turns and leaves.

Henrik and I hurry upstairs to his apartment, and when he closes the door behind us, I feel as though I'm finally able to breathe. I open my mouth to say as much when Henrik's phone rings and he answers it almost immediately.

"Oh, I must've forgotten. Yes, come up. We're running a bit behind schedule. Please forgive me," he explains. I look to him in confusion and he smiles.

"Sarah will be right up. Hurry and change," he instructs.

"For what?" I ask in surprise.

"Shopping, remember? She's going to outfit you properly."

I forgot. With everything that happened, I completely and totally forgot. I hurry off to the bedroom and go through my closet, looking through the clothes that Sarah brought over yesterday, hoping that something fits me and looks good enough for me to be photographed in, since apparently that's what will be happening to me regularly.

I slip on a pair of skinny jeans that hug my ample thighs, hips and thick ass. Looking in the mirror, I wonder if I am indeed *overweight*, or if Henrik thinks me to be.

I'm nothing like the waif thin Eugenie. I have curves, and they're not slight at all. I shake my head, annoyed at the thought. I've never imagined myself overweight, not one day in my life. *I'm curvy*. I have breasts, and hips, and thighs— I'm a woman.

"Are you ready, precious?" Henrik asks, walking into the room. I jump slightly, standing in only my jeans, my torso completely bare. He frowns slightly before he tips his head to the side. "What's this, then?"

"Your grandfather said I was overweight. I'm nowhere near as small as Eugenie, Beatrice, or even your mother," I explain.

Henrik doesn't say anything. He just stares at me, his eyes roaming my body before he closes the distance between us and stands behind me. His gaze meets mine in the mirror and he grins as his hands come around and rest on my belly.

"You're nowhere near their sizes, it's true. It's also what attracted me to you. I may have never been publicly seen with a woman who looks just like you, *like a woman*. But every woman I've had in my bed, she's looked similar to you in body shape. Probably not something you want to hear, but I think you *need* to hear it. I have a type," he grins before he cups my breasts in his big, warm palms.

"I like your gorgeous, full breasts," he murmurs before he slides his hands down to my waist and holds me there. "I like how small your waist is here. Then he slides his hands to my hips. "I like how your hips flare out, and this," he mutters before he takes a step back and grabs handfuls of my ass. "I like how perfectly this, right here, fits in my hands. You're a woman, Caitriona, in every way. You're *my* woman. I choose *you* over and above all other women." His announcement sends me spinning around, and I throw my arms around his neck, pressing my bare breasts into his chest and tipping my head back to look into his eyes.

"I choose you, too, Henny. *Always you*," I whisper before I press my lips against his in a hard kiss.

"Good. Now, go and spend all my money with Sarah," he chuckles against my lips.

I take a step back with a gasp only to find him smiling and shaking his head.

"Go. You need clothes for your new status. I took you from your home, the least I can do is provide you with a proper wardrobe," he murmurs.

"Wait, does this renouncing the title thing, does that affect you monetarily?" I ask, unbelieving that I hadn't thought of it before.

"No," he shakes his head with a chuckle. "I have a trust fund, and I've already been given control of it. Plus, my job does very well. We're just fine there, Riona. Now go and shop," he orders, brushing his lips to mine before he leaves the bedroom.

I spend the next ten minutes finishing getting dressed. I throw on a soft V-neck sweater that is loose and comfortable, along with a pair of knockoff *Toms* canvas flats. Then I brush my hair and re-braid it. I don't bother with makeup, deciding to just bring some clear lip gloss with me.

I walk out of the bedroom to find Sarah and Henrik

talking amongst themselves. When Henrik's green eyes lift to mine, he smiles, and it's blindingly beautiful.

Sarah stands to greet me; she's wearing a brightly colored outfit that rivals the one from the day before—a lime green pantsuit with an electric blue blouse, and orange kitten heel shoes. Her makeup is just as bright and colorful as the day before as well, and it makes me smile. She's eclectic and sassy. In a way, she reminds me of Madison, doing and wearing what she wants, the rest of the world be damned.

"I have my work cut out for me, don't I?" she mutters, turning to Henrik.

"Don't change too much about my wife. I like her just as she is," he says, his eyes never once leaving mine.

"Lovesick, that's what you are," Sarah chuckles. "Move along now, we've got work to do," she announces.

I start to walk toward the front door when Henrik wraps his arm around my waist and pulls me into his chest. His nose runs along the side of mine and his mouth presses against me in a gentle kiss. I inhale his clean scent as I wrap my hands around his shoulders.

"Have fun today. Enjoy it all. Listen to Sarah. I know she looks like she won't know what to pick, but trust her. She will have you outfitted like the princess you are," he murmurs against my lips before he takes a step back. "Hugh will be joining you ladies today. Try not to run him too ragged."

"Hope he can keep up," Sarah announces with her hand on the doorknob.

"Have fun, Riona," Henrik calls out as I walk toward Sarah.

I turn to him and smile, giving him my brightest, shiniest, fakest smile. Mainly because I'm terrified. I don't want him to know that, though. I don't want him to worry about me. He has enough to worry after. A day of me shopping should not be one of them.

Hugh is waiting by the elevator as we walk up, and, as usual, his eyes meet me with a stony face. He doesn't look angry, just very, very serious. I smile at him and he does nothing except dip his chin in acknowledgement.

"I've made an appointment for after lunch at the salon," she announces.

"The salon?" I ask as we step inside of the elevator.

"Personally, I love your hair and your fresh face. Unfortunately, it's not going to work for your position. You need to look poised and put together at all times. The paps will be in your face on a regular basis, and they'll be looking for anyway to drum up gossip. If you have a dress that isn't cut the right way, they'll be on baby bump watch, or they'll be on eating disorder watch. It's just the way it is," Sarah shrugs.

"I hate being the center of attention," I murmur.

"So does Beatrice and Helena, which is why they spend their extra time volunteering for charities and giving back to the world. They use their fame for good," she says.

I think about what Beatrice said, how they use their fame to help people, and I wonder if this is something I could join in on with them. I think I would like something like that, and it would be a way for me to meet new people as well.

We walk silently out of the building, and I breathe a sigh of relief that there are no reporters this time. It's something that I can't guess at, when or where they'll be, which makes me that much more apprehensive about this situation.

Maybe I should have taken Henrik's offer and gone into hiding, becoming his mistress so I could stay away from all of the drama that comes with being his wife in public.

Hugh opens up the back door of the SUV that's waiting at the curb, and I slide in as Sarah shuffles in beside me. Then I watch as he climbs into the driver's side and we're off. Sarah spends the time in the car tapping on her phone, and I'm glad for the break from her attention on me.

I let my mind wander to the charities that I could possibly be involved in. I think I want to do something with children, perhaps childhood cancer and orphans. Perhaps victims of abuse as well. While I don't know what it's like to be physically abused, I do know firsthand the anguish and torment that comes from mental and emotional abuse. I would like to help children who suffer in any way. I turn to Sarah and I explain that.

"I like it. I think that it is a very worthy cause, and even more, the world will love you for it. It clearly comes from your heart," she says.

"What do Beatrice and Helena do for their charity work?" I ask.

"Beatrice works with women and children who have been trafficked—sexual, slave, and drug. She also does some awareness for HIV and AIDS. Helena works closely with breast and prostate cancer foundations. So, your idea, it would round out their causes nicely."

I think about her words, about how it would round out Helena and Beatrice's causes, but also, that what I want to spend my time with comes from my heart. It does, one hundred percent, come from my heart.

I don't think children should have to suffer at all. They are precious gifts to the world. No child should suffer in sickness or at the hand of another person.

My sad thoughts are interrupted by Sarah announcing our arrival. I look up and am in complete shock and awe at the building we've arrived at. It looks like the front of the Pantheon in Rome, the pillars tall, and stone surrounding the front of the building.

"This is a mall?" I ask in surprise.

"This, my dearie, is *The Royal Exchange*," Sarah chuckles as Hugh opens the back door to let us out.

I look around at the people. They're all dressed fabulously, and I look like some country bumpkin that just rolled out of bed in comparison. Sarah tugs on my wrist and the three of us make our way toward the entrance.

"It's unlikely that anyone will recognize you without Henrik at your side. My company card is also in the name of an Alas, so there is no worry about a cashier calling the paps," Sarah informs me as we enter *The Royal Exchange.*

My eyes widen and take in every single detail, with nothing other than astonishment. To simply call it a Mall is insulting. It's *The Royal Exchange,* and it's absolutely stunning.

"Hugh, dear, I love you, you know I do, but our first stop is *Agent Provocateur*. I'm sure Henrik would not wish for you to see the lingerie his wife is purchasing. Can you stand guard at the door of the shop instead of coming inside?"

"Yes, madam," Hugh's deep voice rumbles.

Sarah and I walk into the lingerie store, and I am still in amazement but also apprehension. The pieces that surround me are beyond anything I have seen before. *Victoria's Secret* used to be a splurge, a special treat, but this store blows them out of the water.

Sarah rattles off to the sales girl what exactly we're looking for. I don't understand half of the things she's saying, but

I don't care. I'm too busy taking in the sexy and stunning pieces around me.

"Can I measure you?" the sales girl asks. I turn to her with a smile and nod.

"What size brassiere are you wearing?" she asks with narrowed eyes.

"A 36D," I explain.

"No," she gasps. "You're tiny in the ribs; you're a 34. And your breasts are not a D, you're a DD," she explains. I stare at her slack jawed, unbelieving of her words. No way am I that big, neither could I be that small around.

"Trust me," she chuckles.

I'm guided into the dressing room, and when I try on my first bra, I almost weep. It's the most comfortable bra I have ever put on my body. I exclaim as much, and the sales girl giggles. I ask her name and she offers it as Harper.

I spend the next hour trying on the sexiest pieces of lingerie. Harper brings them to me one right after the other, and Sarah takes them from me to purchase.

I've never liked my naked body, but encased in these pieces, I look hot. They fit my frame perfectly and showcase the best parts of me, lifting what needs to be lifted, whether my breasts or my ass. I'll never wear anything else again.

When it's time for me to finish, I look down at my old bra and panties and frown. Then Sarah throws some more lingerie over the top of the door.

"Wear that out of here, throw your old stuff away," she hollers.

"Really?" I ask.

"Really."

We spend the rest of the morning shopping. We've hit

every single store in *The Royal Exchange*, and I'm starving.

Unfortunately, there's no time to break for lunch as we need to hurry to the salon. When we arrive, my mouth waters at the sight of the little buffet that is set up.

"Knew you would be famished," Sarah says as she loads a couple of plates for us.

I don't listen to her talking to the stylist as I'm too busy shoving small croissant sandwiches in my face.

"Your hair is to die for," the hair dresser mutters as he takes it out of the braid.

"It's wild and so hard to tame," I explain through bites of my food.

"I hate to, but I know that it's what will be most appealing to your new family. I suggest Keratin Hair Straightening."

"What's that?" I ask.

"Some people call it a Brazilian Blowout," he says.

I remember hearing some of the girls at the Medical Spa talk about Brazilian Blowouts. I chew on my bottom lip, wondering if this is going to ruin my hair for life. I don't love my wild mass of hair, but I'm not sure I want it to be straight all of the time, either.

"Caitriona, it will be best for the polished look we're going for," Sarah gently explains.

I nod my agreement, hoping that I'm not making a huge mistake. I close my eyes while the hairdresser does his magic. It takes forever, and by the time he's finished I'm not only tired of sitting but I'm just plain tired. I want to go home, curl up on the sofa with a good book and just *be*.

I've shopped all morning, and we've begun purchasing a wardrobe that is sophisticated, yet still young. It's not quite as conservative as Beatrice's, but still nicer than anything I have ever owned. It's stressful, but I'm entrusting Sarah with whatever she thinks I need.

"You need more clothes. After this, we're just doing clothes, no more shoes or accessories," Sarah announces as the makeup artist is explaining to me about contouring—something I'm never going to be able to do on my own.

"More?" I groan.

"You have some good pieces, but you need some more basics to get you started," she explains.

"I feel like we've bought enough to outfit three women, at least," I whine.

Sarah challengingly lifts an eyebrow, and I shut my whining mouth. It doesn't matter how I feel about spending more time trying on ridiculous clothes. It's what needs to be done, for Henrik.

"Off to *Harvey Nichols*," Sarah announces as we walk out of the salon beside Hugh.

"More?" he questions, making me giggle.

"I said the same thing," I grin.

We spend the rest of the afternoon in the biggest department store I have ever seen. By the end of the day, I have enough shoes, handbags, accessories, and clothes to outfit a small country.

I'm exhausted, completely and totally exhausted.

I even fall asleep in the car on the way home.

CHAPTER
Eighteen

Henrik

MY PHONE BUZZES IN MY HAND AND I GRIN. IT'S A photograph of Caitriona in *Harvey Nichols*, trying on a beautiful evening gown. I send a text to Sarah telling her to purchase it.

Eveningwear is an important part of her new life, and she needs to have a few items in her closet for last minute occasions. Sarah explains that Riona is knackered, and they'll be leaving shortly to come back to the flat.

Then my office phone rings and I answer it, not responding to Sarah but still focusing on the photo of Riona with slicked, straight hair. She looks lovely, but I already miss her curly mane.

"Hello," I mumble distractedly.

"Did you get rid of her?" my father asks, not beating around the bush.

"I've decided I'm not going to," I state.

"Then you'll be relinquishing your title and the titles of your heirs?" he asks.

"I don't want to, and I really don't think that it's something that I should be threatened with. I've not done anything wrong. Though my decision wasn't thoroughly planned or thought out, Caitriona is a good woman. Her mother's past is not the best, but there's been nothing other than her lack of breeding that has come to light in the paperwork you've provided," I explain.

There hasn't, either. Riona comes from a mother who is *trash*—plain and simple. But she is not that. Riona is nothing like that. She's had less than a handful of lovers, all relationships, her one night with me being the only wild thing I've found in her past. She's held steady jobs.

She may not have been able to afford college, but she's always been able to take care of herself, no matter how meagerly she's lived. She's completely self-sufficient, and I like that about her. I respect her, and truly, I admire her.

"Do you think you'll be able to teach her how to be a princess or a duchess? Those are things that are born inside of you. They cannot be taught," he explains.

"If you mean can I teach her to behave like Eugenie? No, I cannot, and I will not. She's a good woman, father. You would do well to give her a chance, privately and without attacking her. I think you would like her. She's sweet and kind."

"I'm not changing your mind, am I?" he asks, sounding exasperated.

"No. Although, last night, you almost did," I chuckle. "Threatening my heir's titles is a low blow."

"I think your grandfather will calm down. Maybe not

today or tomorrow, maybe not next year, but he will, eventually. However, I want you to know that I'm not supporting, nor am I condoning this relationship," he announces.

I almost laugh.

If the whole situation wasn't so fucked up, I just might.

He starts talking to me about the upcoming calendar for Philip and Beatrice's wedding, plus a few other familial obligations that are coming in the next few months.

Then he explains that there will be a tea with Beatrice and mum next week, and that Caitriona needs to be in attendance as well.

I beg off after making a note, then see that a new text has arrived on my phone, informing me that my wife is downstairs and passed out asleep.

I chuckle to myself as I gather my things to meet her downstairs. Knowing Sarah, the Land Rover SUV is weighted down with garment and shoe bags.

Poor Hugh.

Once I arrive on the street sidewalk, I see that Sarah has enlisted the help of the doorman and a few other employees to help her with all of their purchases. I look from her to Hugh and see him standing beside the car, looking puzzled as he peers into the backseat.

"What is it?" I ask, walking up behind him.

"I wasn't sure how to get her out of the car. She's knackered; won't wake up for anything," he murmurs.

I look in and see that she's completely leaning against the car door. If I open it, she's sure to topple onto the hard concrete. I jog around the car and get in from the other side, crawling until I've reached her side. She looks so at peace, asleep in the car. I hate to wake her, but I must.

"Riona," I murmur, shaking her slightly.

"Henny?" she sighs as her head swivels around and she eyes me fresh from sleep.

"Come on up home."

I help her out of the car. She's boneless and dragging. I almost laugh at how tired she is just from shopping. She clings to me as we exit the lift, and I pour her into bed before I help with her purchases. Once I've thanked and excused Sarah for the day, I make my way back to my wife.

I don't bother closing the curtains, as the sun is setting and casting a pleasant glow that surrounds my sleeping beauty.

I frown at the fact that she's still in her clothes for the day, so I go about stripping her so that she can nap more comfortably.

I curse in a hiss when I see what she's got on underneath her clothes. These are definitely *not* the knickers she left with this morning.

What she's wearing now is almost the exact shade of her skin and sheer; so fucking sheer, I can make out every single inch of her delectable skin. I slide my hand up her thigh to her hip, and then her waist before I gently run my finger on the underside of her tit.

I glance up to her face and see that her beautiful eyes are focused on my face.

"I have to apologize in advance," she says, her voice thick and husky from sleep. I grunt, unable to form a fucking sentence.

"I went a little crazy in this lingerie store. Sarah kept bringing me things and they were just so lovely. I've never seen anything like it in my life," she whispers.

I knit my brows together, knowing exactly what she means, but feeling sad. She should have always had beautiful underthings—she should have always had *beautiful things*. But she hasn't, not like this, not ever. It is saddening. It makes me want to buy the entirety of the world's beauty and lay it at her feet, to give that to her, to give her what she deserves.

"Never apologize for wanting lovely things. I'll always approve of anything your heart desires," I murmur, meaning every single word.

She doesn't respond with words. Instead, she wraps her hands around my cheeks and tugs me further down, closer to her.

Then she presses her lips to mine and slides her tongue into my mouth. I take over the kiss, controlling it as I thrust my tongue into her waiting, warm, mouth.

I wrap my fingers around her hip as I break the kiss and back away as I roll her over to her stomach.

"These are truly lovely, but I need them off," I rumble as I tug them down her shapely legs. "Spread your legs, precious."

I watch as she rises to her hands and knees spreading her thighs for me. Her pussy is exposed, and I lick my lips at the soft pink flesh that greets me. I run my hands over the backs of her thighs, then her ass, grasping onto it before I spread her cheeks apart, my eyes focused on her pussy lips.

"Henny," she whispers.

Releasing her, I strip my own boxers off before I align my dick with her sweet cunt. She's slick with her want, and I close my eyes as I ease inside of her. She tenses as I seat myself inside of her, biting back the groan of pleasure at the tight glove wrapped around me.

"Fuck my cock. Show me how badly you want me," I rasp.

Riona shifts forward a bit before she slams back against my pelvis. My hands fly to her hips and I hold onto her as she does it again. Christ, she feels good. I let her control her own movement, my eyes zeroed in on the way my cock disappears repeatedly into the heaven that is her cunt.

My hands circle her waist as I start to shift my hips and meet her thrusts with my own. Cupping her breasts, I feel the soft lace that covers them and her hard nipple poking through. I squeeze them as I pull her up slightly and thrust up inside of her, taking over.

"Play with that pretty clit, Riona," I grunt as I continue to fill her over and over with my cock.

"I'm going to come," she breathes with a whisper.

"Come all over me."

"Henny," she squeaks and then sighs before she moans.

I push her forward until she's lying flat on the bed, my cock still pumping in and out of her tight cunt. I feel crazed with my need for her, my need to be inside of her.

I fuck her with all of my strength, knowing with her sweet little gasps that she's probably tender, but I can't stop myself.

"You feel like nirvana, precious," I whisper into her ear as my cock continues to thrust inside of her, my hips pinning her to the bed.

"Henny," she whimpers.

The simple way she rasps my name has my balls tightening as my orgasm rushes through me. It's here, in this moment, that I realize how she owns me. I fill her pussy with my release as I press my lips to the back of her neck.

I'll relinquish everything for her, just to have her in my arms as mine.

Caitriona

After shopping all day and spending a few hours wrapped in Henrik's arms, I was famished, *again*. He ordered in for us, and I was grateful that I didn't have to try and cook in his pristine kitchen—a place that looked like it was ripped from the pages of a magazine and had probably never been cooked in.

So in bed, me wearing nothing but his shirt, and Henrik wearing nothing but his boxer briefs, we ate dinner together. *Takeaway*, as Henrik called it, from a burger place in North London called *Homeburger*.

I didn't think that London could *do* burgers better than the states. I was wrong. They aren't exactly like home, but they are completely delicious.

"Better than America?" Henrik asks as if he's reading my mind.

"Better? No, I don't think anybody could make a burger better than this little hole in the wall place in Portland where James likes to go. But these come in a very close second, maybe even tied," I grin.

A few minutes go by and we're silently enjoying our dinner when Henrik turns to me. He looks concerned and then he speaks.

"I never thought I would have a wife that I could do this with," he announces.

"Do what?" I ask around the last bite of my awesome burger.

"Sit in bed and eat burgers with after some epic fucking," he shrugs.

I giggle at his words, but feel the exact same way. I never thought that I would have a husband, not really. I always thought I would be this single woman, destined to avoid matrimony like the plague, afraid I would turn into my mother. Here I am, though, married to a prince, a real prince, and I feel absolutely nothing like my mother.

I feel like the luckiest girl in the entire universe, and that doesn't have anything to do with titles or status, and everything to do with the man at my side. The man who tells me I'm beautiful, who thinks I *deserve* expensive, sexy lingerie.

To the world, he's *Henrik Stuart*. To me, he's my *Henny*.

"Oh, you have tea with my mum and Beatrice next week. Tuesday, I believe," he mutters.

"I do?" I ask, surprised that he's changed the subject so quickly.

"My father rang and we went over some calendar items, that was one of them," he shrugs.

I gather our trash and take it to the kitchen to toss it in the bin before I get some waters from the fridge, wondering what exactly this tea will consist of.

I like Beatrice, a lot, and Helena seems very quiet and reserved, but sweet. I hope that it isn't too terrible. The whole situation of even seeing Henrik's family again makes me nervous.

"Riona?" he questions as I hand him a bottle of water I retrieved.

"I'm just nervous about the future, about what's to come with your family," I murmur as I slide beside him in bed.

"Don't be nervous. It will all work itself out," he says.

He doesn't sound quite convinced of his own words, and that makes me even more anxious. I watch as he reaches for his phone before holding up to his ear.

"'ello," Henrik says as he answers his phone.

I didn't even hear it ring. Then I hear him chuckle before he hands the phone to me.

"Madison," he says.

I grab the phone from him and put it up to my ear, feeling like I haven't spoken to her in months. It's only been days, but the days have been long and stressful.

"Hey," I squeal in delight.

"Well, howdy, princess," she laughs. "How's London?"

"Different, but I went shopping all day long today, and you would have *loved* it," I gush.

"Well, it's up to you to take me when I make it for a visit," she says.

We spend the better part of an hour chatting about her job, James, and she also tells me all about her doctor's visit. It's good to hear all about her happenings.

Then she tells me how she went to the MediSpa to tell them about my leaving. She says that Natasha's face turned about five different shades of pissed off and that it was fantastic, that she wishes she would have recorded it for me.

"Tell me the truth. Are you happy?" she asks toward the end of our conversation.

"Right now? Yeah, I really am," I admit.

"Just right now?"

"*For* right now. I honestly don't know what's going to happen. I'm scared for the future, but yeah. I'm happy," I murmur as I lie down and curl up next to Henrik.

We end the call, promising to talk again really soon,

and I feel somber as I press end, missing my friends back in Oregon.

"You okay?" Henrik asks, wrapping his arms around me after he sets his phone down on the nightstand.

"Just miss them," I admit.

"Do you regret leaving?" he asks.

I lift my head and put my chin on his chest.

"No, not at all. If I stayed, then I wouldn't be here, wrapped in your arms," I murmur. "Doesn't mean that I don't miss them, though."

"We'll have to get them out here soon, give you a fix," he grins.

"Thank you, Henny," I whisper.

His green eyes watch me and they start to smolder.

He's it for me.

This is the man I was meant to have.

I knew my life would never be easy, yet I didn't know the types of challenges that would face me. I'm ready for them, though.

One look into his eyes, one look at the way he watches me, and I'm ready. I'll do whatever it takes to keep him right here with me. I'll face it head-on.

CHAPTER
Nineteen

Caitriona

"I'M HEADED INTO MY OFFICE TODAY. I'LL BE BACK later this evening. If you want to go anywhere, just ring Hugh. I left his cell number on the kitchen counter," Henrik whispers into my ear.

I crack my eye open and look at the clock. Six in the morning; way too early for me to comprehend anything he's telling me.

"When will you be back?" I ask, my voice rough.

"I've been neglecting my duties. I'll probably stay fairly late tonight again," he announces.

"All right," I murmur.

Once he's gone, I try to go back to sleep, but I can't. Henrik has been back into the swing of his duties for a few days now. He leaves early in the morning and doesn't come home until after midnight every night. Last night, *Friday night*, he stayed gone until three in the morning.

He left me a cellphone of my very own this morning. Only a few numbers are programed in it, but it's mine at least.

I haven't left the apartment in days. Not since I went shopping with Sarah earlier in the week for my starter wardrobe and my new sleek hair.

I haven't even had a chance to try out my new makeup. I don't see a point in wasting it when I'm home alone all day long. The apartment is spotless, and the laundry, aside from dry cleaning, is all clean.

The apartment phone rings and it surprises me. I hesitate for a moment, wondering if I should answer Henrik's phone, but then I realize that technically it's my phone as well. *I'm his wife.* My last name was even legally changed just the other day. The documents were delivered, and his *people* handled everything.

"Hello," I answer.

"Oh, thank *fuck* you're awake. Turn your television on to whatever gossipy news channel you guys have," Madison shouts.

I'm surprised to hear her voice, unsure of how she even got this number, but then I remember—it's Madison. She probably demanded it before we even left the states.

I reach over for the television's remote control, and I turn it on. I don't know what channel is the gossipy news channel here. It's not like that's something I watch, not even while I've been home and bored stiff. So I flip through them until I see one that looks about right.

I know I'm on the right one when there's a photograph of Henrik with a stunning woman on his arm who is *not* me. It was taken last night. *Last night.*

"Tell me it's all bullshit," she whispers.

The photo will forever be burned into my memory. Unfortunately, it isn't just one picture, either.

It's three.

Three photographs of my husband, dressed in a gorgeous tuxedo. His hair is unruly and messy, just the way I love it; there's even light stubble on his face that is always present. And his green eyes shine brightly into the camera.

The woman is absolutely gorgeous—the likes of which I've never seen before. She's wearing a backless, floor length, champagne colored gown that is adorned with crystals from top to bottom. Her platinum blonde hair is pulled up and away from her face in a sleek up-do.

In the first photo, his hand is resting at the small of her back, and her arm is wrapped up tight around his waist, the side of her body is pressed tightly to his.

The second photo, he is bent down with his lips pressed against her temple while she is smiling at a group of people surrounding them.

The third photo is what sends me over the edge. My husband's *hand* is just above her tight little *ass,* and her hand is wrapped around his neck, as they are so obviously going in for a *kiss.*

"A charity gala," I mutter.

"Talk to me," Madison orders.

"He came home after three in the morning last night, or this morning, whatever it is. He's been working late all week; and when I say late, I mean past midnight. I've only been here a few days, I just assumed he was behind on work, since he took time off to come to Oregon, and took a few days to help me settle in. He hasn't been working, has he?" My lip starts to quiver and I feel the tears well up in my eyes before they start to stream down my face. "I am so stupid," I say softly.

"No, you aren't," Madison assures.

"I am. He promised me everything, then in a heartbeat, he turned to somebody else. He told me no matter what his grandfather said, that he could relinquish his title and he would be at my side. That he wanted us to work. He tried to move me into a separate place to be his mistress, did I tell you that? When I told him no, he fought for me. He said he didn't care what happened, that all he wanted was me. He made me more promises—promise after promise. I should have known," I sob.

"Cait," Madison coos.

"I didn't even know him when I married him. I was happy being alone in Oregon with just you and James. But then he came in, and offered me everything, and I believed every single freaking word of it. Now, here I am, the *fool*, the *mistress*. But the kicker is, I'm his *wife*," I laugh, but it sounds psychotic.

"*He* is the fool, not you. Never you. Cait, do you understand that *he* is the problem? You trusted him, and that is beautiful," she whispers.

She knows everything there is to know about me, every single thing, and she's been at my side for all of it.

"I am a fool. This is my life, huh? Being the prince's whore. How lovely for me," I say, my words dripping with sarcasm.

"Do not *ever* call yourself that again, Cait. You are not the problem, *him*, he is the problem," she says.

"I need to go," I whisper.

"No, I can't let you off of this phone before I know that you're okay."

"I'm a big girl, Mads. I'll be okay. Just, I don't want to know anything else about paparazzi shit," I mutter.

"I wasn't even going to tell you, I swear I wasn't, but then I started thinking about how I would feel if I were in your shoes," she murmurs.

"I know. I appreciate it more than you know. I really do; but yeah, I don't want to know anything else for a while," I laugh, but it sounds strained.

"I love you, Cait," she whispers.

"I love you so much, Mads. Give James a hug for me, and be nice to him."

"I'll try to be nice," she laughs softly.

I sit unmoving, staring at the television. It's on mute. The words aren't important to me, not when I see the pictures. Those pictures, they say a thousand words, every single one of them.

Then I see another photo of myself flash on the screen. It's of me in Oregon. I look terrible. It was taken before he came to get me, in those weeks in between when I was somewhat of a mystery.

I look around the apartment, or flat, as Henrik calls it, and I wonder what I'm still doing sitting here.

Am I really going to sit around all day long and feel sorry for myself?

Or, am I going to call him out on it?

This isn't some tiny thing. This is *huge*, and he went into public with her, wrapped around her tiny little body, while I sat at home alone.

I'm his wife, and he's done something wrong—*very wrong*. I can't just let it slide.

What happens when it's not just some party? Am I really going to allow myself to be shoved to the side, ignored until he wants a piece of my body? No, no I am not.

I might be a nobody from Oregon, but I'm Henrik's wife, and there's no way I can just let him embarrass me like this—in front of the world.

I get up and shower. I do my hair and makeup, just like the people at the salon showed me how, and I make sure that I look *fierce*. If I'm going to be publicly humiliated, I'm going to look damn good during it. I search through my closet next, looking for the sexiest dress I have that isn't eveningwear. I grin when I see it.

I take the dark plum pencil skirt and slide it on before I shimmy on a peridot green, silk, spaghetti strap blouse. I then slide into a pair of nude high heels.

I look at myself in the mirror and grin. Sure, I look nothing like the perfect, slim blonde he was seen with, but my outfit shows off all of my curves—curves that Henrik claims he loves.

"Hello," Hugh answers the phone sounding confused.

"I need to go somewhere. I'll be downstairs waiting," I say before I hang up the phone.

I don't bother explaining anything, yet. I'll tell Hugh when I get into the vehicle. I don't want him to call Henrik ahead of time and warn him of my arrival. This is a sneak attack. I want his real response, not some practiced nonsense he's going to try and feed me.

Once I arrive downstairs, I'm not surprised to see the horde of reporters waiting outside the building. Hugh is at my side seconds after my arrival, and he gives me a look of confusion as he talks to the valet about bringing the car around.

"What's this about, then?"

"We're going to pay Henrik a visit at his offices—but if you warn him, I'm going to be pissed," I say narrowing my eyes.

His brows rise and he looks at me with concern. Luckily, he doesn't question me, neither does he reach for his phone. I see a tabloid sitting on the front desk, and I walk over to it.

There, on the cover, is Henrik, the mystery woman, and me, along with some headline that I can't bring myself to read. I take it and I push it into Hugh's chest as my way of explaining what's going to happen.

"Cait," he murmurs.

"No sympathy. I want answers and I'm going to get them."

"Yes, I do think it's about time for those," he nods.

It's only been days, *days*, and Hugh is right. It's about time for answers because this—this tabloid should *not* be an issue.

My husband wrapped around another woman at a gala should *not* be an issue. I'm pissed as hell, and heartbroken— completely and totally heartbroken.

"Prepare for a barrage of questions," Hugh says as the car pulls up to the curb.

"The only thing I want are answers," I murmur.

"Let's get some of those, then," he grunts.

With Hugh as my shield, we walk out to the car. Reporters scream at me, hurling question after question in my direction, but I ignore them. I don't wish to hear them talk, nor do I wish to waste any more time getting to the bottom of my own questions. I have a one-track mind, and my focus is to get to Henrik and demand he tell me what is happening.

We arrive at his building, our car ride completely silent. Hugh walks me inside and talks to the front desk clerk before he tells me which floor Henrik is on and wishes me luck. I smile, too nervous to even respond. I walk toward the elevator and press the button that leads me to his office.

Apparently, some days he works from the actual palace, but today he's working his job instead of taking care of duties for the crown so he's in an office building just down the street from the palace itself.

I am a ball of nerves, but I have to do this. Henrik has been playing with my heart, and I don't appreciate it one single bit. Pushing aside the embarrassment and humiliation, he's playing *me,* and it's just plain cruel.

The elevator doors open, and I step outside of the car. I walk into his reception area and smile at his little receptionist. She is very petite, young, and extremely adorable, which doesn't do anything to ease my already extremely active imagination.

Walking right past her, I vaguely notice that she's talking, but I don't have time for her. I march right into my husband's office, noticing his name on the door before, throwing it open and then slamming it closed behind me. Henrik jumps up and his eyes look to me in disbelief.

"Riona, precious, what are you doing here? Has something happened?" he asks, worry marring his features.

I close my eyes and re-open them, trying to calm myself.

I walk right up to the front of his desk and throw the

tabloid down. His eyes flick down and then come back to me. I see regret and guilt swimming in them.

The asshole.

"Where did you get those?" he asks quietly.

"Madison called me this morning to enlighten me on the gala photos from last night, and then I turned on the television," I say calmly, even though inside I am full of anger, hurt and all-consuming rage.

"Riona," he whispers.

"I want a divorce." I announce.

I watch as his face pales as he stares at me.

CHAPTER
Twenty

Henrik

I DON'T SAY ANYTHING. MY EYES LANDING ON THE tabloid she's thrown on my desk.

What is there to say? *It's not what it looks like?*

I want a divorce.

My breath is stolen just by the words she's said, by her demand.

Those photographs are unfortunately exactly what they look like. I went to a gala on the arm of another woman. Nothing happened, the pictures look a little more intimate than reality, but I still went in public with a woman who was not my wife, all because of family pressures.

"No," I growl.

Thinking about her leaving me, divorcing me, that makes my chest ache, and I will refuse her.

"No?" she asks, arching a brow.

"That's right, *no*. This was a party that I was obligated to attend. Eugenie, of course, was my original date; but since I've cut ties with her, grandfather set me up with a Dutch Princess Nicoline. It wasn't a date, nothing more than pleasantries were exchanged," I explain.

"And why wasn't *I* your date?" she asks as tears swim in her eyes.

"I caved, Riona. Grandfather pressured me. I was just going to show my face for a few hours. I was ambushed, and Nicoline was thrown at my side," I murmur.

"You're nothing but a pussy," she says before she covers her mouth, as though she's surprised herself by saying the words. She probably has. My Riona doesn't curse often.

"Riona—," I start.

"No, please, just don't. That right there," she says pointing to the tabloid. "That makes me look like a fool. You've made me look like a fool to your entire country, and not once did you think about that. You say you've been here night after night *working*. In reality, I don't know *what* you've been doing. You've lied to me, Henrik." She sniffles and then a tear falls from her eye.

I rush over to her and reach out for her, but she takes a step back.

"I don't want you to touch me right now. I don't trust you and I don't really like you," she whispers. Every single word breaks my heart.

I fucked up.

I fucked up *royally*.

"You don't understand the pressures, precious," I murmur, knowing that my excuses are pure shit.

"It's been a week, Henrik. One week, and you're out with another woman. Innocently or not, it doesn't change the fact that I simply cannot trust you, at all."

"I'll make it up to you, I swear to it. I'll tell grandfather today that it doesn't matter. He can renounce my titles and the titles of my heirs. I'll do it, just don't leave me," I plead, sounding exactly like the pussy she's proclaimed me to be.

Her eyes look up into mine and they look nothing other than completely haunted. I did that to her, *me*, nobody else. I've broken my sweet Caitriona.

"Don't come home," she whispers.

"Riona," my voice cracks.

I watch as she turns around and leaves. I stand completely still, frozen inside of my office as she walks away from me. I fought for her to be here. I brought her from her home, and then I fucked up. And all for what? *A title?*

My office phone rings and I stomp over to it and yell my greeting, completely angry at whoever is interrupting my moment of shock.

"She must have seen the news," Philip mutters on the other end.

"She's asked me not to come back to the flat. She wants a divorce," I admit. If anybody will understand my plight, it will be Philip.

"Meet me at my place. I'm sending Beatrice over to talk with Cait," he offers.

I agree and close down my office, not able to do another minute of work. My mind is spinning out of control; my thoughts are of nothing but loneliness and despair, regret and self-loathing.

"Is everything all right, sir?" my secretary questions.

I don't even look in her direction, my mind too busy thinking of Riona.

"It's fine," I murmur.

"That woman, I tried to stop her. I'm sorry," she whispers her apology. It makes me stop in my tracks.

"That woman has complete access to this floor and my office. That is my wife," I announce.

"Your wife?" she gasps.

"Caitriona Stuart, my *wife*."

The words tumble from my lips, sounding lovely. She is my wife, and I aim to keep her just that. I'm not losing her, not over my stupidity and my grandfather's stubbornness—I refuse.

I leave my office, offering no explanation of where I'm going. It doesn't matter. It's Saturday and nobody should even be here, yet here they are. All because of me and my family.

Fuck it.

I walk out of the building and toward my car. I catch my security detail out of the corner of my eye, and they watch me. They'll be on my tail following me, and that's fine. Philip's building isn't a far drive, and by the time I pull in front of it, my detail is parking behind me. One gets out to escort me to the front door, like a child.

"I'll be here for the remainder of the day. I'll phone once I'm ready to depart," I murmur.

Robert nods his acknowledgement and leaves as soon as Jasper, Philip's security, answers the door. I brush past him, murmuring a greeting as I go and make my way toward Philip's home office.

Unlike me, Philip only works from home. His entire staff is in and out of his personal residence all day long. I wonder if that will last once Beatrice has moved in. I can't imagine she'd want so many people in and out of her home throughout the entire day, every day.

"You're a right fuck up," Philip announces as soon as I close the door to his office behind me.

"Yeah," I sigh as I sit down on his plush leather sofa.

"Grandfather?" he asks, arching a brow.

"Grandfather."

"How will you fix it? Or do you even want to?" he asks, eyeing me suspiciously.

"I made a mistake. I went to that gala last night thinking I would stay for a few hours and then go home to Riona. Grandfather had Nicoline waiting for me. I couldn't just abandon her, not like that. So I took a few photos and ate next to her at dinner. We didn't speak more than ten words to each other the whole evening," I sigh.

"You had me right until the point where you agreed to take pictures with her, pictures that were public, that you knew would raise speculation," Philip says.

"I wasn't thinking," I practically shout.

"You're going to have some serious groveling to do, brother."

"I don't know how to make it up to her," I mutter running my hand through my messy hair, tugging on the ends in frustration.

"Ask her out on a proper date. Woo your wife," he suggests.

"She'll say no," I firmly state.

"Women are different than us. You can't always tell what they're feeling or guess their next move. If I were you, I'd move forward to make this right before she's not as easily attainable and moves back to her friends in the states."

"Date her, then? That's all I need to do?" I ask hopefully.

"Oh, you'll need to wear some holes in the knees of your trousers as well, but I think a good start is to date her, *publicly*. Let not only her, but the world *see* how much you care for her."

"Are you sure you're not a marriage counselor?" I ask on a chuckle.

"Go home to your wife," he shoos.

"Thank you, Philip, truly," I say, lowering my voice.

"If you want her, absolutely want her, then you'll put in the work to keep her."

I leave without responding to his parting statement—there's no need to speak. He's right. If I want her, then I'll put in the work to keep her. And I do—I want her. She's my wife, and there is no other woman for me.

I start to head toward my car before I decide on a detour. I text Robert my plans, and I head away from home and on toward my next stop—Grandfather.

I look at my watch as I ring the bell to his private residence. He should have already eaten and is probably settling down to watch some tele before bed.

Grandfather is an early riser and is always in bed by seven in the evening. I'm positive this will rile him up and he'll be annoyed by me, but I don't care. This issue needs to be resolved before I commence wooing my wife.

"Henrik, what's this about, then?" my grandfather says on a cough as I enter his sitting room.

"I've made a decision and you're not going to like it. I hate that I have been put in the position to make it," I say.

I'm standing in the middle of his sitting room, too

amped up to even try to take a seat. He sits up and his beady eyes narrow slightly.

"I'm going to stay married to Caitriona. I'll not be annulling my marriage, and she will not be hidden, nor sent away. She's my wife," I say before exhaling a breath that I didn't realize I was holding throughout my short speech.

"Your decision is final, then?" he asks.

"It is, grandfather."

I'm standing firm and tall. For the first time in my life, I'm not cowering down to him. I've always been the screw up, mucking up everything, but not today. My choice in a wife is not approved by any of the family, save Philip and perhaps my mum. The fact is, I don't care anymore.

My title doesn't define me. It never has. Sure, I'm a prince, but at the end of the day, I'm only a man; and I only want one woman to lie beside me, and that's Caitriona.

"I won't touch your trust fund, nor will I require you to quit your work for the crown. However, I will be petitioning for your title to be stripped, renounced, along with any heirs you produce with the embarrassment you've chosen to be at your side," he announces. "Is it all worth it, Henrik? All the things I've said?"

"Is Riona worth it?" I ask. He nods and I grin. "She is. She's everything," I admit.

I watch as his lips quirk and he nods.

"As a grandfather, I'm happy for you. You have to believe that. As a king? I'm disappointed as hell. My original statements about her stand. She's unpolished, comes from trash, and is overweight. But if she makes you happy, and you're willing to give up not only your title but your legacy, then Godspeed."

217

I don't say anything else to him. Nothing else needs to be said. He's already voiced his opinions.

I don't know if what I have for Riona is love yet. I do think that just the basic lust I had for her is gone, and as each day passes, it begins to morph into more.

Seeing her hurt, because of me—again—it crippled me in a way that I never want it to happen again.

I've made my decision, and my decision is her.

I just hope that it isn't too late.

Caitriona

I stand at the entrance to my personal walk-in closet and stare. None of the items in here are mine, not really. My clothes are still neatly packed in my suitcase, just another reminder that all of this is nothing but a dream—*a bad dream*.

A knock on the door startles me, and I hurry to answer it, looking through the peephole before I do. It's Beatrice. She looks nervous as she twists her fingers together, waiting for me to open up.

I sigh heavily before opening the door, knowing that none of this, absolutely none of this is her fault. I'm not mad at her—I'm angry with Henrik.

"Beatrice," I murmur as I hold open the door.

Her head comes up and she gives me a shaky smile before she makes her way inside of the apartment.

"I didn't know if you'd allow me in."

"Of course, come and sit," I offer, waving my hand toward the sofa.

I follow Beatrice and sit across from her in a chair. She opens her mouth as if she's going to speak and then closes it. She does it a second time, and by the third, I tell her to just spit it out.

"He's an arse. A rightful arse."

I'm unable to hold it in, to stop myself from giggling, and then from that giggle turning into a full on belly laugh. Once I've controlled myself, I catch my breath and I smile.

"He is," I agree.

"I was there. I didn't agree with it, but it wasn't a planned thing on his part. He looked absolutely miserable the entire time," she murmurs.

"He didn't look miserable for the pictures."

"We're all taught how to turn emotion off, or how to play up our features when the cameras are pointed at us. It's PR 101. I know it doesn't take any of the pain or the anger away, but I thought you should know," she says softly.

"I should leave him, go back home," I announce.

"You could, or you could stay. Make him beg, make him *work* to be back in your good graces. In the meantime, meet with Helena and I next week and we can get started on your children's charities," she offers.

"How'd you know?"

"Henrik was so excited, he told me what it was you wished to do. I absolutely love the idea, and Helena has already found some wonderful charities. She has meetings and ideas already gathered for you. You round us out nicely, Cait. You're strong, independent, and you have a heart, which is so important," she says with a smile.

"If I stay, if I want to stay married to Henrik, he has to give up so much. I don't think I can ask him to do that, no matter how angry I am with him right now," I confess.

"You're worth it. And if he doesn't believe that you are, then he doesn't deserve you," she states before she stands. "Now, I expect to see you for tea on Tuesday. Helena is most excited."

She doesn't give me a chance to tell her my answer before she is walking out of the door. When it clicks closed behind her, I think about her words.

If he doesn't believe that you are, then he doesn't deserve you.

I can't help but think that if he gives all that up for me, if I allow him to do so, does that truly mean that it's me who doesn't deserve him?

I stay seated on the sofa as the first tear falls, then the next, until I'm sobbing uncontrollably. I don't think that the answer is clear here. Not at all. I don't know what to do. I don't know what is right or wrong.

CHAPTER
Twenty-One

Henrik

I WALK INTO THE FLAT QUIETLY. I DON'T KNOW EXACTLY what I'm going to say, so I'm being contemplative as I set my keys and wallet down on the kitchen bar. I start to walk toward the Master Suite when I notice something out of the corner of my eye. It's Riona; she's curled into a ball in the corner of the sofa.

With quick strides, I make my way over to her and sit down on the sofa where her middle curves, placing my hand on her hip. She doesn't move. Instead, she stays silent, sleeping.

I take a moment to look at her face, really look at it. Her lips and eyes are swollen, and there are red streaks on her cheeks. She's been crying, for a long while, and it's all my fault—*mine*. I did this to her. I'm a bastard of epic proportions.

I decide to carry her to bed, sliding my arm under her knees, and the other underneath her back. Picking her up, I look down at her face again, needing to see her, and I feel a tug on my heart. Knowing that I've caused her this pain, it hurts me in a way I have never felt before.

She's right. I've been a pussy. I let my grandfather push me, push me into hurting her. Not anymore. She'll never feel pain like this again—I won't let her.

"Henrik?" she asks once I set her down on the bed.

"You're not leaving me," I murmur.

"I can't talk about this right now," she whimpers.

I run my fingers down the sides of her face and shift her soft hair over her shoulder. I miss her wild curly hair, and the thought dawns on me that I miss it because it was her, one hundred percent her, and not a fake persona.

"I've spoken to my grandfather. He'll be petitioning to have my titles stripped. As a king, he's most disappointed in my choices. As my grandfather, he wants me to be happy," I explain.

"All those things he said about me?" she whispers.

"He said those as a king. Regardless of how my family behaves, at the end of the day, without the pomp bullshit, they want me to be happy. You do that, Caitriona, *you* make me happy."

"I wish I could pretend that I never saw those pictures, that I didn't know. But I can't," she whispers.

"I know. A mistake that I will always regret. You don't have to welcome me with open arms, Riona. However, I would be eternally grateful if you wouldn't completely close the door on me—on us," I murmur wrapping my hand around the side of her neck.

She closes her eyes for a moment, and when she reopens them, they're full of fire. If I weren't so worried she was about to tell me to fuck off, I'd be hard as a rock. She looks damn sexy. Then she opens her mouth to speak and blows me away with every word.

"I'm so damn angry with you, Henrik; but beyond that anger, I'm hurt. I'm crushed and devastated by your actions. These are feelings that will not just go away, not anytime soon. But there's a reason I'm here at your side. There's a reason I married you. Maybe, one day, we can get back to where we were, but that day is not today, and it will not be tomorrow either."

"I'll jump every hurdle you throw at me, Riona. I'll take every test to earn your trust and your heart again," I murmur. "Just give me the opportunity."

"I'm not asking you to jump over hurdles, and I won't be putting you through any tests. I'm asking for time and loyalty, nothing else," she offers.

"You have it. They're yours. You also have space. I would like to court you, properly. I would like to have you by my side, to take you out and get to know you the way it always should have been."

"Okay," she says hesitantly.

"Sleep," I murmur, pressing my lips to her temple before I stand and leave the room.

I decide to go to my home office and do some work. I also call Sarah and my publicist to schedule a meeting. I have statements that need to be made and a wife to completely claim and support, not only personally, but publicly as well.

I also have to make a statement about the renunciation

of my titles. I have to figure out how to word that, how to do that, without making my grandfather look like the arse he is.

Caitriona

I stare at the empty doorway and wonder what on earth has just happened.

Henrik just told me that he's accepted his titles being stripped from not only him but his heirs as well. It's too much, too much of me to ask.

If I were less selfish, I might just leave in the middle of the night and never look back. I don't think I could do that, though. I don't think that I could just leave, never knowing what could have been between us. When it's just us, not anything from the outside, but just the two of us—it's heaven.

I know that I cannot just forgive, accept, and move on from what he did. He didn't just go to a party without me; that would be hurtful in and of itself, but I could get over it. He wrapped his arms around another woman, he touched her and he socialized with her, all while hiding it from me.

I don't think of myself as one of those crazy jealous people, but that, what he did, was enough to drive the calmest woman to crazy.

I close my eyes and try not to think about the pictures, about the media or the tabloids. I know that the next time I'm in public I'll have to deal with it. But for right now, all I want is sleep.

"I don't care. I need to issue a press release, and I'd like to have you look over it before I do. Unless you want me to just issue it without your approval?" Henrik's voice floats through the room, waking me from my slumber.

I sit up slowly, looking at the windows and seeing that the sun is up. A sunny Sunday morning has never felt so gloomy. The weight of yesterday settles down on my shoulders again. I look over and Henrik is lying beside me, the sheet pulled up to his waist and his chest bare.

I wonder if he slept in this bed last night. It appears as though he did, and if so, it's the last time. I may be willing to work on things and accept his vow of courting me properly, but I'm not accepting him back inside of my body *anytime* soon.

"I'm holding a press conference tomorrow morning, grandfather, time is of the essence," he murmurs. "Yes. Right," he mumbles before he ends the call and tosses his phone onto the nightstand.

"I hope I didn't wake you," he sighs without even looking in my direction.

"You slept here," I announce.

"I did," he admits as he turns his head to face me.

"We're not together, not like that, anyway."

"I'll not be sleeping anywhere other than beside my wife. That is non-negotiable. However, I'll never pressure or force you into anything, Riona. We're married, we sleep in the same bed, but I'm giving you time and loyalty just as I've agreed to."

I hate that he makes logical sense. I want to tell him to get his own room, to leave me alone, but the determined look in his eyes tells me not to even broach the subject.

"Henrik," I whisper.

I watch in fascination as he maneuvers himself, rolling to where half of his body is pressed against mine. I can feel his hard muscles above me, pressing against my softer body. The green in his eyes has intensified, and the look on his face is sheer determination.

"*You're mine*, my wife—my Riona. I will give you time and loyalty, as you've asked. I'll not be giving you space to retreat from me, from us. We're here, in this bed, in this marriage, for a reason. I believe that with my whole heart. You're my precious girl, and I'm going to win all of you back."

I feel my nose tickle as my eyes sting with tears. I didn't know that I had anymore tears left to cry, but here they are.

Without thinking about my actions, I wrap my arms around his shoulders and bury my face into his neck.

I cry.

I cry out of a mix of emotions, but one of those is happiness. Out of everything that's happened the past couple of days, happiness is not an emotion I thought I could feel anytime soon, but here it is, bubbling to the surface.

"Precious, what is it?" he murmurs as his fingers comb through my hair.

"I want to hate you so badly, but I can't. Your words are too beautiful, Henrik. I just hope that you mean them," I whisper hopefully.

"Every *fucking* word. I mean every single fucking word, precious."

We break away from each other and Henrik stares at me. He looks like he's lost in thought, and I wish I could read his mind. I wish I knew what he was thinking while he's looking at me the way he is. There's something working behind his green eyes, and when he grins at me, it's confirmed.

"Spend the day relaxing, my Riona. I want to take you out, but I'm afraid the paparazzi will be insane. I'm making a statement to them tomorrow, so perhaps I'll order some food in and we can eat dinner outside on the balcony?"

"Are you asking me out on a date?" I ask, arching a brow with a smirk.

"Indeed, I am. Candlelit dinner with a beautiful woman; I can think of no other way I'd rather spend my Sunday evening," he grins back at me.

His green eyes sparkle, and I find that I couldn't deny him even if I tried.

"Then, yes, I accept."

"Take a bath, read, watch the tele, or do absolutely nothing. Whatever it is that you find relaxing, spend your whole day doing it."

"Is this your way of saying that tomorrow may not be so relaxing?" I ask.

"Perhaps, not so much; at least, not after the announcements I'm going to make."

"I wish things could be different," I say, furrowing my brows.

Henrik presses his thumb between my brows and grins down at me, shaking his head once.

"The fact that you wish things could be different convinces me so much more that this is exactly what *needs* to be done. Who knows, maybe one day my grandfather will overturn his decision, or perhaps my father will if he's ever King; maybe even Philip could.

"I was never going to be a King, Riona. The most I could hope for is a Dukedom, perhaps an Earldom, and our children would be Lords and Ladies. Stripping that from me, it doesn't make me feel good, but it doesn't cripple me, either.

"So I'm forever known as Henrik Stuart and you Caitriona Stuart. What does that do? What does that change? Nothing, absolutely nothing. Right here, in this bed, in this flat, all that matters is that you're my Riona and I'm your Henny," he murmurs.

"You need to stop trying to make me cry," I hiccup.

Henrik presses his lips to mine in a swift and gentle kiss before he stands up and starts to walk away from me, toward the bathroom. Then he stops and turns around to face me.

"I'll never stop telling you how amazing you are, how lucky I am to have you, and how much you mean to me," he murmurs before he closes the bathroom door.

I hear the shower start, but my eyes are glued to that closed door, knowing he's behind it and naked. I can't deny that my body still wants him, especially after he's said such lovely things to me this morning. All of it combined, his bright eyes, his grins, and his words of loyalty and devotion, I want it—*forever*.

I hope that I've made the right decision to stay by his side. Maybe I'm foolish, but when he says the things he does and looks at me with intensity and passion, I don't feel like it's a mistake. I feel like I'm exactly where I'm supposed to be.

I spend the day exactly how Henrik has instructed me to. *Relaxing*. I take a bath and then I comb through Henrik's books to find something to read. I enjoy reading, though I haven't had the time to do it as often as I would like. Maybe that will change now. Maybe *everything* will change.

Henrik spends the day holed up in his office. He does

venture out a couple times, and every time he's on the phone talking.

Later in the afternoon, I watch as both Sarah and a man walk past me and into Henrik's office. They don't notice my spying them from the sofa, and I don't interrupt their obviously determined gaits as they hurry past me.

By the time the sun goes down, Sarah and the unidentified man have left. Henrik informs me that dinner will be arriving within the hour and to dress. I thank him and hurry to the bedroom.

I don't know what to wear to a candlelit dinner on a balcony with my husband. Jeans and a t-shirt seem too casual for the occasion.

I decide on an off shoulder, loose, cream sweater and a pair of skinny jeans, slipping my feet into a pair of suede wedge booties. I leave my hair straight and my face makeup free. Henrik has seen me at my worst, my face splotchy from crying all night, and it's just the two of us tonight.

I walk toward the balcony and I gasp at the table. There is a candelabra set in the center; cream tapered candles are lit, and there are two plates with domes covering them awaiting us. But that isn't exactly what has me at awe, though it is very lovely.

Henrik is standing, his hip resting against the edge of the railing, and his eyes pinned straight on mine. He quirks his lips in a smile before he walks toward me. Wearing a pair of dark jeans and a light blue sweater, he looks every bit as handsome and devilish as he did the weekend we met.

"Good evening, precious," he murmurs. "Dinner awaits."

"This is beautiful," I rasp.

"I can't take credit in the set-up or the cuisine, I ordered it all; but I hope that you'll enjoy the company."

I smile as I sit down in the chair that he pulls out, watching as he walks to sit across from me. His green eyes are completely focused on me, nothing else in the world exists. Somehow, I know that we'll work, we have to.

We start to eat and the whole scenario is a bit awkward, conversation being stinted until I take a sip of my champagne, then millions of memories flood back to me.

"Thank you for my second taste of champagne," I whisper. His head shoots up.

"Riona," he rasps.

"Tell me your most embarrassing moment as a teenager," I say with a grin.

"Never," he chuckles. I arch my brow at him and he rolls his eyes. "I was away at boarding school. A bunch of us decided we were going to get snockered and snuck out. One of the guys had some booze, so here we were, fifteen and pissed off of our arses. We finally picked ourselves up and stumbled back to the dorms, only to be separated. Everybody else went into their regular dorms, but for whatever reason, I ended up in the girl's dorms," he grins.

"You didn't!" I gasp.

"I did, and I fell face first into the bed of the girl I had a major crush on. She screamed before kicking me out of her bed, and I tossed my cookies right there on the floor at her feet," he chuckles.

"Henny," I breathe as I laugh.

"You now," he says, taking a bite of food and lifting his chin. "Tell me about your happiest moment," he murmurs.

"My happiest moment, ever?"

"Yeah," he urges.

I bite my bottom lip, wondering if I should admit to him what my happiest moment is. Then I decide to just go for it.

"Becoming your wife," I whisper.

"Riona," he rumbles.

Henrik stands and walks over to me, wrapping his hand around mine before he tugs me up and in his arms. I gasp when his lips crash down against mine and he consumes me, completely and totally consumes me as his tongue fills my mouth. He breaks the kiss and moves his lips across my cheek until they're against my ear before he speaks.

"Marrying you was the best decision I ever made," he whispers in my ear.

CHAPTER
Twenty-Two

Henrik

I STAND IN THE CONFERENCE ROOM OF MY OFFICE building. It's empty this very second, but in about ten minutes, it will be full of gossip rag and news outlet reporters.

I don't feel ready, even though my speech has been written by my team and approved by my grandfather's team. To say that he's unhappy I'm doing this is a big understatement—but I don't care. I'm doing this for Riona and me, for us. It has little to do with him when it comes down to it.

"Are you ready?" Paul, my publicist, asks.

"Not really," I shrug.

"This is big for you, a very big step," he murmurs as he sips his espresso.

"It is; yet, in actuality, it feels like it isn't enough," I say.

"She's worth it all, then?"

"Every single part of it. She truly is," I nod.

"I'm glad that you have that, then. Rules be damned," he grins.

Paul, an adviser turned great friend. A colleague. He's exactly who I want at my back today, and I'm grateful to have him right there.

"Shall we begin?" I ask, arching a brow.

"Yes, Sir," he nods once before he turns and opens the doors to the room.

The meeting itself won't start for another five minutes or so, but the reporters need time to set up, so I stand behind their podium and I watch them.

The reporters push and shove their way in, looking like the blood thirsty animals that they can truly be at times. I stand at the head of the table, a podium in front of me. I'm glad to have the small piece of wood there.

It serves nicely as a barrier between them and me.

"Good morning, ladies and gentlemen of the press," I begin. "I've brought you here today to discuss a multitude of things happening, mostly in my personal life. I've prepared something to say, and then I'll open the floor for questions. I'll take, and answer, as many as time allows."

"As most of you know, I have indeed married a woman from America. It was a whirlwind affair, and one that we didn't realize was legitimate until a couple of weeks ago. Since discovering the truth, Caitriona has moved here and taken her place as my wife. My engagement with Lady Eugenie subsequently ended.

"My family has not been pleased with my actions, nor with my decisions in handling this marriage. I will not be separating or divorcing my wife. A few nights ago, I attended a gala, where I was seen in the company of a friend, Princess Nicoline. There is no romantic relationship with us, nor has there ever been. I'm deeply regretful of my actions that night, as they hurt the feelings of the woman whom I care very deeply for—my wife.

"I am wholly devoted to my wife, and as such, I have made the very difficult yet needed decision to relinquish my title, along with the titles of my future heirs with Caitriona."

The crowd's low buzz turns into a roaring flame, and the cameras begin to flash in my eyes. None of it bothers me, though. I feel calm and at peace. I know that this is the right thing to do, that my Caitriona is the right decision for me—always her.

"Now, if anyone would like to ask me a question, feel free," I say as my closing.

I didn't want to blame renouncing my title on my grandfather. What good would that do? It would serve no real purpose, but rather cause more drama that he does not desire.

"His majesty, does the renunciation of your title stem from pressures from the crown?" one reporter asks.

"My renunciation stems from the fact that no matter how it is viewed, Caitriona is a foreign commoner with no ties to any royalty. To thrust her into this position with expectation would be wrong of me; not only for the crown, but also for the people," I respond, earning a nod from Paul.

A few more minutes go by and questions are being hurled toward me from every direction. Not one person asks questions about Riona, nor are they tearing her down at all. I must admit that I'm pleasantly surprised, surprised that there aren't any digs coming her way. They can say what they want about me, about my screw up, but I don't want them to say anything about my precious Riona.

"Will your wife be joining you at your brother's nuptials in two month's time?" someone asks.

"If she will accept my request to have her at my side, I would very much like to escort her as my date," I murmur.

Paul closes the questioning down after that one and ushers the reporters out of the room.

"You did very well," Sarah clucks.

"They didn't ask me anything about Riona. I'm surprised," I say, voicing my confusion.

"They don't know her yet; she's been fairly hidden during this whole thing. You're the cad who took another woman out," she says, arching her brow.

"Don't worry, Riona is not letting me off the hook easily for it either," I grunt.

"I knew I liked her," she grins before she pats my cheek with her palm and walks away from me.

I spend the rest of the day in contemplation.

I think about everything that has happened. It *has* been a whirlwind couple of weeks; and honestly, I wouldn't change any of it for the world.

Caitriona is still of the utmost importance to me, as is her happiness, and I aim to make her as happy as possible. She is the strongest woman I have known, and more forgiving than any person I've ever come across. When she smiles, it feels like she's giving me a gift, every single time.

Riona is my other half, not just because our bodies fit so well together, but because when she's not next to me I feel the loss of her like a living breathing thing. She makes me feel whole. I just hope that I can make her half as happy as she makes me.

Caitriona

I gape at the television, my ear pressed to the phone, listening to Madison shout as Henrik speaks. I can't believe he's come right out, and said everything that he's said. I'm still completely and totally in shock at his words.

"He's wholly devoted to me," I whisper as I finally speak.

"Shit, yeah, he is," Madison mutters. "He's deeply regretful for being a fucked up asshat too, did you hear that part?"

"He didn't say that," I chuckle.

"No, but he meant it. You know he did."

"Am I stupid for staying here, after all that's happened?" I ask, wanting her completely and totally biased opinion.

"I want to say you're dumb, because I'm selfish and I wish you were back here with me. But as selfish as I am, I can't say that to you," she sighs before she speaks again. "He's saying all of the right things, he always has. I think that's part of his training or some shit.

But he's saying them, and only time will tell if he's going to back them up. He fucked up, *royally*—pardon my pun, but he did. Though, I can't imagine the pressure he was under. He did something that wasn't very nice, however, he didn't cheat on you, right?"

"He says he didn't," I say, nodding my head like she can see me.

"Let him prove it to you. If he wants to prove it like he

claims he does, let him," she suggests.

"He's refusing to sleep in another room," I blurt out.

"*Ha!* Henrik knows the allure of the D, but you have the V and it's all up to you what happens and what doesn't. Leave his balls blue for a few weeks. He'll live," she laughs as though she's hysterical.

"Madison," I sigh.

"Seriously, Cait. You're in control now, nobody else. Move your entire relationship at a pace you're the most comfortable with. If you're planning on staying married, you have the rest of your life to make this work. Don't rush anything," she advises. "I do have something else important that we need to discuss, though."

"What?" I ask, almost dreading what she's about to day.

"Your mom contacted me. I ignored her calls for a while, but she wouldn't stop. She wanted me to tell you that she's homeless now, living in a shelter. She also said she saw you on the news," Madison says, sounding as though she's cringing.

"Shit," I hiss.

"I'll let you know if I hear anything else. I didn't give her money or anything. But Cait, I'm worried about her going to the paparazzi or something," she says, voicing her concern.

"I'll talk to Henrik about it. Thanks for letting me know," I say, closing my eyes.

Luckily, she changes the subject and starts to talk about everything else going on in her life—her job, her new baby that is making her ill and fat all at the same time. And, of course, there's James, who is not only a pain in her ass, but also the sweetest man to have ever lived all rolled into one. By the end of the conversation, I feel better, lighter than I have in a week.

"Make good choices," Madison giggles as we end our call.

This is something her mother said to us, every single time we left her house on a Friday night and went out with James and partied. It's become a joke between us, because we hardly ever made good choices.

"Riona," Henrik murmurs from the doorway of the bedroom.

I wonder how long he's been there.

"I watched your speech," I blurt out.

He nods, making his way toward me and sitting down at the edge of the bed.

I don't bother keeping my distance. He's got his head in his hands, and he looks completely miserable. I crawl over to him and wrap my arms around him from behind as I press my cheek to his back. I breathe, enjoying his warmth and the stillness and calm surrounding us.

"I meant every single word. I am wholly devoted to you, Riona. I want so very much for this to work between us," he rasps.

I release him before I move around him and onto the floor, kneeling between his thighs and looking into his sad face.

"Henny," I whisper.

His hands reach out and cup my cheeks before he crashes his lips to mine and sinks down to the floor in front of me. His tongue snakes out and swipes across my lips. I can't stop the moan that bubbles up my throat, and when my mouth opens, he dives inside of me. He fills my senses as his tongue fills my mouth and makes love to me. It isn't hard and fast, it's soft and sensual as he devours every part of me.

"I want all of you, Riona," he whispers as he nibbles on

my bottom lip.

"Henny," I sigh.

His hands fist in my sweater as he pulls it over my head, then his mouth is on mine again, his tongue filling me again in a soft, sweet, wet kiss.

I don't stop him when he unhooks my bra. My hands tug at his shirt, pulling it out of his pants before I start to unbutton it, then slide it off of his shoulders as his lips travel down my neck to the tops of my breasts.

"Need you, Riona," he whispers against my nipple.

I don't say anything, my moan being the only thing that's able to escape my lips.

Henrik unbuttons and unzips his pants, letting them fall past his hips before pushing his boxers down too. My eyes are transfixed on his cock, his long, hard cock. I watch as he wraps his hand around it and strokes himself, my eyes flying up to meet his, noticing he's got a grin on his lips.

"Take off your pants and knickers, play with yourself for me," he murmurs.

I slip my pants down my legs along with my panties and watch him stroke himself. He's so bold, so unashamed, so uninhibited. I don't know if I could do that, if I could be that.

"C'mon Riona, show me your beautiful cunt," he rumbles.

"Henny," I whisper.

"For me, precious," he whispers.

I stay on my knees, not willing to lie down and spread my legs, not willing to be quite that vulnerable. But I spread my legs as wide as I can and let my fingers trail down my stomach to my pussy, swirling them around my clit before I let them run along my slit. Henrik moans as I dip two fingers slightly inside of me, dragging them back to my clit to stroke myself.

"Fuck yourself for me," he mutters.

I look up at his face and notice that he's totally focused on my hand.

With a heavy sigh, I slide my fingers inside of my pussy on a moan. Grinding my palm against my clit, I start to gently glide my fingers in and out of my center.

"Christ, yeah," he mutters from a few feet away.

I close my eyes and let my head fall back as I start to thoroughly enjoy myself. My free hand slides up my body and I wrap it around my breast, squeezing as I continue to pleasure myself.

"Fuck this," Henrik shouts, startling me.

He wraps his hand around my wrist and tugs it away from my body. Pushing me back, gently but firmly, to the ground, holding my wrist above my head.

"Henny," I gasp.

His cock fills me with one swift move, and we both groan.

"Lift your legs, tuck them high against my ribs, precious," he orders. I quickly do as he demands, feeling him slip inside of me a bit deeper. "I'm going to fuck my gorgeous wife now."

"Okay," I whisper, looking into his eyes, unable to look away even if I wanted to.

Henrik rears back and then pounds back inside of me, his pelvis hitting my clit at just the right angle. His cock slams inside of me, hitting the most perfect spot with every thrust.

The second time I lose my breath, and I wrap my free hand around his neck to hold on. He doesn't stop. He thrusts inside of me with long, deep, *hard* strokes. I whimper as I climb closer toward my release, knowing its coming and just bracing myself for it.

"Fucking hell, Riona, my precious—*fucking hell*," he grinds out as beads of sweat form on his brow.

"I need to come," I practically cry.

"Yeah, you do," he grunts before he starts to erratically pump in and out of me.

The jerky, sudden movements mixed with the heat and fire in his eyes sends me over the edge. I feel myself clamp down around him, squeezing and pulsing against his dick.

"Fuck," he curses before he plants himself deep.

He buries his sweat soaked face in my neck with a long groan as his hips continue to thrust in and out of my pussy.

"Henny," I rasp.

"I never want to leave your perfect cunt," he whispers against my neck before he lifts his head with a smile.

"This wasn't supposed to happen," I whisper with a grin.

"Yes, it was," he says, his smile growing. "Let's get off the floor and get in bed."

I do as he suggests, quickly curling into his side and draping half of my body against his chest and side.

"Tomorrow is tea with mum and Bea?" he asks, changing the subject.

CHAPTER
Twenty-Three

Caitriona

I'M WEARING A LAVENDER SHIRT DRESS. PURPLE ISN'T my favorite color, but it always looks so nice against my skin, along with my dark hair. I secure the brown belt around my waist, highlighting my natural hourglass figure, the way Sarah instructed me to do.

Then I slide my feet into the nude high heels I've become particularly fond of, mainly because I know that I can literally wear them with anything and they *match*.

I've curled my hair with a curling iron, something I've never done before; but with the Brazilian Blowout treatment that I've had done, it's now possible. The curls are loose and pretty. I look at my face, noting that I have more makeup on than usual, and I hope that I applied it all the right way.

I walk around the apartment but I can't find Henrik, so I

start to look room by room and find him in his weight room. He's lifting weights, concentrating on his reflection in the mirror, his tongue poking out slightly as he does.

"Stunning," Henrik announces as his eyes shift to mine in the mirror.

"I could say the same," I breathe. "I'm leaving for tea."

"Not yet. Come here," he says. I watch as his eyes darken slightly.

I walk over to where he is on the bench and turn to face him when I arrive. He scoots forward to the edge and I suck in a breath when his fingertips skim up the outside of my thighs.

"Henny, I don't want to be late," I whisper.

"I'll be quick," he rumbles. "Turn around."

"Henrik, we talked about this," I whisper lamely as my body breaks out with goosebumps from his touch.

"Riona," he says in what sounds like a warning.

My entire body shivers, I want him, and I shouldn't. I should walk away from him right now, but I don't. I turn around, my heart racing as I do. I see myself in the mirror, his hands under my dress. He then tugs my panties down my legs and taps my ankles so I lift each one, my eyes skirting down as he tosses my panties to the side.

"Unbutton your dress. I want to see all of you," he rasps.

I bite the corner of my bottom lip as I unbutton my dress and unbuckle my belt, sliding them off and setting them down to the side. Then I unhook my bra without him telling me to, only to have him groan from behind me.

My body trembles as he slides his hands up my body and cups my breasts, lightly pinching my nipples before he skims his fingertips back down to my hips.

"I want to watch you in the mirror. I want to watch you take my cock, and I want to watch your tits bounce as my fingers play your clit just the way I know you like," he rumbles.

"Henny," I whisper.

Turning my head slightly to see that he's completely naked, his sweaty gym clothes thrown to the side and his cock hard, and waiting.

I back up, widening my legs before I start to slowly sink down. I straddle his lap, but I don't take him inside of me. He widens his thighs beneath me. I look at his reflection in the mirror in surprise.

"I want to play for a minute," he rasps as his lips touch my shoulder.

I watch as Henrik's hands move from my hips, sliding to my belly. Then one slides up my chest while the other glides down to cup my pussy.

"Henny," I whisper.

"You'll ride my hand first, *then* my cock," he declares as he slips two fingers inside of me.

I let my head fall back against his shoulder as he pumps his fingers inside of me, his other hand playing gently with my breast, kneading it and then plucking my hard nipple before switching to the other side.

"Look at yourself, Riona. Look at how fucking stunning you are," he demands.

I lift my head and I look at myself in the mirror. I don't know that I'm *stunning*, but my cheeks are flushed and his tanned arms are around me, his fingers inside of me.

When I glance at the way *he's* watching *me,* I suddenly feel absolutely beautiful.

"You feel so good," I admit on a whisper.

"You ready for my cock, precious?"

"Yes, so ready," I say with a shiver.

He grins as he slips his fingers from my body and swirls them around my clit before he taps my thigh. I lift slightly, watching as he positions his cock at my entrance.

Then I watch myself sink down on him, taking him inside of me completely, his cock disappearing into my body.

"Do you see just how amazing that is, Riona?" he asks.

I lift my eyes to meet his in the mirror and I nod with a jerk of my head.

"You're my gorgeous wife. No other woman could make me feel the way you do, precious," he murmurs.

His hand returns to my pussy and he starts to stroke my clit. He pinches my nipple, instructing me to move. I start to move on his cock, my eyes slowly drifting from his to our connection.

I lick my lips at the sight of his glistening cock as it disappears and reappears over and over again inside of my body. It's amazing and stunning, just as he's said it to be. My pussy flutters as I climb closer toward my release. The constant strum of his fingers against my clit, making it impossible to hold off at all.

"Henny, I'm close," I rasp.

"Yeah, precious, I know," he grunts. "Get there so I can fill you up."

I throw back my head as his fingers stroke me harder, and faster. I come with a long moan, my body tensing, and then shaking, with my climax.

Henrik's hands move to my hips and he guides me as he lifts my hips, fucking me with all of his strength until I watch his jaw clench and his head fall forward against my shoulder with his own groan. His release does just as he promised, filling me with every jerk of his cock.

"I need to get dressed," he mutters against my back.

"Why?" I ask my chest heaving as I try to catch my breath.

"I wanted to escort you to tea. The paparazzi have been dying to get your take on the situation, and I don't want them to bombard you. I didn't want you to feel overwhelmed."

I blink my eyes at him in surprise. He's taking care of me, and that thought alone makes me smile. He places a sweet kiss against the side of my neck as he slides out of me. I gather our things and we hurry to the bedroom. I redress and fix myself, as Henrik showers quickly and gets dressed himself.

A few minutes later, we look pressed, prim, and proper as he wraps his hand around mine and together we walk silently out of our apartment and toward the elevator.

"I have tickets to an Opera this evening. Would you care to join me?" he asks as he presses the button that takes us to the lobby.

"I… I've never been," I admit.

"Say you'll join me. It's a date that requires one of your evening gowns," he murmurs, pressing his lips against my temple as the car travels down.

"Really?" I breathe.

"Yes, Riona, really."

"Okay."

"I may not be available to bring you home from tea, but Hugh will escort you. However, this evening, I will pick you up at five for an early dinner, and then we'll head to the Opera House," he announces.

I nod in agreement, but my breath is simply stolen from

my body as we walk toward the front doors of our building. The mass number of paparazzi are more than I have ever witnessed.

"Henny," I whisper.

"I have you, Riona. I have you," he murmurs, sliding his hand around my waist.

Together, we walk toward the door, and Hugh is there with a serious look on his face, parting the throngs of people as we try to walk toward the curb where the car waits for us.

People are shouting, but I don't hear what they're saying, what they're asking. The blood is rushing through me and pounding in my ears so loudly that I couldn't hear a siren if it were next to me at this exact moment.

Henrik helps me into the backseat of the car, and I slide to the other side while he climbs in behind me. I tell myself to breathe, to take in deep breaths and then release them. I have to, or I'll stop altogether.

"I'm sorry it was crazy. It will die down, eventually," he shrugs.

"That was the worst I've ever seen it," I murmur.

"It's a big deal, me renouncing my title and telling the world the way I did," he offers, wrapping his arm around my shoulders.

"I know," I nod.

I don't say what I want to. I don't ask him why he's done all of this for me—just little me. He could find a beautiful Lady, Duchess, Princess or whatever to be at his side, and all of this drama, it would be gone. But he wants me; he says that he's wholly devoted to me, and I still don't understand it.

I know why I'm drawn to him. He's the sexiest man I've ever met. He oozes charm, sophistication, and confidence.

His confidence alone simply astounds me. He's also kind and caring in a way that I've never had before. He messed up, but none of it was to intentionally hurt me, not really.

"We're here, my worrier," Henrik chuckles before he gets out of the car and then helps me out as well.

I look around, thankful for the fact that there are no paparazzi hiding. I'm so lost in my own thoughts, I don't need to worry about them, too. Then it registers that Henrik has just called me his worrier.

"Do you really think I'm a worrier?" I ask as I follow him up the walk to the door.

"I know that you are, Riona. That's okay, though. I'm typically not much of one, so we balance each other."

"Typically?" I ask, tipping my head back to look into his eyes.

"I've been worried I'll lose you since day one. It's the first time I've felt such a way, and it's hard for me to completely comprehend it," he murmurs, pressing his lips to mine in a whisper of a kiss.

"You have been?" I ask, though I should know the answer, because I've almost left him twice now.

"You know it to be true. But I'm not going to let you leave me, not ever," he rumbles.

Just as he presses his lips to mine, there's a sound of somebody clearing their throat. We break apart like two teenagers caught making out on the front porch.

"Madam is ready for tea with the ladies?" Jasper asks, arching a brow.

"Yeah, right," Henrik mutters, cleaning his own throat.

"If I'm not here to pick her up, please ring Hugh to escort Mrs. Stuart home," Henrik instructs.

Jasper nods. Then Henrik turns to me and cups my cheek in his palm, his thumb skirting over my bottom lip.

"Be good today. I'll see you this evening for dinner," he rumbles. Then he turns and leaves.

I unabashedly watch him go, enjoying the view his straight leg slacks offer me of his ass. I bite the corner of my lip thinking about last night, thinking about the way he held my arm down and fucked me hard on the floor. I swore we weren't going to have sex again anytime soon, but we did, and it was completely fantastic.

"Are you ready, Madam?" Jasper asks, interrupting the ogling of my own husband.

"I am," I sigh.

I follow Jasper inside and then toward the same receiving room where I was berated by the elder of the Stuart family. I hold my breath as I walk into the room, but the only people I see are Helena and Beatrice. They're sitting separately, Helena on the sofa, and Beatrice in a chair, but they're both offering me kind smiles as I enter the room.

"Welcome," Helena says as she stands and walks over to me, embracing me in a warm hug. "Beatrice has told me of your plans for charity work, and I am so excited."

"Oh, I'm glad," I mutter as she clasps her hand around mine and pulls me toward the sofa to sit down next to her. "I'm also thrilled you aren't letting my son walk all over you," she announces, arching one of her brows at me.

"He's very charming," I mutter.

"Indeed, he is."

We spend the rest of the afternoon talking, not only about the charity work that Helena has brought for me, but also about the family, and then about Beatrice's wedding. I'm told it's a two-week affair, and there will be activities and parties for days. It sounds like fun and hell all at the same time.

"So I've thought, perhaps, we can put together a tour for you," Helena suggests.

"A tour?"

"I thought you might need some time away, away from it all. If you don't, that's okay too; we can just come up with something else," she says.

"Oh, actually I kind of like that idea. How long would it be for?"

"Only a month. You'd be touring different children's hospitals and women's shelter safe houses; it would give exposure, and you'd be able to meet people, talk to the people that run it about needs. The news outlets would be all over it, which would bring awareness to the charities," Helena explains.

I'm instantly in love with the idea. Henrik won't be thrilled with it, but maybe Helena is on to something. Maybe I need the space to breathe. Four weeks isn't *that* long, not in the big picture, and I know where my heart lies.

I know that I would come home to Henrik no matter what. But we've been through so much in our extremely short time together that it would be nice to think and focus on something else for a time.

"I'll do it," I affirm.

"You don't want to talk to Henrik?" Beatrice asks.

"No, I don't think I will. Please, Helena, I love the concept, and I really want to go forward," I say, looking at my mother-in-law in the eye.

"You'll be leaving this Friday," she warns.

"I'll be home for the wedding festivities?"

"You will," she confirms.

"Then yes, let's do it."

I leave tea late in the afternoon. I'm thankful when Hugh rushes me home to get ready. I have thirty minutes to look Opera ready. I don't know if I can pull it off, but I plan on trying.

I grasp the pale pink shimmery gown that's hanging in my wardrobe and smile. I hope that it looks as good as I remember it looking in the dressing room when Sarah and I found it, and that Henrik likes it.

I slip it over my body and shift slightly to look at the absence of the gown's back in the mirror. It dips well below my lower back, leaving me entirely bare from neck to just above my ass, except for across my middle back, where my bra line is. That is covered with fabric, as it's a strapless dress.

I hope and pray that it all stays in place for the evening. I've never worn a strapless gown, other than the tiny dress Madison poured me into the evening I married Henrik in Vegas.

"Riona, are you ready, precious?" Henrik calls out.

I take one last look in the mirror and I nod to myself, my dress is so pale pink I look almost nude in the mirror, my red shoes standing out, the only competition being the fact that every move I make causes my dress to shimmer in the light.

My high heels click on the hard floor and Henrik looks up before his mouth gapes open slightly at the sight of me. I probably look at him the exact same way, as he's wearing a tuxedo and he looks fantastic.

"Go back in there and put a rubbish bag on," he mumbles as I step in front of him.

"Absolutely not," I laugh.

"You look completely stunning," he whispers as his hand slides around my back. It freezes and he hauls me into his chest as his eyes peer down my back.

"What's happened to your dress? It's missing," he announces.

"It's made that way," I grin.

"*Un-fucking-bloody-believable*," he curses.

"Do you really hate it?" I ask, feeling self-conscious.

"No, it's stunning, as I've said. It's just sexy, and now I know for certain that every man will have his eyes on you," he grunts before pressing his lips to mine.

"You're jealous?" I ask, arching a brow.

"Of every single man that looks in your direction. All of you is mine, and nobody else should even look."

"That's absurd. Do you know how many women ogle you?" I ask as we walk toward the elevator.

"Doesn't matter," he shrugs.

"Well, I feel the same. Doesn't matter," I shrug back at him.

He smiles but doesn't respond. I wonder if there will be a good time this evening to tell him of my plans to leave for four-weeks on Friday. I don't think there will ever be a good time to tell him that. I'm nervous and scared.

Maybe I'll just wait until Friday morning.

No, I'll tell him sometime this evening, maybe after the Opera.

I agree with my self-banter and relax next to him.

This is going to be a great evening. Even if it ends up in an argument, I don't care. I'm going to a fancy dinner and a fancy opera with my husband, our first real date. I'm so excited, I can hardly stand it.

CHAPTER
Twenty-Four

Henrik

CAITRIONA IS A SIGHT TO BEHOLD. I WASN'T LYING when I said that every single man would look in her direction. Walking through the restaurant at dinner, every man's head was turned, and at the Opera, the same. She was a vision the entire evening, and now that we're headed home, she's a vision who is tense and obviously worried about something.

I don't say a word; I want to wait until we're in our flat to broach whatever it is that has her completely and totally stressed out. I unlock the door and usher her inside. As soon as I walk through a doorway, I throw my keys down on the kitchen counter and I face her.

"What's happened, then?" I ask.

She doesn't bother denying that it's something, because

she and I both know that it is. We're in this weird, fragile, limbo state, and there is a lot of tiptoeing. But there is obviously something up with her, and I aim to get to the bottom of it.

"I don't think you're going to like it," she practically whispers.

"I don't like a lot of things, yet I survive them. So what is it?" I ask, making my way toward her and cupping her cheek in my hand.

"I'm leaving for a month," she blurts out.

I freeze. Dead frozen in my tracks like nothing else I've experienced before. I feel like I'm on the outside looking into this conversation, as though this cannot be *real*.

"Where will you go?" I ask, grinding my jaw together, clenching it so that I don't say something out of heated anger.

"At tea this afternoon, your mother—she made a tentative tour schedule for me. I will be touring children's hospitals and women's shelter safe houses, bringing attention to the causes and also speaking with the people of the organization staff," she explains.

My anger depreciates a bit and I look at her, really look at her. She's apprehensive, but underneath all of that, she's excited.

"You want this," I whisper.

"I think it would be a great experience," she says with a nod.

"Then you'll go."

"You're not upset?" she asks, looking up at me with wide, scared eyes.

"Do I want you to stay here with me? *Absolutely*. Am I going to miss you? *Naturally*. Do I want you to be happy?

Definitely," I murmur running my nose alongside hers. "You'll come home to me?"

"Of course, there's nowhere else I'd rather be."

"Then you need to go," I whisper before I press my lips to hers.

Caitriona

Henrik's lips press against mine, and I swear the world rapidly spins beneath my feet. This evening has been magical, and then when I thought it would be destroyed, he surprised me.

He always surprises me.

He releases me and takes a step back, but I quickly wrap my arms around his neck and step forward, closing the distance he's tried to create.

"Riona," he practically chokes.

"I want you, Henny," I whisper, my eyes completely focused on his sparkling green ones. "I'm leaving on Friday. I want you was often as I can get you until then," I confess.

"Friday?" he chokes.

"Friday, so that I'm back in time for all of Philip and Beatrice's wedding celebrations."

"Mum has thought of it all, hasn't she?" he asks with a humorless laugh.

I open my mouth to respond, but he doesn't let me speak. He presses his lips to mine before he leans down and picks me up at the backs of my thighs, carrying me into our bedroom, my heart racing with each step he takes.

"You want me as often as you can have me before Friday.

Prepare, precious, because I'm going to be inside of you for the next three fucking days," he growls, sending shivers up my spine.

Without another word spoken, he peels my dress down my body, leaving me in my shoes, panties, and bra. I hold my breath when he breaks our kiss and takes a step back. His eyes scan my body, and his teeth sink into his bottom lip with a slight grin.

"Magnificent, precious," he murmurs.

I watch with bated breath as he slowly removes his tuxedo. I wish I could do it for him, because watching him is making me anxious, making me want to rip it off of him in a hurry and take him inside of me.

"I had plans tonight. I was going to bring you pleasure then put you to bed, asking nothing in return," he rasps as he steps out of his pants.

He's now in nothing but his boxer briefs, and I can make the outline of his cock out from beneath the thin fabric. He's hard and ready, *waiting*.

"But?" I ask on a wheeze as he grips his hard length in his palm.

"Now I don't think I'll be able to fall asleep without making you scream," he announces with a shrug.

I want that.

I want to scream his name as I come.

I want him to *make* me come.

I want it all.

Henrik arranges me on the edge of the bed, my legs dangling with my feet still firmly planted in their red high heels. His finger grazes up my thigh and across the center of my panties to the other side of my thigh and down. I hear him hum before he grasps the edges of my panties and yanks them down my legs.

"Very pretty knickers, but very unneeded." I shiver. "Take off your bra and show me your tits, Riona."

I do as he commands, ready to do whatever he wishes. I watch him with wide eyes as he pulls his boxers down his legs, leaving us both naked—not touching any part of our bodies, but completely bared to each other.

Henrik lifts his chin to the bed and tells me to get in the middle, sitting with my back to the headboard. I do as he asks, bringing my knees to my chest to cover myself, though he's already seen every inch of my body so I'm not sure why I feel the need to keep myself from him. He makes a clicking noise with his tongue before he crawls up, grasping onto my ankles and pulling my legs apart.

"Don't ever keep yourself from me, Riona," he rasps.

"Henny," I whisper.

"Let me have a taste," he rumbles.

I gasp when he lowers his mouth and his tongue thrusts inside of me. My hands automatically fly to his messy brown hair and tangle in his strands.

"Delicious, now ride my face," he grunts as his hands wrap around my thighs and he widens them even more, fitting his broad shoulders between them.

I let my head fall back, hitting the wall behind me as I lift my hips, moving close to him as his lips wrap around my clit before moving back to my center, sliding inside as his fingers hold onto my thighs even firmer.

He feels so good, his mouth and tongue so damn warm against me. I can't hold back. My body moves, and I'm unable to control it as his mouth takes over, consumes me, and as always—owns me.

"I'm close," I whimper.

I climb higher toward my release and my hips jerk. He pulls back, leaving me on the edge, and I cry out in surprise and irritation.

"I'm going to take you, Riona," he whispers.

I hold my breath as he moves closer to me, his dick easing inside of my center, filling my pussy and stretching it like only he can. His hands grab onto the headboard at either side of my face, his thighs pushing my knees even higher beside me, and his eyes focused completely on mine.

"Henrik," I sigh.

"That's *not* who I am to you," he growls, as he gently eases out of me and then slams back inside with a hard, deep, fast, thrust of his hips.

"Henny," I cry out, lifting my hands to his sides.

"Fuck. *Yes.*"

He buries his face in my neck, his lips pressing against my skin, his breathing heavy as he fucks me hard and fast. My legs start to shake, his pelvis grinding against my clit with each down thrust of his hips.

My entire body is on edge, sweaty, and primed for its release. Then I feel his teeth against my neck, sinking into my skin, and I fall over the edge, my climax taking over as my nails dig into his sides.

"Fuck, yes," he growls. "This cunt of yours, this perfect fucking cunt, makes my dick ache, precious," he murmurs against the side of my neck as he wildly pounds inside of me.

His hips are moving jerkily, and I watch as he rears his head back with a long deep, groan, his eyes finding mine when he comes inside of me.

"Come again, for me," he murmurs as he continues to slide in and out of me, his head tipped down to watch.

"Henny," I whimper.

"Now, Riona, I want to watch you touch yourself," he demands

I lift my hand and slide it between my legs, shivering at the feel of his cock's lazy strokes. I'm still sensitive from my first orgasm, but I want him to have his pleasures as well, and I know how much he loves watching me touch myself and watching as he takes me.

"You're so beautiful," he mutters. He starts moving a little faster, his hips moving with precision, a little harder with each thrust.

"More," I beg as my finger furiously works between us.

I'm so close, on the edge again, needing something else to help me topple over.

One of his hands leaves the headboard and moves down to my breast, pinching my nipple, tugging on it, and repeating the move until I can't hold back.

I come on a scream.

I beg him to stop, plead with him, but my words fall on deaf ears as he continues to take me, harder than before, through my orgasm and after. I move my fingers, my clit is so sensitive it's painful to touch.

Henrik slaps the outside of my thigh and orders my hand between my legs again. I comply, tears welling in my eyes, knowing that it's going to be too sensitive. I bite my bottom lip and I do as he's ordered, and in just minutes, the pain is forgotten as I climb toward a third release.

"Yes, come for me again," Henrik chants as he continues to pound into my body.

He's sweating now. It's dripping down his face and his chest, and it's the most beautiful sight I've seen. I feel my legs quiver, and he grins, his eyes clashing with mine as he drives into my center, moving inside of me and filling me.

"Riona, precious," he groans.

His groan reverberates throughout the room, and it's then that I come. My body shakes uncontrollably, and I scream at the top of my lungs. I scream out his name as I sob, my body spent, wrung out, and completely exhausted.

"Fuck. Yes. *Fuck*," Henrik roars, planting himself deep inside as he comes, again, filling my body with even more of his release.

I feel his cock twitch, then he collapses against me. His sweat soaked chest presses against mine, and I wrap my arms and legs around his body, holding him to me, needing his closeness.

"Are you okay, precious?" he asks as he nuzzles my neck, his arms reaching behind him to remove my shoes, which are still on my feet, and pressed against his lower back.

"I am. I truly am," I murmur.

"I'm glad for it. I've missed my precious Riona," he murmurs.

"I'll never get enough of you," I shamelessly admit as my fingers stroke his back.

"You'll come back to me, and we'll move forward when you do."

He doesn't ask me; he states it as a fact. That I will indeed come back to him and we'll be past Nicoline and the relinquishing of his title. We'll just be Henrik and Caitriona.

I close my eyes, hoping that his statement is correct, I want that; I want it more than anything. When we're here, wrapped in each other's arms, everything feels so damn right.

"Yes," I whisper. "I want that."

We take a long, hot shower together in silence. The evening feels uneasy, the foreboding of what the next few days will bring hanging over our heads like a dark shadowed cloud. When we finally dry off and crawl into bed, Henrik wraps his arms around me and pulls me into his chest his mouth at my neck.

"Four weeks is a long time," he murmurs.

"It is," I whisper, staring into the darkness of the room ahead of me.

"You do this, you don't ever leave my side again."

"Henny," I say with a warning tone. He squeezes me before I can say another word.

"Non-negotiable. You're my wife. Your place is in my bed, on my cock, and at my side," he announces.

"Henrik," I hiss, trying to wriggle out of his grasp. He only tightens against me to keep my body still.

"You know you like it, my precious girl, don't act like you don't. Now, get some sleep."

I huff out a breath of annoyance, making him chuckle behind me. He's right. I do like it, but he shouldn't have said it out loud. Henrik owns me, every part of me, and I love it when I'm with him, including when he's inside of me. That doesn't mean that my only focus in life is his dick, though.

I like the fact that this trip will give me a chance to give back to the world, to do something that is for me, that doesn't have to do with anybody but me wanting to bring awareness to these children, to visit with them, and to hopefully raise money for them in the future.

CHAPTER
Twenty-Five

Caitriona

M Y SUITCASE IS LAID OUT ON THE BED, AND I'M
finding it difficult to pack. I know that I need to
leave, and I want to, but—Henrik. Leaving means
being without him for a full month, and although I'm still
very much hurt and upset with him, he's still very much in
the forefront of my mind.

I'm folding a pair of jeans when I hear his grunt come
from the doorway.

"Yes?" I ask without looking in his direction.

"You're really leaving."

"I am," I agree.

There's a moment of silence as I continue to try to busy
myself with packing, trying my very hardest not to look at
him. If I do, I might not leave. I need this space and time

away. I also need this experience. I pause when I feel his arm encircle my waist and his hand flatten against my stomach.

"I'm going to miss you, Riona," he murmurs as his lips graze my neck.

Slowly, I straighten my back, still afraid to turn around and look into his eyes. Those green eyes of his, they capture me and hold me hostage.

"I'll miss you, too," I whisper, looking straight ahead.

"Say you'll stay."

"I can't," I sigh, closing my eyes.

It pains me to say it, to leave him, but it's only for a few weeks—it's not forever.

"When you come home, we'll be good again?" he asks as his tongue snakes out and tastes my neck.

I shiver in his arms, and his hand tightens against my stomach when he feels it. He knows how he affects me. He keeps asking me if we're going to be good as soon as I return. I keep telling him yes, to placate him; but in reality, I don't know. I don't know how I'm going to feel.

"I hope so," I murmur.

My breath hitches when both of his hands shift and move to the outside of my thighs, dragging up my dress as they come to my waist. Then he wrenches my panties down my thighs in one swift move.

"Bend over," he orders.

I close my eyes, inhaling deeply before letting it out and then doing as he's demanded. I bend over. I'm leaving in a few hours, and selfishly, I want to feel him inside of me one last time before I go.

Without a word spoken, Henrik's hand lands on my ass with a sting and a smack. I gasp, but before I can say anything—*think* anything—he pushes completely inside of me with one swift thrust.

"Henrik," I squeak.

"I suppose you must need reminding of how you feel when I'm inside you, since you're suddenly only *hoping* we'll be good after your return," he announces.

I'm not able to respond as he pulls out and then slams back inside of me with a punishing force. He doesn't stop, he doesn't slow, but continues to fuck me with wild abandon. It's as if he's branding me, marking me as his so that I won't forget him—*as if I ever could.*

My climax erupts with no warning, my legs shaking and giving out simultaneously. Henrik doesn't slow his rough, brute, force as I cry out with my release, not until he's chased his own; and only then does he plant himself deep, freezing as he groans.

"Precious," he murmurs, folding over me, his cock still completely inside of me, and his mouth hot against my ear. "Come back to me."

His words are just above a whisper before he pulls out of my body and walks away. I'm left bent over my opened suitcase with his cum leaking down my thighs. I stand and hurry to the restroom to clean up. Once I've taken care of myself, I look in the mirror.

I've hurt him by using the word *hope*, as if I may not come back to him. He's given up so much for me already, announced it to the world, and yet I'm not committing fully to him—not in the way that he wants me to. I'm not ready, though, and that is another issue.

I'm not ready to forget that my husband went on a date with another woman and was planning on keeping it a secret from me. I'm not ready to forget that he posed for the media with her, while I waited at home for him.

So, while I understand his insecurities and I comprehend why he's upset, he's going to have to be understanding with me, and with my feelings, as well.

I finish packing my bags, no longer questioning my decision to go on this trip. I need this, for my own sanity; and if Henrik can't handle a few weeks of being apart, then he's got bigger issues at hand that have nothing to do with me.

I need this time to reflect, and I aim to take it.

An hour later, I'm packed with my suitcase next to the front door. I'm still in the dress I wore earlier, a navy blue with white polka dot fabric. It's sleeveless with a V-neckline and hugs my waist before it flares out to an A-line skirt and brushes the tops of my knees. It's very fifties style, and paired with a white cardigan, I feel classy and demure in it.

"Hugh will accompany you the entirety of the trip?" Henrik asks from the sofa. I jump slightly, not having realized that he was even in the room.

"Yes, he will," I agree with a nod.

"Best get a move on it, then," he grunts.

I ignore his words and, instead, walk over to him, sitting down next to him when I've reached his side. Lifting my hand, I cup his cheek and force his head over to me, to face me, needing to see those green eyes on mine. When I do, I'm left feeling terrible. He looks so damn sad.

"Henny," I murmur.

"Just go," he croaks.

"Four weeks, Henrik. Only four weeks," I whisper.

"You *hope*," he grunts, down casting his eyes.

"Don't be this way."

"Go, precious. Be good and have fun," he mutters.

"I'll be back in four weeks."

I press my lips to his, but he doesn't attempt to deepen the kiss, and neither do I. It isn't needed right now. We've already had our moment in the bedroom, and last night—last night we truly made love. It was beautiful, our real goodbye. When our kiss breaks, I press my forehead against his and just inhale his scent.

"If you don't leave, I'll be forced to take you to the bedroom and tie you up to keep you here with me," he whispers.

"You're terrible," I respond with a giggle.

"I'm not kidding," he grunts.

I shake my head, smiling at him. He's sullen and irritated, sulky like a child. My Henrik isn't used to not getting what he wants, and apparently that makes him act extremely childish.

I press my lips to his one last time before a knock on the door interrupts us. Standing, I walk over to the door and see Hugh on the other side.

"You'll watch over her, keep her safe?" Henrik asks walking up behind me.

"With my life, your Highness," Hugh nods.

"No more of that, Hugh. It's not my station anymore. Henrik is fine," he shrugs.

"Sir," Hugh murmurs, taking my bag and walking toward the elevator to wait for me.

"Come home to me," he mutters, wrapping his arm around my waist and pulling me into his chest for a hug.

"I will," I whisper.

We break away from each other, but we don't kiss. The tears are starting to well in my eyes, and I need to get out of here, or I'll allow him to tie me up and keep me with him, without hesitation.

I walk away, leaving half of my heart behind me with him. I know that this is needed, but it still hurts with each step that takes me further from his side.

"Four weeks," Hugh mutters as the doors close.

"I'm being a baby."

"You aren't, but after everything…"

Hugh knows it all, everything that's happened, and he's been at my side, protecting me from the media with every step I've taken.

He knows what people are saying and he knows how the family works. He also knows what a large sacrifice it was for Henrik to relinquish his title.

"I need the space."

"You need the space," he agrees.

"We're going to become besties, Hugh, you and me," I say, grinning up at him.

"Perhaps Jasper would wish to accompany you on this trip," he grunts before he winks at me.

"You're terrible," I huff as we walk toward the waiting car.

There are no reporters or cameras today, and I'm grateful. I climb into the passenger seat, not wanting to sit in the back all by myself. We have a bit of a drive to our first destination, where I'll be staying for just a few days, then we'll be jet setting on airplanes for the rest of our schedule.

"Do you like American Country music, Hugh? Please tell me you adore it," I smile.

Hugh only grunts, trying to ignore me. I don't let him, though; we've got three hours in the car alone together. It's road trip time, and I need to do something to keep my mind off of Henrik.

I plug my phone into the port and I crank up some George Strait. I let him sing about his ex's from Texas, and I sing along, annoying the hell out of Hugh—but I notice that he's smiling while I do it.

I try not to think about last night, about our goodbye, and I fail. It was absolutely beautiful. Henrik and I ate a delicious meal inside the apartment, silence deafening and sadness filling the air, but then we went to bed and we were desperate for each other.

It hadn't mattered that we'd had sex so many times I'd lost count; that we'd both come until we exhausted ourselves. We needed more of each other.

"Four weeks isn't so long," Hugh says, interrupting my memory.

"Yeah," I whisper, my eyes shifting to the passenger window.

Henrik

I close the door after I've watched her go. I feel empty inside. I look around my flat, realizing that Caitriona has only been here for a few weeks and yet, she's part of the space now—part of *me* now. She's worked her way into my heart, into my soul, and I couldn't be happier.

I had to go and fuck it all up, all of it, and now she's gone. She says it's only for four weeks, but what happens when she comes back and realizes she doesn't want me anymore?

I call the only person I can think of to take my mind off of it all. I call my brother.

"Henrik?"

"Want to go to the club, play tennis or golf, or fucking *something*? I need out of this flat," I grunt.

"She's left, then?"

"Yes, she's fucking *left*," I growl.

I'm in a piss poor mood, and I don't even try to hide it.

"Right, okay, you big bear. Let's play eighteen holes."

After agreeing to meet at half past the hour, I make my way into the bedroom to change into my golf attire. The room seems smaller than it did yesterday, void of life and excitement. It seems so quiet—so still.

Riona brings such vibrancy into my life that I didn't even realize, not until she left. Even when she's doing nothing, she's still lighting up rooms just by walking into them.

I don't know how I'm going to last the four weeks without her. I fucked up—I fucked *us* up. I want her to come back to me and tell me that she loves me, that she can't live without me, that she was miserable the entirety of her trip.

In reality, none of that will probably happen. Her trip will be a grand success because she'll be helping people, and her cause is close to her heart.

Then there's love—I don't know if we're in love yet. I know that what I gave up, I wouldn't do for just *any* woman. The way I feel right now, without her here, I wouldn't care if I didn't have romantic feelings for her.

Thinking about being without her makes me feel nauseous. I want to have a family with her one day and to keep her at my side always. If it's not love, then I don't know what it is. It's definitely not just lust, although I do lust after her.

I leave the empty flat, knowing that it will be void of life and vibrancy for the next four weeks and feeling absolutely ill about it. Perhaps a day with my brother is exactly what I need to lift my spirits.

Making my way to the club, I think about everything, unable to get Riona off of my mind for even a split second. I have a feeling that I'll be burying myself in work, completely and totally, just to keep my mind off of her.

This afternoon, however, golf awaits.

CHAPTER
Twenty-Six

Caitriona

I FOLLOW THE WOMAN DRESSED IN A BEAUTIFUL CREAM pantsuit through the Children's Hospital. The walls are brightly painted with cartoon looking animals throughout each and every hall we turn.

Hugh is at my back, keeping a fair distance from me, but also being close enough to do his job, which is to protect.

The woman prattles on about budgets and such. I don't have money to donate, that's not why I'm here. I'm here for my time, to meet children, and to just listen to them.

Although, an idea springs to the front of my mind. *A charity gala.* I make a mental note to text Beatrice and ask about it. If she can help me organize one, then maybe I can donate all of the proceeds to finding a cure for childhood cancer—not necessarily each hospital individually, but toward the research itself.

"This is the terminal floor; we'll skip that and I'll take you to see the babies," she announces.

"Why would we skip it? This is exactly where I wished to go."

"Why?" she asks, actually looking baffled.

I don't bother explaining a thing to her. She obviously wouldn't understand. I walk past her, Hugh a little closer to me now, and make my way toward the nurse's station. The nurse freezes when she sees me, and her mouth gapes open slightly.

"I'd like to visit with some children, if that's possible," I say, trying to sound as poised as I can.

"You're *Princess Caitriona*," she whispers. "Oh, I've been following you."

I don't know what to say. I don't know if her following me is a good thing, or a bad one. I've yet to actually speak to many people since I've moved here. I've been pretty isolated, except for Sarah, Henrik's family, and Hugh.

"I hope you gave Prince Henrik an earful when he went to that gala without you," she says as she stands and walks around the counter. I giggle at her words and nod.

"I did," I confess with a grin.

"Good. Now, are you sure this is the floor you wish to visit? It can be very depressing here," she says quietly as she looks around to make sure no passerbys have heard her.

"It is, please."

"Right. This way then," she motions. "I know the perfect first visitor for you. Elizabeth is the sweetest child, and I think she knows more about the royal family than the King himself," she giggles.

We walk inside of the dark room, and the first thing I notice is the smell—it's awful. My stomach turns, but I try to ignore it. I see a woman sleeping in the corner and realize that she must be the little girl's mother.

Then I look over to the girl. She's nothing but skin and bones. She has a scarf wrapped around her head, and she looks like she's about to disappear into thin air, she's *that* small.

"Elizabeth, dear, wakey wakey. You have a visitor," the nurse calls out.

I take my eyes from the girl briefly and turn to her mother, who has now sat up and is looking around in confusion. I decide to introduce myself before I just start talking to her daughter.

"Hello," I say, holding out my hand for her. "I'm—."

"I know who you are," she says dipping her head. I can't tell if she's angry about my being here or not.

"I was wondering, if it's okay with you, could I spend some time with your daughter?"

She looks around and her eyes snap to Hugh.

"He the man who's going to be takin' pictures?" she asks with a snarl.

"No pictures. He's my security," I say with a smile.

I understand her hesitancy now. She thinks that this is nothing but a photo op and I'm using her daughter for it.

"No pictures?"

"I'm here just to visit and talk. Nothing more," I murmur.

She gives me a nod but keeps her eyes on me in suspicion.

I spend the next twenty minutes chatting with the gorgeous little Elizabeth who is beyond excited to meet a real royal member of the family. I laugh her off, because though

I technically am married to Henrik, I'm nothing special, not really.

"Did Prince Henrik really renounce the crown for you?" she asks.

"*Elizabeth*," her mother hisses.

"It's okay," I laugh. I hear Hugh cough out a laugh behind me as well.

"He did," I say. Then I whisper very closely to her, "It's all very sordid. See, we married without proper approval, and this upset some people. So, instead of fighting with his family or anybody else, Henrik decided to relinquish his title."

"To keep the peace," she says with a nod.

"Yes, to keep the peace." I agree.

"And Princess Nicoline?" she asks with wide eyes.

"A surprise set up," I admit with a smile.

"Weren't you terribly hurt?" she asks.

"I was very hurt, yes. But when Henrik discovered how hurt I was, he apologized immediately."

"Did you take him back?" she asks. I love how she's quite the gossip. She's smart as a whip, too.

"I'm not sure yet. *Should* I take him back?" I ask, raising my brow.

"He *is* very handsome," she says, as though she's truly mulling over her advice for me. "I think that if he begged your forgiveness, crawled on his knees for you, then yes, you should."

I giggle and take her hand in mine.

"You're amazing, Elizabeth," I whisper.

"Thank you for coming to visit me. I won't be alive to see you have children with Henrik, but when you do, I hope you have dozens," she grins.

I don't stay much longer, as Elizabeth begins to drift to sleep. I walk outside of her room, her mother following behind me. Then she throws her arms around me in a hug. I return the hug, hers much tighter than mine. She sobs in my arms, this mother of this beautiful, yet very sick child, sobs in my arms.

"Thank you," she whispers.

"I feel like I haven't done anything," I say as she takes a step away from me and begins wiping her eyes.

"But you have. You made her smile, and just that alone is worth a million pounds," she says.

"How long does she have?" I ask, feeling a weight settle down on my heart.

"Days, hours, minutes. We aren't sure exactly," she whispers.

I give her one last hug, holding her close as I do, and whispering that she and Elizabeth will both be in my prayers.

I leave them and continue down the corridor. I visit every single terminally ill child in the hospital. I spend a minimum of thirty minutes with each of them, and my heart aches with every single child's situation. I cry with every single parent who is at their child's side, and when I leave the hospital, it is with a new determination.

I will be part of this cause. I will use my name as *Caitriona Stuart* to help find a cure.

"You were very poised," Hugh says as we walk out to the car.

"This was the most difficult thing I've ever experienced," I whisper.

"It will only get more difficult as we go. I doubt it will get any easier. This has a place in your heart. You're doing what you are meant to be doing," he murmurs.

"Why do I feel like I've done absolutely nothing?"

"What feels like nothing to you is everything to them," he says with a nod.

"How do you know?"

"I was one of those parents once. My daughter died from cancer. So I know that sometimes, watching a stranger smile and engage your sick child as though they are completely normal, that can mean everything. I also know that just giving a parent a hug, showing your support, that can mean the absolute world."

I don't stop the tears from falling at Hugh's confession. I take his hand in mine and I give it a squeeze as he drives toward our hotel for the evening.

"I'm so sorry to hear that. It makes me want to do this even more," I say, keeping my head forward and my eyes aimed out of the window.

"You're a good woman, Cait," he says as we pull into the hotel's valet.

"Your daughter's mother?" I ask out of curiosity.

"She couldn't handle it. We split about a year after she died. I tried to help her, but she didn't want the help," he murmurs.

"You're a good man, Hugh," I say repeating his words.

"I could be a better man. I could have been a better husband and father. The situation, when you're in it, you're so invested that you can't see anything else. There is no bigger picture, because your only picture is sick and you're helpless to fix it."

"All you can do is your best," I say softly.

"Exactly. But when people like you, and you're special

even if you don't believe it, take time to visit with them, especially the way you did it with no press, that's so touching and special. You're married to a prince, relinquished crown or not, he'll always be a prince to us. You're a princess by default, and you're giving them your time, not because you want cameras to capture it for publicity, but because you truly just want to. That means so much. You'll never know how deeply you've just touched all of those people."

Hugh doesn't wait for my reply. He exits the car as the Valet attendant opens my own door. We don't speak of the conversation again. It's said and done. I know a piece of Hugh's past that most people probably don't know, and I feel honored that he trusted me with that.

We're all people. We all have pasts. We all hurt. If I can ease that pain for somebody, even if it is just for fifteen minutes, then it all becomes worth it.

The paparazzi and the news stories, the pictures and the name calling, I'll take it if that means that I made a sick child smile because they know who I am and I've made them feel special.

Henrik

Sarah walks into my office for our monthly meeting. She usually informs me of royal business, telling me about certain events coming up, different obligations that I'm required to attend, things of that nature.

Today, she walks in with a grim look on her face. It surprises me, as she's always chipper for our little chats.

"What's happened, then?" I ask as I turn away from my computer to face her.

"I'm absolutely *stunned*," she whispers. Then her lips curve into a big smile.

I wait for her to continue, but instead of saying anything, she tosses a gossip rag on my desk. I pick it up and scan the front page. It's a picture of Caitriona walking out of the Children's Hospital that she was scheduled to visit a few days ago. She's clearly wiping a tear from her eye.

"What's this?" I ask, not reading the article, knowing that Sarah already has.

"They love her. They absolutely *love* her," she beams. I arch a brow waiting for her to continue. "She's the princess with a heart. She's done all of these appearances, in a way that's never been done before, and the public is eating it up."

"How's that?" I ask in confusion.

"No media coverage at all. No reporters or cameras following her around. Just her and Hugh, going straight to the terminal hall and visiting every single terminally ill child in the hospital. This was taken after somebody from the hospital alerted the paps."

"I thought mum had set up media coverage?" I ask in confusion.

"Cait cancelled it, almost immediately after they arrived. Helena said she didn't want to take a bunch of people into the hospital with her. It's genius and genuine all at the same time."

"So, they love her?" I ask, my lips quirking in my own smile.

"Indeed. I would even venture to guess that as time goes by, they'll adore her completely."

Sarah and I continue our meeting, and once she's gone, I pick up the gossip rag and look at the picture. My Riona looks absolutely lovely, and every bit the princess. Hugh is at her back, doing his job to precision.

But it's Riona I'm entranced with. Her hair is straight, not the way I prefer it, like when we met, but it's all a part she plays now, so I know she must wear it this way. Her dress is classic, demure, yet because of her figure, it is also naturally sexy.

I miss her.

I miss everything about her, but she's doing wonderful things right now.

Important things.

She's letting her heart lead her, doing what's expected of her but in a nonconventional way, in her own way. That's what the people love about it.

Hell, that's what I love about her. She's completely and totally genuine. She's never been entranced by my title, not even after she found out who I was. She's always just been Riona and treated me as though I've always just been Henny.

My precious girl is magnificent, and I can't wait to see her again.

CHAPTER
Twenty-Seven

Caitriona

I'M EXHAUSTED. HUGH AND I HAVE BEEN ON THE ROAD now for three weeks. We've visited all of the children's hospitals on our list, and now we've begun visiting women's shelter safe houses.

The entire trip has been humbling and eye opening all at the same time. I didn't have the best life growing up, or the best mother, but I've lived a privileged childhood and life in comparison to some.

"You look pale," Hugh announces as we're leaving the safe house we visited for the day.

"I'm tired," I admit on a sigh.

Hugh doesn't say anything else, he just continues to walk beside me until we're at the car. He drives us to a store and tells me to stay inside, that he needs to pick something up.

I could care less as long as I'm able to just sit here and close my eyes for a few moments. I think that being away, traveling and then the emotional toll of each visit I make, it's causing my body to wear down a bit.

Once Hugh is back in the car, we make our way to the hotel. He parks and throws a paper bag on my lap. I open it and promptly close it, my eyes shooting over to his in question.

"Take it," he grunts.

"Why on earth did you buy this?" I ask in a shrill shriek.

"Just take it. If I'm wrong, I'm wrong," he shrugs.

I slide out of the car and stomp my way toward the hotel's lobby and then to my room, slamming the door behind me. I don't know why I'm so irrationally angry that Hugh bought me this at the store, but I am.

I fish my phone out of my purse, something that Henrik slipped into my suitcase before I left. Something he has yet to call me on. I try not to think about *that* as I scroll through the few names I have listed, then I find what I want.

"You better have a good damn reason for calling my ass at this hour," I hear her grumble into the phone.

"Oh, no, I forgot about the time difference," I gasp.

"Cait?" she mutters. I can hear rustling, and I'm sure she's sitting up in bed. "What's wrong?"

"Hugh bought me a pregnancy test," I whisper, afraid to say the words out loud.

"Your security bought you a pregnancy test? Isn't that a little personal, Cait?" she laughs. "Does he know your cycle, too?"

"Shut up," I snap as she giggles in the background.

"I'm sorry, I really am, do you think you are?" she whispers, all joking aside.

"I don't know."

"How long has it been?"

"I haven't had my period in a while. I just thought that it was stress," I admit, feeling stupid.

"Take the test, you crazy bitch," she orders.

"Will you wait with me for the results? I can't do it alone," I murmur.

She agrees and I put the phone down as I run to the bathroom to take the test. Then I hurry back to the phone.

"Have you heard from my mother?" I ask, trying to distract myself from looking at that test.

"Not again. I think she's gone, or who knows. I keep searching the gossip sites to see if she's trying to claim crazy shit, but there's been nothing as of yet," she explains.

I take a deep breath. I'm unable to talk about anything else, the results of this test consuming me.

"What am I going to do if it's positive?" I panic.

"Our babies would be so close in age. I'm making James move to England. That's it. *It's decided*," she announces.

"*Madison*," I hiss. "I can't have a baby. I'm not even sure what is going to happen with Henrik and me."

"You're going to go back and live happily ever after. He fucked up. He didn't sleep around and he didn't kiss her. He was an asshole, but he fixed his shit really fast. Don't be crazy. You're so in love with him, it's ridiculous," she says.

"Says the woman whose husband has never fucked up," I snort.

"He's fucked up," she mutters.

I don't bother asking her when, I know she's about to tell me. When she does, she leaves me completely and totally shocked.

She tells me about the time in their lives when she was studying for the bar exam; she was totally neurotic and stressed, a complete basket case. I remember the time well.

James would stay away from the apartment they lived in for as long as possible after work because she would complain every time he made any noise at all. He had taken up going to a bar after work and having a few beers with co-workers.

Then she tells me about this waitress that had become interested in him. Nothing happened, but James started questioning his devotion to Madison, started wondering if they were really meant to be. He came to Madison as soon as he started having second thoughts.

"So what did you do and why do I not know any of this?" I ask.

"I told him if he wanted some nasty bar slut, then he could have her. I also apologized for being crazy. I was under a lot of pressure, and I had put everything on the backburner in my life," she murmurs. "I was embarrassed, that's why I never told you."

"What happened?"

"Nothing. He stopped going to the bar after work, and I stopped screaming at him over every little thing. Eventually, we worked everything out and it was fine, but it took me a long time to be able to feel as though I could trust him again," she admits.

"That's where I'm at right now. The trust part," I murmur.

"Well, I follow the tabloids religiously, and I've only seen what a saint you are lately, nothing about Henrik," Madison announces.

"He hasn't called," I mutter.

"You said you needed space and time. Men are literal to a

default. It's obnoxious."

"I don't know what's going to happen between us, and now that being pregnant is a possibility. I *really* don't know what's going to happen," I admit.

"Look at the test," Madison encourages.

I pick it up and look at it.

The word *Pregnant* is right there on the screen.

I mutter it to Madison and she screams in my ear, almost causing me to drop the phone.

Pregnant.

It doesn't seem real. This can't be reality.

"Madison," I whisper.

"Be happy, you're an adult. You're married, to a *prince*, I might add. This is not a bad thing," she explains.

"I'm married, but it's rocky," I point out, even though I shouldn't have to.

"Yeah, well, it won't be. Next week, when you're back, I bet it'll be perfect. He's probably scared shitless to call you, in all honesty."

"Probably," I admit, thinking about the way I left.

He didn't want me to go, and I think about how he was afraid I wouldn't want him when I returned. He probably *is* scared; he's probably worried that our relationship is over.

"What's your next step?" she asks.

"After I return?"

"Yeah."

"Tell him, I guess," I sigh.

"First, tell him that you only want him, and that you missed him," she suggests. I nod as though she can see me, agreeing with her words. "Then tell him that he popped a biscuit in your oven."

I laugh at her words and thank her for being there for my drama, even though she was halfway asleep.

"Any time you need me, Cait, I'm here. Anytime at all," she murmurs. I can tell she's getting sappy.

"I love you," I whisper.

"I love you, too."

We end the call and I just hold the test in my hand, staring at the word—*Pregnant*.

Children aren't something I have ever thought about. Just like marriage wasn't anything I thought about until Henrik came along.

Now, though—now there's Henrik, and I want to give him children. I want him to have everything. He really is giving up so very much for me. This trip has shown me just how much the titles mean to the people.

Titles that I thought were kind of silly, they're not.

The titles, the positions, and the lineage of the family, they stand for something; they can also be encouraging to people. This family, they're not just celebrities or political figures, but they're a legacy, an entity.

I press my hand to my stomach as a wave of sadness washes over me. This baby will not be part of the legacy that Henrik was born into, because of me. I now understand exactly why he wasn't sure he wanted to relinquish his title for his future heirs.

I wonder if perhaps this pregnancy won't be such a joyous thing for him? Will he be reminded of the fact that this child will not be a Lord or Lady, or whatever it would have been?

Then, when Bee and Philip have a child, will it just rub salt in his wound all over again? It makes me sad to think about this child not being treated the same as his cousins.

I can't think about it anymore. I decide to go to bed.

In just five short days, I will be back on a plane and headed toward Henrik. I hope that he will take what I've just discovered in stride, that he'll be happy and that we're going to make it. I can do anything on my own, but I can't deny that having Henrik at my side is what I want.

Henrik

I hang up the phone with Hugh. My daily update on Riona is complete. I haven't called her once since she's been gone. I'm trying to give her the space and time that she requested of me. But that doesn't mean that I've not been kept briefed of her whereabouts and safety.

Hugh says that she's tired but good. She's been in good spirits and has truly enjoyed her time away, visiting with people in the hospitals and safe houses that have been on her itinerary. I just hope that when she returns, she'll still want me—*want us.*

My office door opens and I look up, surprised to see my father, accompanied by my grandfather, waltzing through as though they own the place. It's ridiculous how they behave some days. I lean back in my office chair as I watch them each take a seat in front of my desk.

"How may I help you gentlemen?"

"Have you seen the publicity on *her*?" my grandfather asks as his eyes cut to me.

"Sarah has kept me briefed, yes," I say, nodding my head,

wondering what on earth they're doing here.

"They love her," my father mutters in surprise.

"Who?" I ask, knowing good and damn well who loves Riona. Everybody loves her.

"The entire country, and America as well," my grandfather grunts.

I sit in silence, looking at them and wondering why they're in such piss poor moods. They should be *happy* that the people love Caitriona. She should be less *embarrassing* to them now.

It should please them that she's not the trash they originally thought her to be. Unfortunately, they look anything but pleased right now.

"Perhaps we could get her some proper etiquette training, get her out in the public eye a bit more?" my father murmurs, easing into the real reason they're here.

"We can truly play up this rags to riches bit, give her training, and then she can continue her work. It will be favorable for all of us," my grandfather grunts.

"Want to know what I think?" I ask.

I'm about to be brutally blunt, and if they want to know, they're going to hear everything I have to say about the subject. This is my wife, and they've made a big deal about my chosen partner, to the point where they wanted to strip my titles. I gave them up, and now they're here and they've realized, maybe, that they were wrong.

"I think that Caitriona doesn't need any etiquette training. I think that the world likes her as is, which is also the way I prefer her. I don't want a poised to perfection, ice cold wife. I want my sweet, funny, and kind Riona.

"She's behaved lovely while on this trip, not one

embarrassing or unsavory thing has happened. She didn't want cameras following her around because this wasn't a publicity stunt, this was simply her wanting to be a good person and help people in any way she could. I think you've both realized what arseholes you were to her, and now you're wanting to try and save face. I also think that I don't give a flying fuck, either. I don't want my title back. You can keep it."

I stand and walk past them, over to the door, and I open it, standing as I wait for them to leave my office.

"You're being ridiculous, Henrik. Don't cut your nose off to spite your face," my grandfather says, raising his voice.

"I'm not, grandfather. I simply don't want all of the conditions placed on me or my family that the crown and titles demand. I've a taste of a more normal life, and I enjoy the serenity that it offers. I won't ever be out of the spotlight completely, but I have to be honest, it's nice not having to do and be perfect at everything. I enjoy my work for the crown along with my regular job, and I like that visiting with my family is just visiting with my family and not some diplomatic pomp bullshit. So, I'm sticking with my statement, with my relinquishment," I say, standing firm.

The weight that has been lifted from my shoulders since I relinquished my titles has been tremendous, and I honestly have no desire to have it added back on.

"You're not thinking. What about your children?" my father asks.

"I can't make decisions for unconceived children. You made those for me as part of your statement weeks ago."

"I'm amending it. The people love her; let's not continue this in haste. Your wife could be a princess or a duchess, and your children lords and ladies. Don't take this from them just because you're stubborn," my grandfather says.

"I'm not *taking* anything from anyone. Obviously, title or no title, Caitriona can continue with her passions. It's just formalities at this point, and I've made my decision, with my wife at my side. We made the decision together. I'm standing firm in that."

My grandfather huffs out a puff of air as he stands and walks past me. He's irritated, but it will pass. He's my grandfather and no *title* changes that. I know that he loves me, and in time, he'll also love Riona as well.

My father begins to follow, but stops right in front of me, placing his hand on my shoulder with a squeeze. His green eyes look up and into mine, and it's as though I'm looking in the mirror. They are the exact same shade.

"I am proud of you, son. No matter the politics, the seemingly poor decisions you made, which perhaps weren't so poor after all, *I'm proud*. You're a man who knows what he wants and knows his convictions. Even if you're not making a decision I would necessarily make, I'm proud of you," he says before he releases my shoulder and then follows my grandfather out of my office building.

I close my door behind them and forego walking back to my desk but instead over to the sofa that is against the wall. I sit down and bury my face in my hands, wondering—*hoping* that I just made the right decision.

The decisions I've made in the past few months have altered and impacted my life greatly. I've not only myself to think about, but Riona as well, and our future, plus our children, whenever we decide to have them.

It's not just me anymore. It's so much more than just myself.

CHAPTER
Twenty-Eight

Caitriona

"ARE YOU NOT TELLING ME YOUR RESULTS FOR A reason?" Hugh asks as we board the plane to head for home.

It's been a week since I've taken the pregnancy test he shoved at me. It's been a week since I found out that I am, indeed, *pregnant*.

Henrik and I are going to have a child, and it scares the hell out of me. It scares me to the point where I don't want to say it aloud because then it will be in fact, a truth.

"I don't want to think about it," I mutter as I sit down and fasten my seatbelt.

"You do realize that in a few weeks, it won't matter. It will be common knowledge," he chuckles.

Hugh and I have developed a friendship during this

month together. I've learned things about his past and shared aspects of mine as well. He probably knows me, my past, and my personality better than Henrik does. He's kept me sane, and helped me learn about the monarchy, history, rules and traditions that I didn't quite understand.

"I have to tell Henrik as soon as we get back," I mutter, looking out the window as our plane begins to move.

"You're not going to put it off, are you?" he asks, quirking his brow and his lips all at the same time. It's frustratingly annoying.

"No," I lie.

I'm going to put it off as long as possible, though I don't know how that's going to happen. My boobs are already tender and fuller than they were even last week.

"You're a terrible liar."

"Whatever," I mumble.

"He's called every day, you know," Hugh rumbles. I turn to him with shock clearly stamped all over my face. "He has. He's checked on you, asked about your welfare, and worried over you as well."

"He hasn't called *me* once," I whisper.

"I'm not a marriage counselor. I'm just telling you that he's called. Perhaps he wanted to give you the distance you so adamantly desired?"

I peek up at him through my lowered lashes and hate that he's probably right. I was adamant about needing space and time away during this trip. I probably wouldn't have contacted me, either.

I bite my bottom lip and close my eyes, regret swimming through me. I said some hurtful things to Henrik before I left. I kept him at a distance, at arm's length when he only wanted reassurance that we were okay. Now, he's been wondering for weeks what our status is; now, I don't know if he'll still want me, want *us*.

"Sleep, he'll be at the airport awaiting your arrival," Hugh murmurs.

I don't respond.

I let out the breath I hadn't realized I'd been holding and lean my head against the back of my seat. I hope that he's there when we arrive, and that he's happy to see me, truly happy. I've missed him so much. I don't want to be away from him like that again.

I realize that he's it for me—the man I was meant to be with. We're not going to have a perfect marriage, that's impossible, but we're going to have one full of chemistry and hopefully *love*. I feel like I love him *now*, but I want more time with him before I say the words out loud.

I wake up with a jolt and look around, only to realize that we're landing already. Hugh chuckles beside me, but I ignore him and turn my head toward the window.

I see him standing on the tarmac and I smile.

There he is.

My husband.

My prince.

My Henny.

I could spot his mass of messy hair anywhere in a crowd, and there is quite a crowd gathered on the tarmac.

"Are you ready?" Hugh asks as I hear the stairs being dropped and the door opens.

"No," I whisper.

"He waits for you, apprehension written all over his face, which he is definitely not accustomed to," he murmurs. "Put him out of his misery, Cait."

"I need to reassure him that I'm his," I say more to myself than to Hugh.

"Indeed."

Hugh stands and walks away from me. I watch him descend down the stairway, and I know that he is waiting at the bottom to help me down the narrow staircase. I also know that Henrik is waiting just beyond the stairs, waiting for me as well, for my reaction to him.

I stand and make my way toward the stairway. Suddenly, I feel this pull to him, this need to see him. He's the only thing on my mind as I descend the stairs with a smile.

I hear the background noise, the people yelling, and there are flashes of lights, but when my eyes land on Henrik's green gaze, intense and unsure—

I run.

I run straight to him, uncaring that there are dozens of people around us. When I'm close enough to him, I jump into his strong arms. Henrik catches me, taking a step back and making a grunting noise, but he catches me.

"Precious," he whispers as he rests his forehead against the crook of where my shoulder and neck meet.

"I missed you, Henny," I sob into his neck.

He doesn't say anything back in response. Instead, he slowly lets me down on my feet and then cups my cheeks in his palms and presses his lips to mine. The kiss is slow, soft, and closed mouth but it's beautiful, sensual, and sexy all at the same time.

"I missed you too, Riona," he whispers against my lips.

I'm in a completely lusty daze when he lowers his hands and wraps one around mine as he tugs me toward the waiting car. My body moves on its own volition as he guides me into the backseat and then climbs inside after me.

Hugh drives us away and pretends not to give me a questioning glare in the rearview mirror. My news is the only thing on my mind as I look into his eyes. I want to tell him now, I don't want to wait at all, like I thought that I would, but I want it to be special.

I need it to be special and sweet and romantic. I'm suddenly extremely anxious for his reaction, hopeful that it will be one of happiness. Looking at him, the panic eases and instead excitement fills me.

"You look so beautiful. I've missed you," Henrik murmurs low enough so that only I can hear him.

"I'm pregnant," I blurt out, my eyes flying to his as I cover my mouth in shock.

Hugh swerves the car slightly before he straightens it.

Henrik's eyes blink slowly, so slowly that I'm curious if he's even going to reopen them. Then he does, and I see something close to anger flash in his green gaze.

"*Pregnant*?" he asks, his voice deep.

"Yes," I whisper.

Suddenly, I'm not nervous or even excited anymore, just scared.

This is not how I expected his reaction to be. I expected shock and surprise, but not the anger that he's throwing in my direction, nor the hostility that's filling up the car, making it hard to breathe.

He doesn't say another word. The rest of the ride to the apartment is bathed in uncomfortable silence, and then we arrive.

The media is outside of our building again. I don't care,

though; I just want to know why Henrik is suddenly so angry.

Hugh parks and then opens the door for us to get out, assuring that my luggage will be right behind us. Once we've made our way upstairs to our apartment, and Hugh has dropped off my bags and left, Henrik locks the door and then turns to face me, fire still very much alight in his eyes.

Henrik

Pregnant.

The word floats around in my head, and while initially I felt excitement about her proclamation, I now feel dread—a mix of anger and dread.

This child, it isn't necessarily something negative, and it's not as though we can't financially support it. I'm more than able to do so, but I've just relinquished my title and that means that I relinquished this little one's as well, something that was just in theory until now. The repercussions of my actions settle on my shoulders like the heaviest of weights. I feel as though I'm suffocating.

"Henny?" she asks. Her voice washes over me, so fucking sweetly.

I grab the lamp next to me on the side table and I pick it up, hurling it across the room and watching it smash against the wall with satisfaction at the many pieces it breaks into.

I could have had my title back, this baby would have had a title, but I did exactly as my grandfather and father warned me of, I cut my nose off to spite my face. I made another fucking mistake.

Caitriona gasps as she brings her fingers to her plump lips—lips I kissed just moments ago, lips I already miss. She looks shocked at my reaction, completely and totally surprised.

"Why are you so angry?" she asks me just above a whisper.

"My grandfather and father offered my title back to me, and I turned them down. Now you're pregnant and this baby won't have its legacy, all because of my fucking stubborn pride," I yell.

"It's okay, Henny, it's going to be okay," she says, taking a tentative step toward me.

"Maybe for you. You're American. This hasn't been your life. This is something you stumbled into, you will *never* understand," I say, sounding crueler than I mean to.

None of this is her fault at all, yet here I am, practically blaming her.

"I'm sorry," she whispers placing her hand on her belly.

She turns and walks away, toward the master bedroom. I'm stuck, frozen to my spot, watching her walk away from me.

I am a bastard.

I pick up my lead weighted feet and rush after her. When I walk into our bedroom, my knees threaten to buckle. Riona is sitting on the edge of the bed, her face in her hands, and her body shaking from her sobbing. I quickly step toward her, right in front of her, and I sink to my knees. I'm a complete arse.

"I'm a complete arse," I tell her.

She doesn't respond, she just cries. I've hurt her—*again.* It's all I seem to do when it comes to Riona.

"I've hurt you again," I mumble my thoughts. "None of it matters. It isn't your fault, precious. It wasn't something I was prepared for. I thought we had time until I had to think about children and titles and everything. I overreacted," I murmur, cupping her cheeks in my hands and wiping her tears away with my thumbs.

"I didn't plan for this to happen," she whispers.

"I know, precious. I know. Apparently, I don't always react well under stress and surprise. Apparently, I'll need to work on it in the future," I offer with a small smile, tipping my head to the side. "Fuck the titles."

"Don't say that. They're important. Your initial reaction proves that," she says, looking into my eyes; thankfully, her tears now dried.

"None of it is as important as us, as you, as this child. This is a happy thing, and I am happy. I swear it. I just panicked," I admit truthfully. "I acted liked a fucking arsehole. My initial reaction was selfish and uncalled for, precious. I'm sorry," I apologize.

I stand and bend down to pick her up and place her in the center of the bed, her arms wrap around me and I fit myself between her thighs, wishing she'd worn a dress instead of these infuriating tight jeans.

I look down on her pretty face and take in all that is my sweet wife, my Riona. Then without a word, I press my lips to hers. I snake my tongue out to taste her mouth, and when she opens on a moan to let me in, I know that we're fine—we're good.

"Henny," she whispers as she melts into the mattress below me.

"I'm sorry," I murmur against her lips.

I shift my hand and slide it under the loose shirt she's wearing. My palm touches her warm skin and I can't hold in my own groan.

It's been so long since I've felt the silkiness of her body. I move my hand up her small ribcage to her bra and wrench the cup down, needing to feel her breast.

"I missed you, Riona," I murmur as my lips pepper her neck with kisses and my fingers swirl around her peaked nipple. I gently pluck at the hardened bud and she shivers. "Missed your tits, too."

I quickly divest her of her shirt and bra, throwing them across the room so that my eyes, then my mouth, can feast on her generous tits. I suck one of them in my mouth as much as I can, letting it go with a pop before I begin to lavish her hardened nipple with my attention and my tongue.

"Oh, god," she whispers as her fingers dive into my hair.

She tugs on the strands, and I know that this, this is where we're the best. This is where we thrive as a couple. When we're together physically, our chemistry ignites.

"What do you want from me, my wife?" I murmur against her skin as I make my way toward her other breast.

I repeat the attention I gave to her first breast on her second as I wait for her answer.

"Just you," she whimpers, her fingers gripping me tightly.

"My mouth or my cock?" I ask, lifting my head and looking into her hungry eyes.

"Both?"

"They're yours," I murmur. "Only yours, Riona." I mean every single word as I kiss her belly on the way down to her sweet cunt.

I make quick work of her jeans, unbuttoning and peeling

them down her luscious thighs, along with her knickers. Then I spread her legs wide and just stare at her sweet center. It's mine, all of her is mine, and I'm going to reclaim it tonight—remind her who she belongs to, who her husband is, and make her scream my fucking name.

I bury my face in her cunt, devouring her sweet taste as I listen to her moan and gasp every time my tongue works her clit. When I feel her legs shake next to my ears, I know that she's close. I move back on my haunches, not giving her the release she so craves.

"Henny," she whines.

"I want your mouth on me, precious," I grunt as I strip my pants and underwear off.

I didn't know she could move so quickly. She's on her knees and then sinking her chest down to the mattress within seconds. Her eyes meet mine under her hooded lids as she envelopes my cock with her warm mouth.

"Fuck," I curse as I twist my fingers in the back of her hair.

I don't control her movements. I want her to take over, but I can't *not* touch her.

She hums around my dick, and I have to grind my teeth together to keep from coming in her mouth. It takes all of my restraint not to. I gently lift her off of me, because with her tongue, her warm mouth, and the obvious way she's enjoying herself, I can't keep myself contained much longer. The only place I want to come is her cunt.

"Lie down," I murmur.

She grins as she makes her way to the center of the bed and lies down. I crawl over her, pressing my lips to hers as I begin to slowly sink inside of her waiting, warm, wet heat.

"I love you, Riona," I whisper against her lips.

Her breath hitches as she wraps her legs around my waist, and her arms around my neck. She's all around me, surrounding me completely, and I don't want to be anywhere else in the world. I roll us over so that I'm on my back and she's above me.

"Oh, Henny," she whispers as she begins to ride me.

"My gorgeous wife," I murmur, tucking her hair behind her ear. "Come on my cock, precious."

I don't say anything else as she searches for her release. I watch the light sheen of sweat on her body appear, the sway of her tits as I thrust inside of her.

My thumb presses against her hardened clit, all of it combined takes my fucking breath away. Then she squeaks and throws her head back in a long moan, and I feel her pussy flutter around me before it clamps down on my cock.

I try my damnedest to let her ride her release out, but it's too much, and it feels too fucking good. I wrap my arm around her waist, my fingers gripping into the flesh on her side as I lift up slightly. I use her body to fuck my dick. I move her dead weight as she bonelessly lies back, her eyes focused on me and watching my face as I take her.

"You feel incredible," I murmur.

"So good, you feel so good," she whispers.

It doesn't take me long, sheer seconds before I'm stilling with my own climax and coming inside of my stunning wife.

I fall back, taking her with me so that she's on top of my chest, my cock still buried inside of her sweet cunt.

"I love you too, Henny," she whispers against my neck.

CHAPTER
Twenty-Nine

Caitriona

I SIGH AS WARMTH ENVELOPES ME, AND I CURL DEEPER into it. Henrik groans beside me, and I can't help but smile. He's cuddling with me. We've not woken up together often, usually he's up before me and heading off to work. But since my return yesterday, he informed me that he was taking the rest of the week off to spend time alone together.

"What is it that you actually do?" I ask, turning my head to the side to nuzzle his neck.

I don't know why I never asked this question before; I guess I just assumed he did something for his grandfather, something *princely*. However, he spends his days in that big office building of his.

"You don't know?" he chuckles, as he pulls me even

301

closer into his front.

"No."

"I'm a Counsellor of State, which means my grandfather delegates some state functions and powers to me when he's unavailable. I also run my own venture capitalist firm, investing in start-up companies," he explains while his fingers gently trail up and down my side.

"Wow," I breathe.

He's successful and smart.

Not that I didn't already know that he was, but his career is so much more than I expected.

"Plus, I have a lot of appearances to make; though, now, those will probably diminish since I no longer have a title."

"Do you *want* it back, your title?" I ask, turning in his arms to face him.

After last night, we didn't talk. We just fell asleep; but his reaction to the baby, about the titles, was intense. I haven't forgotten one second of it. I watch as his eyes roam over my face and his fingers shift to play with the ends of my hair.

"You know, it was offered to me just a few days ago, along with yours and our children's," he murmurs as his hand moves to my belly to caress my still flat stomach.

"Yeah." I stay silent, watching him, waiting for him to continue.

"I declined it," he announces. "When you told me about the baby, I had a sudden pang of regret at my actions and that's why I became angry. It honestly had nothing to do with you, precious, and everything to do with me."

I suck in a breath and hold it, listening and waiting for more, knowing there *has* to be more to it.

"I don't want it anymore, nor do I desire to have

everything that comes with it. I thought about it after you fell asleep last night. I thought about it for a long time, and you know what?"

I shake my head, wanting him to keep going, enjoying the fact that he's talking and telling me all of this.

"I'm happy just as we are, precious. Declining the offer lifted the heavy weight of duty from my shoulders. They'll always be my family; this will never change. We'll always be a topic for the paps. We'll always, *always* be sought out. But we'll also have more freedoms and less pressures without the titles and the added duties.

"Our children will have less pressures and more freedom as well. They'll be able to marry who they want, go to whatever college they want, and just be whatever it is they desire, something I've never experienced. You can do your charity work and I can focus on my own work—*work* I actually like."

I think about his words—about everything he gave up for me. It was all offered back to him, but he didn't want it, even if he had a moment of panic, he didn't want it, not after he truly thought about it.

I lift my hand to run my fingers over his full lips, knowing that this man is mine. He was meant for me like no other could be. He's the father of our child, and he was born into a life of luxury, a life that came with heavy burdens and duties. It wasn't something he chose, but now, now he's making a decision and he's choosing what he wants.

Just like the life I was born into, with the mother I had, it was not chosen. But I made a decision and I left that life, and then I chose to leave Oregon to be at his side.

"I love you, Henny," I whisper, unsure of what else to say.

"And I adore and love you, Riona," he murmurs before

his lips touch mine.

There's nothing else to say between us. The decisions and choices we've made have shaped our future. We'll have his family at our side, but he's no longer *His Majesty Prince Henrik*, and he's happy with that fact.

He rolls my body until he's between my thighs and hovering over me; then he slowly slips inside of my center, his cock hard and warm. I lift my legs to wrap them around his hips, locking my ankles behind his lower back.

Henrik makes love to me, slow and gentle, and his green eyes never once leave mine. I come as his lips touch mine and swallow my cry. After he's climaxed, I expect him to leave, but he doesn't. He stays above me, inside of me, and his mouth continues to take mine in a slow sensual, devouring kiss.

"You need to get ready," Henrik announces a few hours later as he walks into the bedroom.

I'm lounging against the headboard, still completely naked, eating a croissant and plate of fruit. After we made love, I needed sleep, then I woke up and needed food. I felt like my stomach was going to eat itself. I'd never felt so hungry in my entire life.

"Where am I going?" I ask around the heavenly buttery bread.

"Mum wishes to have a meeting with you, something about a gala?" he asks, arching his brow.

The gala. I completely forgot. It's scheduled for next Saturday. Beatrice and Helena have been organizing it for me, especially since I have zero clue and even less contacts on how to put something like that together.

"Oh, that," I mutter.

"What's it about, then?" he asks as he starts to get dressed.

I take him in and see that his hair is damp from the shower, he's dressing in a pair of dark washed jeans and a solid white, tight t-shirt. I haven't seen him look this casual, *ever*, and I love it.

"Oh, uh, I thought since I did all of those visits to different hospitals that I would try to raise some money for children's cancer research instead of trying to raise money and then distributing it amongst the different hospitals," I shrug as I take a bite of cantaloupe from my plate.

"That's brilliant, Riona," he murmurs. "Truly, I love that idea."

I beam up at him, glad that he is supportive of my idea. My breath hitches when he reaches out and tucks some fallen hair behind my ear before he cups my cheek.

"You're a very beautiful person, inside and out. I adore this about you."

"Thank you," I whisper.

"Hop up now, and we'll go together to your meeting. I'm very interested to see how this gala will be," he grins.

I place my plate on the nightstand and then make my way toward the bathroom to shower and get ready. Henrik groans before he leaves me to, presumably, go to his office and get a little work done.

I know he's taken some time off, but I also know that he'll want to check in a few times as well. I like that about him; he's been taught to be responsible no matter how wild his youth was. And I have a feeling, the way his family has been, was complete, downright insanity.

Once I'm fresh from the shower, I take a look in my closet. I haven't unpacked a single item, but I still have a few things I can wear to see Helena and Beatrice. I decide on a simple pair of coral jeans and a white top, paired with a navy blue cotton blazer; then I slip my feet into a pair of shimmery gold high heels. When I'm ready, I make my way toward Henrik's office.

I stand in the doorway and watch him work. He's concentrating on his computer, his tongue poking out slightly as his brows furrow. He looks younger, his hair a mess, him dressed in a t-shirt. I like him this way, so comfortable looking, and it reminds me of the way I saw him at the pool in Vegas.

"Ready?" he asks without looking up.

"How did you know I was here?"

"I can feel when you walk into a room, precious," he smirks as he looks up at me, his green eyes sparkling.

"You heard my shoes?" I ask, tipping my head to the side.

I watch as he powers down his computer, stands, and then skirts around his desk, making his way toward me in silence. He wraps his hands around my hips and pulls me flush against his body, his head tipping down so that his nose runs along mine.

"I heard your shoes, Riona, but I also know when you're in a room. My body knows its desire is present," he murmurs before he brushes his lips against mine.

"You sound like one of those werewolf's in a paranormal book."

"I have no clue what you mean," he chuckles.

"You know, they always say that they can sense their mate and stuff," I murmur, realizing I sound completely silly.

"I don't know about werewolf's, precious, but my cock knows when you're around. It's in a constant state of semi-arousal whenever you're in the same space."

"Henrik," I murmur.

"Are you wet?" he asks, moving his lips to my ear.

"No," I lie.

"I could take you quickly against my desk," he offers, pressing his length against my belly. "Bend you over, pull down those sexy-as-fuck pants, and take that sweet, sweet cunt of yours."

"Please," I whimper.

I want that. We've had sweet sex since I've been home, but I want what he's growling about in my ear, right *now*.

Henrik picks me up, pressing his lips to mine and thrusting his tongue in my mouth as he walks us over to his desk. Without a word, he sets me down and spins me around, ordering me to place my hands flat on the desk. I do so without question. I'm so ready for his touch, for him to take me, I'll do whatever he demands right now.

I shiver when I feel his fingers at my jeans, unbuttoning, unzipping and then yanking them down my legs, stopping at my mid-thighs, along with my panties.

Henrik's strong hands grip my ass and squeeze before one his hands slides to my center and his finger presses against my clit. I'm already wet, and by the sound of his hum behind me, he's pleased.

"Are you ready for my cock?" he asks as he thrusts two of his fingers inside of me.

I tip my hips back a little more and whimper at the quick

intrusion. I'm ready for him, all of him, and I want him now.

"Yes," I moan, dropping my head.

Henrik removes his fingers from between my legs and both of his hands grab hold of my hips with a firm grip, digging into my flesh. Then I feel his cock pressing against my center and he slowly sinks inside of me.

"Henny," I sigh once he's fully seated.

"Precious Riona," he murmurs before he pulls almost completely out of me and then slams back inside with such force I lose my breath.

He does it again, and again, not stopping, or slowing, or easing his thrusts. It's perfect. I let my body relax as I take him inside of me. Every single stroke, every thrust, I accept. My body is loose and pliable for him as he brings me toward the height of pleasure I know that he will deliver.

"Touch yourself, Riona," he grinds out.

I can tell he's close. His rhythm is changing, becoming more erratic with each thrust from his hips.

I slide one of my hands between my thighs and shiver when my figures initially touch my clit. I'm so close, I can feel my body on the edge, but I just need a little bit to push me over. I brace my forearm on the desk and let my forehead rest against my arm. Then I begin to rub circles against my clit as Henrik continues to pump vigorously in and out of my body, with wild abandon.

"Come, Riona. Fuck, precious, *come*," he practically begs behind me, his voice so strained it's almost unrecognizable.

Within seconds, I do as he's begged. *I come*, and when I do, it's with a sob. Henrik freezes inside of me, and I feel his dick twitch and then his climax.

"Fuck," he curses as he presses his chest against my back.

The only things holding me up are the desk and his tight grip on my hips, otherwise, I would be a sweaty, messy, pile of flesh and bones on the floor right now.

"How am I going to look your mother in the eye in a few minutes?" I ask breathlessly.

Henrik chuckles but offers zero advice for me, except to tap me on the ass and tell me we're leaving in five minutes.

I hurry to the bathroom to clean up, fixing my hair and makeup before I follow him out the door. Henrik wraps his hand around my hip and tucks me into his side before he nuzzles my neck as we ride the elevator.

"Love you, Riona," he murmurs, pressing his lips to my skin.

"I love you, too, Henny," I whisper.

We walk to the waiting car together, and to my surprise, Henrik drives us to his parent's home. He keeps one hand on my leg the entirety of the short distance to his parents' house. Even when we exit the car, he meets me at my side and slides his hand around my hip again, tucking me in close and keeping me there. I love it, the affection, the simple touches. It's absolutely perfect.

Henrik

I listen to my mother and Beatrice prattle on about the gala, and all of the plans they made. Riona seems most interested in everything, and even asks a few questions, none of which I'm paying attention to.

All I can think about is the fact that she's here next to me, home, in my arms and my bed, and that she's pregnant with my child. I feel like I'm living in a daze—a dream.

"Sarah put the event on your calendar, did she not?" my mum asks, breaking my daydreaming.

"I don't know what's on my calendar, mum. I'm sure she did."

"Well, then, Caitriona you need a dress. I've had my assistant contact some exclusive designers, but unfortunately, their samples were all *otherwise occupied*," my mother says, whispering her last words.

She's trying to be delicate and nice. She's not telling Riona the truth, though. Sample dresses are in miniscule sizes, something that I know because Eugenie talked about it incessantly the few times I was in her presence.

"Don't fret, I'll take care of it," I murmur, kissing the side of her head before I stand and walk away.

I take myself outside on the back patio and call Sarah.

"Sir," she murmurs, obviously busy.

"There's a gala next weekend," I announce.

"Yes, your lovely bride's event. It's on your schedule," she says.

"My lovely bride doesn't have a dress. Mum just informed her that all the designer's samples are *otherwise occupied*."

"That's a load of bolloks," Sarah mutters.

"I know, which is why I'm calling you. What can you do?" I ask, hopeful that she'll be able to find something, or someone to design a dress.

"Do you know what I think would be smashing?" she asks.

I can tell she's smiling extremely wide, and she's

probably feeling a bit sneaky, which is Sarah and one reason I truly adore her.

"Go on."

"She needs a dress from a department store. *People will love that.* Of course, it won't be something inexpensive, it will still be exquisite, but it will also seem as though she's more down to earth," Sarah explains. It sounds like my Riona, so I agree with her plan.

"I'll pick her up at ten tomorrow morning," Sarah announces before she ends the call.

I grin to myself, pleased that I have Sarah at my side to help with such matters, knowing that she's going to take great care of my Riona.

CHAPTER
Thirty

Caitriona

I LOOK AT MYSELF IN THE MIRROR, COMPLETELY SHOCKED at how elegant I look. I've never looked elegant in my entire life, and yet here I am. My hair is up in a massive bun, away from my face, and sleek. Not one hint of its natural, uninhibited wildness is on display.

My shoes are gold, shimmer high heel pumps, with gold studs around the edge—*Valentino*, a brand I never thought I would ever have the opportunity to see in person, let alone own.

My dress is electric blue, with a wrap bodice that is sleeveless. There is a tiny cut out at my waist with a twist of fabric, both in front and in the back. It hugs my waist and then falls freely to the floor.

I look down at my wedding ring and smile, my only piece

of jewelry, but the only piece I require. I grasp my shimmery gold clutch in my hand and make my way toward the living room, where I know Henrik is waiting for me.

He's waiting for me all right.

Standing with his hip against the counter and a cocktail in hand, he looks every bit the prince he is.

Henrik is dressed to perfection in a tuxedo that I know is specially made for him, and designer. His hair is its usual messy mop, and his face has a bit of stubble, but he looks absolutely—

"Stunning," he says, taking my exact thoughts.

"I agree," I nod, not taking my eyes from his.

"You're missing something, precious," he murmurs as he sets his glass down.

He then makes his way toward me, his gait slow and sexy as sin.

"What's that?" I whisper.

I watch as he reaches inside of his jacket and pulls out a small velvety box. Then he opens it and it takes my breath away. Nestled in the dark blue velvet is a necklace—and not just any necklace, but a diamond necklace. Each diamond is so big, I couldn't guess the total carat weight even if I tried, and they're surrounded by a rose gold setting.

"Henny," I wheeze.

He doesn't say anything. He removes the necklace before tossing the box onto the sofa and walking around me. Then I feel the weight of the jewels touch my neck and my hand automatically goes to it, touching the magnificent stones as he clasps it at my back. Then, he grasps onto my shoulders and spins me around to face him.

"You look like royalty," he murmurs before his lips gently

touch mine, careful not to mess up my lipstick.

"It's so beautiful, Henny, thank you so much," I whisper.

"Expect so much more from me in the future, Riona. You're very deserving of beautiful things."

I open my mouth to oppose his words, but his hand presses against my lower stomach and his green eyes meet mine as his lips tip.

"How are you feeling?" he asks.

"Good. Wonderful, actually," I whisper.

"The doctor?"

Henrik set up an appointment for me today, my first doctor's appointment, and he couldn't make it. There was an emergency at his office, and he had to go to a meeting, something he was not thrilled about. He voiced his unhappiness very boisterously about it as well.

I open my clutch and reach inside before I take out the little slip of paper the doctor gave to me. It's the first picture of our child, a sonogram that confirms I am indeed pregnant—six weeks pregnant, in fact.

The doctor told me that all of the stress I'd had recently made it simple to write off any symptoms as stress related instead of pregnancy related. I asked him about morning sickness, and why I hadn't had any, and he told me to count myself lucky so far, and that it could come at any time or not at all.

"What's this?" Henrik asks, taking the paper from my hand.

"This little blob is our baby," I murmur, pointing to what the doctor told me was our child.

It looks like a blob to me, but the doctor assured me that it was, indeed, *a child.*

"Yeah?" he asks as he studies the sonogram photo.

"It's beautiful, absolutely beautiful," Henrik murmurs, his eyes completely focused.

A chime on his phone alerts us to the fact that the limousine is waiting downstairs. Henrik takes the picture and puts it in the breast pocket of his jacket, the place that held my necklace just moments ago.

"This is mine, yeah?" he asks as he pats his jacket pocket.

"Yeah," I confirm.

"Good," he grunts as he wraps his hand around mine.

Together, we walk out of the apartment and toward the elevator.

We ride in the limousine in silence, me tucked close to Henrik's side as we pick up the rest of our party, Philip and Beatrice.

"Your dress is so pretty, where'd you find it?" Beatrice asks as we drive toward the event.

"Sarah and I decided to go to some of the major department stores to see what we could dig up at the last minute. She said next time I could try and talk to a designer about having something made, like perhaps for your wedding," I say.

Beatrice looks at me a little funny but then schools her features and gives me a warm smile.

I don't have time to question her as we've arrived at our destination. My eyes widen when I see a red carpet and the paparazzi littering each side of it, along with news cameras and reporters.

"Ready, precious?" Henrik whispers into my ear.

"No," I murmur truthfully.

"Get ready, because there's only one way out of the limo,"

he chuckles and then the door opens.

I'm bombarded with bright lights flashing, but I try to ignore them as I smile and allow Henrik to help me out of the car. He tucks me in close to his side, and together, we begin to walk the red carpet.

Philip and Beatrice are in front of us, and we all end up stopping to take pictures every few steps. It feels so surreal that I can't believe this is really my life.

"It's rumored that all of this was your idea, Princess Caitriona," one reporter calls out.

"I had an idea to put together a gala for childhood cancer research, yes. But it was Princess Helena, and Beatrice that really did all of the organization and hard work," I smile.

We continue on our way when the last reporter in the line blurts out.

"How do you feel about Princess Nicoline being in attendance?"

I try not to show emotion at the question. Inside my stomach drops and I feel ill. Henrik's hand tightens around my waist, and I watch him open his mouth, about to say something, but I beat him to it.

"I look forward to meeting the lovely princess," I hurry and say before I begin to walk away and inside of the building.

"I swear, I didn't know," Henrik quickly says.

"Is there a reason for me to be upset about her being here?"

"I just, it's your night, and I don't want to upset you," he rambles.

"Are you going to ditch me to be with her?" I ask with a smirk on my lips.

"*Riona*," he hisses.

"Henrik, it's fine. You're mine, right?" I ask, reaching up and wrapping my hands around his neck.

"Always, every second of every day," he murmurs as his hands go to my hips and bring my body closer to his. Then his lips touch mine in a sweet but brief kiss.

We walk into the ballroom, and I'm glad to have had the warning about Princess Nicoline, because she happens to be the first person who greets us.

"Nicoline, meet Caitriona," Henrik says, gesturing to her with a sweep of his hand.

"Pleased to meet you, Caitriona," she says sweetly.

"Yes, it is very nice to meet you as well," I say with a smile.

"It was nice to see you again, Henrik. Very nice to meet you, Caitriona," she murmurs before she walks away.

It's a small exchange, but not unpleasant. I don't know what he was so worried about. It almost makes me giggle. She was a woman he spent a few hours with against his will, at the wishes of his grandfather. I can't hold that against him forever; nothing even happened.

We spend the rest of the evening dancing, eating, dancing some more, and then there's an auction at the end. I look at the auction sheet and gasp at all the things that are up for bidding.

There are week vacations at villas all over Europe, spa days, meals prepared by a few famous chefs, jewelry, and even a specialty designed suit up for grabs.

"Beatrice, how did you get all of these things in such a short period of time?" I ask on a whisper.

"People can be very generous, especially when the

royal family, children, and a much loved new princess are involved," she grins before she turns away.

"Much loved new princess?" I ask, turning to Henrik.

"The world adores you, Riona. You must have seen the paps or the news. You're quickly becoming a favorite amongst the people," he explains. I stare at him in surprise and shock. "All the visits you made, the way you did it all so privately, and with true compassion in your heart? It's made you endearing to millions."

"I just didn't want it to be a big production," I murmur.

"Which is exactly why you're endearing to so many people, precious. You're just being you, and you're sweet from the inside out."

"Henny," I choke.

"Don't cry. Enjoy every second of it," he whispers, placing his lips at my temple.

Henrik

Spending an evening at a gala is not my most favorite thing to do in the world.

However, watching how the elite take in my beautiful wife, that is a favorite thing. They loved her, everybody I introduced her to, young and old, simply adored her.

I made the absolute best decision of my life when I was pissed as fuck in Las Vegas and married a girl I didn't know.

Caitriona isn't royalty, not even close to it. And yet, she's loved and accepted by not only every person she's met in my family's circle, but also every single person she meets. She was definitely meant to always be at my side.

Some people may think giving up my title, and the title of my heirs, wouldn't be worth doing just for a woman. Then again, they haven't met my precious Riona.

"I'm so tired, Henny," she whispers, cuddled into my side on the way home.

"Let's get you home, then," I whisper, pressing my mouth to the top of her head.

"I love you," she sighs on a yawn.

"I adore you, my love."

EPILOGUE

Six Months Later

Henrik

"**H**ENRIK!*" PHILIP SCREAMS AS HE COMES BURSTING through my conference room. I'm in a meeting with my entire management staff and have asked not to be disturbed, at all, until it's been completed. "Henrik, *fuck*, Henrik," he rants.

"Calm down, what's happened?" I ask, knowing that it must be huge if it's elicited such a grand response from my normally mild mannered brother.

"Cait, she's in the hospital. *Fuck*, Henrik, we have to go," he says. I freeze. I can't move. "She's had the baby, Henrik, six weeks early. Nobody has been able to reach you. Hugh is there, but nobody will update him. Something is wrong, and they won't tell him anything." He continues to ramble, but it sounds as though he's underwater.

My feet won't move. Nothing will move. My Riona, and my baby, something's wrong.

Philip grabs me behind my neck and physically pushes me toward the door.

I can't think. I don't even know if I'm breathing properly. But as I'm led by my brother out of my office and into a waiting car, I look at the seat next to me and see Beatrice. She's crying, and she wraps her hand around my forearm.

"Bee," I croak as the car lurches into traffic.

"It will be all right, Henrik. Babies are born early every day. It will be all right," she assures.

The drive only takes a few minutes but it feels like an eternity. I don't take a breath until we pull into the hospital's parking garage.

Luckily, there is parking close to the exit, and I jump out of the car and jog toward the hospital's entrance, without a care, if Philip and Bee are anywhere near me.

I hurry into the hospital and notice that it's so bright, *too bright*, and I catch Hugh leaning against the wall, a solemn look on his pale face. I know, right then and there, that everything is *not* going to be all right, as Bee had tried to assure me in the car.

"Hugh, what am I walking into?" I ask.

My voice cold and devoid of anything remote of feelings. When in reality, I'm completely and totally panicked and downright terrified.

"They won't tell me much, but I know she had to have emergency surgery and a blood transfusion," he states as the doors to the lift ping open and we all step out.

My girl, my beautiful precious Riona had surgery, a blood transfusion, and a baby six weeks early, and I was sitting in my fucking office holding a meeting where I announced to my secretary I did not want to be disturbed.

I am a right bastard, as usual.

I step straight up to reception, and all I can think about is finding out how Riona is and when I can see her. The nurse looks up at me with wide, shocked eyes and gasps, but I only vaguely notice. Right now, I just want answers.

"I am here for Caitriona Geneva Grace Stuart. I need to speak to her physician about her condition immediately," I state as professionally as possible.

In my mind, I'm screaming—*get off your ass and get me a fucking doctor.*

I have to know how my Riona is.

"Uh, yes sir, your highness, sir," she stumbles.

Usually, I would smile and perhaps give a wink; but right now, I don't have time for this shit. I need to see my wife.

"Prince Henrik," a man says, coming toward me in a pristine white lab coat. I know he must be the doctor.

"Henrik is fine, doctor," I say.

He motions for me to follow him into his office.

"Just Henrik in here, please," he states to my entourage of Hugh, Philip, Bee, and Jasper at my back. "All right, then. Caitriona has delivered a baby today, which I am sure you are well aware of. As far as I can see, she had no signs initially of premature labor.

"I have called her primary physician, and he confirmed this for me. He's on his way over as well to evaluate her. Her water broke at home, and her guard brought her here. Less than an hour later, she was already dilated to an eight.

"Normally, this wouldn't be a big deal; she's early, but not terribly so. However, there was a very small placental abruption, where the placenta has partially separated from the uterus. That's what caused the premature labor. It was likely so small that it went unnoticed, but unfortunately, during the delivery, Caitriona's uterus ruptured, and I had to repair it," he explains.

I only understand a quarter of what he's saying. I'm not a damn doctor, and all I can think about is my wife, alone in a room.

"Your child, he's in the NICU, and seems to be doing well on the ventilator," he informs me.

"Is Caitriona going to be all right?" I ask, my voice just above a whisper, as I feel so completely overwhelmed.

"Usually, if we can't stop the bleeding, we have to perform an emergency hysterectomy, but I want to avoid that as much as I can, and I think I have. We have given her a blood transfusion, and though her healing time will be much greater, I anticipate a full recovery. It won't be an easy one, but I have high hopes that she *will* recover. She is asleep now and should be waking up shortly. You may also visit the baby," he says with a smile and a nod, as if I am to leave.

"Are you saying she and the baby almost died?" I ask, still in shock, still processing everything he's just told me.

"Yes, Henrik. It was touch and go there for a while, but she is healthy and strong. She rallied."

I nod and stand. I need to see her, to hold her, to know that she is all right.

"The baby, is he going to be all right, too?" I ask, my hand on the doorknob.

"Yes, he will be just fine. He will probably have to stay here a few days, maybe a week. As long as he is able to breathe and eat on his own, he should be free to go home fairly soon."

He... my baby... he. I have had a boy. I should be shouting from the rooftops and passing out cigars, not fearing for his and Riona's life—*my son*.

I run from the doctor's private office, ignoring the questioning looks from Philip, Hugh, and Jasper. I have one place to be, and one place only.

My wife's side.

I storm toward Riona's door, throwing it open to find my precious girl.

She is pale, her hair in complete disarray and wild around her pillow. She looks so fucking fragile in that bed. I run to her side and drop to my knees, taking her hand in mine and kissing her fingers one by one.

I close my eyes and take in the sounds of the machines, the rhythmic beep of her heart. I hate myself for not being here at her side. I've always known that I didn't deserve her—now it's confirmed.

I'm a shit husband.

Caitriona

I am vaguely aware of a presence around me, my hand engulfed in a familiar warmth, and I can hear beeping next to my ear. I try to roll over, to move, but my body is heavy, and my limbs seem tied down.

The smell is making me nauseous, and I try to calm myself so that I can understand the murmurings and buzzing around me.

"Riona, my precious, please wake up, wake up," I hear Henrik's voice murmur. I want to tell him that I *am* awake.

"Cait, you need to open those eyes," I hear Hugh say from somewhere far away.

I wonder just how many people are in this room. I wish I could just open my eyes and see for myself.

"Precious, I love you, please wake up," Henrik whispers.

I feel my eyes fluttering open what seems like seconds later, and the room is shrouded in darkness. I can feel a slight breeze on my hand and look down to see a mass of wavy hair resting on my bed.

His face is next to my hand, and his breath is tickling my fingers. I twitch them to try and wake him. All of a sudden, his head pops up and his eyes lock with mine. I give him a lazy smile and I watch as his furrowed eyebrows relax.

"Precious," he mutters.

I let that one-word wash over me with his raspy voice.

"Henny," I croak, my throat dry and tired.

"Sshh, Riona, don't talk. I'll get the doctor," he says as he picks up my phone.

I want to ask him what has happened. Why would he have to get a doctor? And where is my baby?

I remember my water breaking, not being able to reach Henrik by phone, and having to call Hugh. But everything after arriving at the hospital is a blur, a complete blur. I tentatively touch my stomach and notice that I am, in fact, no longer pregnant.

I want my baby, and I want to know that he is all right.

Just as I begin to freak out, a handsome older man in a white lab coat arrives.

The doctor starts asking me questions about pain level

and such as he takes my vitals. He starts telling me about the delivery, talks about ruptured uteri, blood transfusions, and my baby being in the NICU. My heart starts to pound inside of my ribcage at his talk of the NICU.

"I want to see my baby," I say softly.

The doctor nods and tells me he will send a nurse in with a wheel chair to take me to him and walks out.

"Have you seen him?" I ask Henrik. He shoves his hands in his pockets, looking down at his shoes.

"I have not. I was worried about you. I wanted us to go together," he murmurs.

"Henny?" I ask in confusion, not understanding why he hasn't seen his new child. I've been out for almost an entire twenty-four hours.

"I couldn't, not when you hadn't held him first," he explains as his eyes tear up a bit.

Just then the nurse comes in and helps me into the wheelchair. It is probably one of the most painful experiences of my life. Henrik helps, but nothing can dull the pain of simply moving.

I am wheeled down a bunch of hallways, and I notice that there are police officers and guards everywhere. I look over to Henrik in question, and he just winks and shrugs.

Once I'm taken inside of the NICU, I know it's my baby before I've even gotten close to him. When my eyes meet my beautiful, tiny baby boy, the tears flow. God, I haven't cried as much as I have this past year in my entire life. It is draining.

The NICU nurse says that I may hold him, so she places the tiny bundle in my arms. He is so small and weak looking, I don't ever want to let him go. I want to hold him to my chest and protect him forever, from everyone who would ever cause him any pain.

I wonder how I will protect him. My own body couldn't protect him long enough to deliver him healthily. How will I fair for the rest of his life?

"He's beautiful, Riona," Henrik whispers from my side.

He's crouched down and taking in the sight of our beautiful boy.

I nod my agreement, words failing me.

"What will you name him?" The nurse asks.

I look down at my boy and close my eyes. He looks so much like his father already.

"Only one name will suit him, don't you think?" I ask, looking to Henrik.

"That is?" Henrik asks, a smirk on his lips.

The bastard knows, he's just making me say it out loud.

"Henrik George William Richard Stuart II."

"Are you sure?" he asks.

I nod, unable to say anything else without crying even more.

"That going to be his name, then?" the nurse asks, her eyes gleaming with excitement.

"It is," I nod.

This beautiful boy in my arms, and this beautiful man at my side, they are everything to me in the world. Without them, I would be a lost soul.

"I love you both, so much," Henrik exhales.

"I love you more than you could ever imagine, Henny. Thank you. Thank you for this treasure," I whisper, looking down at our boy.

"I'm so sorry I wasn't with you during everything," he mutters.

"You're here now," I say softly.

"I am, precious, I'll always be here for you."

Henrik is the man that loves me and I—I love him with all of my heart.

Every single part of me loves every single part of him.

Our family is anything but conventional. We're spread out overseas, with James and Madison in Oregon; and Henrik's family is literally royalty—but there is more love than I could have ever imagined possible in the people around us.

Henrik's family may have been surprised by our Las Vegas nuptials, and initially they disapproved, but over the past few months they've been fantastic.

Henrik's father and even grandfather have accepted this new dynamic, the fact that Henrik relinquished his royal title, and it seems that the bond between the three of them is stronger than ever.

Bee, Helena and I have also grown very close together, working alongside each other and becoming more than just relatives, but also friends.

The story of our life isn't over—it's just beginning. I honestly cannot wait for more. I can't wait for what awaits us, for the ample love that will fill our lives, for the craziness that Madison will bring when she comes for a visit with her own little family, for the roller coaster that is our life, and has been since I met him poolside in sin city.

My prince—my *Henny.*

Also by Hayley Faiman

MEN OF BASEBALL SERIES—
Pitching for Amalie
Catching Maggie
Forced Play for Libby
Sweet Spot for Victoria

RUSSIAN BRATVA SERIES—
Owned by the Badman
Seducing the Badman
Dancing for the Badman
Living for the Badman
Tempting the Badman
Protected by the Badman (May 2017)
Forever my Badman (2017)
Betrothed to the Badman (2017)
Chosen by the Badman (2018)
Healing the Badman (2018)

NOTORIOUS DEVILS MC—
Rough & Rowdy
Rough & Raw
Rough & Rugged
Rough & Ruthless
Rough & Ready (Summer 2017)
Rough & Rich (2017)
Rough & Real (2018)

STANDALONE TITLES
Royally Relinquished

Follow me on social media to stay current on the happenings in my little book world.

Website: www.HayleyFaiman.com

Facebook: www.facebook.com/authorhayleyfaiman

Goodreads: www.goodreads.com/author/show/10735805.
Hayley_Faiman

Signup for my Newsletter:
hayleyfaiman.us13.list-manage.com/
subscribe?u=d0e156a6e8d82f22e819d1065&id=4d4aefaf0b

ABOUT THE
Author

As an only child, Hayley Faiman had to entertain herself somehow. She started writing stories at the age of six and never really stopped.

Born in California, she met her now husband at the age of sixteen and married him at the age of twenty in 2004. After all of these years together, he's still the love of her life.

Hayley's husband joined the military and they lived in Oregon, where he was stationed with the US Coast Guard. They moved back to California in 2006, where they had two little boys. Recently, the four of them moved out to the Hill Country of Texas, where they adopted a new family member, a chocolate lab named Optimus Prime.

Most of Hayley's days are spent taking care of her two boys, going to the baseball fields for practice, or helping them with homework. Her evenings are spent with her husband and her nights—those are spent creating alpha book boyfriends.

SPECIAL NOTE

I want to give a special thanks to all that have supported me along this journey that I have taken.

Thank you to The Green Pen, Pink Ink Designs, Champagne Formats, and Enticing Journey—without you this book would have never been published.

I appreciate every single reader, fan, and blogger that has taken a chance on my writing, on diving into my little world, and enjoyed themselves!!

Thank you to my Husband, Mom, Rosalyn, and Crystal who are always there for me, always lending an ear and supporting me. I truly appreciate you all!

Printed in Great Britain
by Amazon